Sarah Whitman, Mary Catherine Lee

A Quaker Girl of Nantucket

Sarah Whitman, Mary Catherine Lee

A Quaker Girl of Nantucket

ISBN/EAN: 9783337398941

Printed in Europe, USA, Canada, Australia, Japan

Cover: Foto ©Andreas Hilbeck / pixelio.de

More available books at **www.hansebooks.com**

A QUAKER GIRL OF NANTUCKET

BY

MARY CATHERINE LEE

BOSTON AND NEW YORK

HOUGHTON, MIFFLIN AND COMPANY

The Riverside Press, Cambridge

1889

CONTENTS.

A QUAKER GIRL OF NANTUCKET.

CHAPTER I.

THE OLD HOME AND THE NEW BOY.

In Nantucket town, on one of the streets which is more properly restrained, more certain than others where it wants to go, stands a house more ample than its fellows, and farther back from the cobble-stone pavement, so as to give it a few feet of grass plot in front, when other houses stand flush upon the sidewalk. It is a drab house, well furnished with drab shutters, inside and out, whereas most of the Nantucket houses have no shutters at all.

These differences give it an honorable distinction. It is a foregone concession that the people who live there are to be very highly regarded.

Three generations of Swains had passed quiet lives under the roof of this exceptional dwelling, and the fourth was represented by one little girl, Miriam Swain, some twenty odd years ago.

Nantucket town is the slowly pulsing heart of Nantucket island, and its history is the history of other hearts, — hope, the high tide of full experience, and at length placid repose. Alas for that repose since the world has come to buy it, and its contagious fever has started the calm pulse into abnormal throbbing! Alas for that sweet and wholesome serenity!

More than two hundred years ago the Puritans, having fled from persecution, became themselves oppressors, and put to flight some Quakers of Plymouth Colony, who sought peace and refuge in that almost desert place.

The spirit of peace itself may be said to have founded the old town, which in later times, after a hundred and fifty years of busy enterprise, slept on its tranquil harbor, dreaming of the past, and quite content with an early and comfortable decadence. Through its bland atmosphere the infrequent stranger walked in those days as if spellbound, so entrancing was the calm, and seemed to sleep while he waked, and knew not whether he saw or dreamed he was seeing queer old homesteads and dear old people, who beamed upon him with loving kindness from regions of waxen neatness if he only had the happiness to be ever so remotely related. Sometimes these old homes looked stiff and uncordial, with a thoroughly prudent air, but they were always sweet and simple, always and altogether delightful with the purest essence of hospitality at heart.

This is as they were years ago, before the invasion of the summer visitor. Some of them remain so to this day.

And the summer visitor has, perhaps, not yet appropriated those miles of open moorland, wild and heath-covered, that stretched beyond the town, whose gently undulating surface was broken at long intervals by clumps of odorous pines. Far apart stood the ancient farm-houses, and lonely, but sweet, were the pastures, far from human habitation, where fat sheep and lambs grazed, and if they had each borne a golden fleece, it would have seemed, as you looked at them in those solitudes, that they were safe from any Jason.

Following the deeply-rutted, sandy roads that straggled across the moors, you would have found a quaint little fishing village. The fishermen's cots stood in zigzag rows, and the doors had wooden latches. Their bright little dooryards blinked at you cheerily, and the inmates of the cots peeped at you wonderingly through the tiny greenish window panes, or around the corner of a doorpost. In one of these dooryards stood the figure-head of a ship, — an heroic female *statuaire*, clothed in gorgeous hues, and bearing aloft a standard. This came ashore after a night of storm, and a bas-relief representing some flying creature, which garnished, not to say covered, the front of one cottage, was also the figure-head of some unhappy ship, towed home by fishermen. The whole village glistened and smiled with trophies which the false sea had cast at its feet.

At one end of it stood the very patriarch of town pumps, looking as discouraged as if all the debts that have been charged to town pumps, since ever town pumps were, had come back upon this one, as the original and last-remaining and most responsible one of all.

One day a boy was tugging at the handle of this pump, making it shriek and groan with weary protestations, and pour forth what might have been a flood of tears, so thoroughly unhappy seemed that ancient fountain; and the boy appeared to be in perfect sympathy with it, for floods of tears poured also down his pale cheeks, and great sobs shook his thin chest.

"Oh, oh!" he moaned with every tug at the pump-handle, as if the burden of life were far too heavy for him.

He was one of those trophies with which the sardonic sea had enriched the little fishing village some years before. From one of the ill-fated ships that came ashore there, were saved two sailors and this child. John Dagget, a fisherman, said, "Leave the boy here. I shall need one to help me a-fishin' by 'n' by. I'll make a fisherman on him."

But the child was frail, and cried, and refused the strange food of the fisher-people. A sad child, foreign in every way to those stern toilers of the sea, they came to despise him, and the boy became sullen as well as sickly. As it seemed evident that he would never be fit for a fisherman, he was frankly pronounced a burden that they would gladly be rid of, and John Dagget applied to the overseers of the poor at Nantucket to have him admitted at the town farm.

Miriam's father, Obed Swain, one of these overseers, harnessed up Jerry one fine morning, and jogged off " 'cross island " to see this peculiar case of a boy who was n't wanted. Boys, to him, seemed a very rare and choice article, partly because in Nantucket there were three or four feminines to one masculine, and principally because the only child Heaven had bestowed upon him was one precious little girl, and although he would not have changed her for all the boys on the island and the main-land together, yet he would have been most thankful for a son. A great warmth crept into his heart as he thought of a boy who belonged to nobody, whom nobody wanted, and as he drove on to the fisher village, his mind received a suggestion, — a leading of the spirit, he called it, — and by the time he came within sight of the town pump, his mind was very clear as to what he would do with this underrated article.

The poor fellow, who was mingling his tears with those of the pump, wiped his eyes with his sleeve, and gulped down his sobs, as he saw some one approaching, and was very busy stooping over to rinse out his bucket when Obed Swain called out, —

" Whoa—a, Jerry !   Will thee tell me, my lad, which is John Dagget's cottage ? "

The boy stared up astonished at this unaccustomed tone and Obed Swain's beneficent face.

" What ! thee ain't a-crying, — not this fine morning, I should hope," said Obed.   " What 's the matter, my son? Anything I can do for thee?"

The words "my son" tasted sweet in Obed's mouth, and they were the open sesame to the boy's suppressed woe. He threw himself on the ground and shook with misery, and filled the air with moans. Obed stepped out of the "shay," and stooping over him pressed his hand gently on the boy's head.

"My child," he said, "tell me, thy friend, what is the matter?"

"O-o-o, *e-e-e-verything!*"

"*Everything*, hey? Umph, this is the worst case I ever did see. There, take my handkerchief, my boy, and wipe th' eyes and th' nose and let's begin somewhere to make everything right again. Whose boy is thee?"

"N-n-no-nobody's!"

"*Nobody's?* Why — *thee ain't the boy that lives with John Dagget!*"

"Ye-yes, I be."

"Well, then, thee get right up and get into my shay, my son. Thee's nothing more to cry about. Thee's somebody's boy from this minute; that's to say, thee's *my* boy."

Directly the boy was seated in the corner of a real equipage — a fine equipage for Nantucket. He could not remember that such an extraordinary thing had ever happened to him before. His grief gave place to wonder, and his sobs hushed themselves into long quivering sighs.

"What's thy name?" asked Obed.

"Joe."

"Joseph what?"

"That's all — only Joe."

"Does thee remember thy father and mother?"

"N-no. I dunno," replied the boy, looking wistfully out to sea.

Obed stroked his smooth face in silent satisfaction, gazing at the sea too. And the sea smiled back upon them blandly, as if it had been the best of friends.

At this time Dame Dagget, since something was taking place that she did n't know all about, threw her apron over her head and came forward. She wore a face which was also bland, like that of the sea, and took pains to show that she, too, had been the best of friends.

"For a gentleman's boy there was n't no fault to be found with him," she said; "but he was dretful sing'lar 'bout his victuals, and was n't the sort of boy for fisher-folks to keep. Look at them hands!" she added scornfully, pointing at the boy's long, thin fingers. "No, she did n't know about the child's belongings more than Obed Swain did himself, except — why, yes; there was that thing he had on when they took him, and there was the bit of a ring on one of his fingers, — she'd got 'em laid away somew'ers. She'd look and see."

Away went the dame, and returned with a little embroidered flannel wrapper fluttering in one hand, and a tiny bit of gold pinched between her broad thumb and finger. "She kept them carefully," she said, "thinking some of his folks might come a-looking for him. It was well known,—it was in the newspapers,—that a child was saved off the Aurory."

Obed put the ring into his wallet, tucked the little wrapper into his capacious pocket, and took his seat in the chaise with the look of a man who has made a successful stroke.

Directly the boy was sailing away in a land-boat, as the carriage was to him, from all his woes. Over fields came the soft lowing of kine, and the scent of pines, and heath, and bayberry bushes; over sea came the fainter and fainter murmur of its waves. He sailed slowly above the little yellow star flowers that made the roadside golden, and he might have been sailing above the stars themselves, he was so bewildered and so happy. His head dropped lower and lower until it rested, with the helpless trust of unconsciousness, against Obed's arm.

Miriam Swain, while her father was ploughing 'cross island, sat on a low stool, having said her lessons to Aunt Hepsy, reading for diversion the life of Ann Millet, a young person who began to have "leadings" at the age of four years, who never cared for play, never laughed, and always waited to be "directed" before she even washed her hands; whose wonderful piety led her to pass all her leisure hours in devotion, and who died at the age of thirteen, an accomplished saint. Every book which came into Miriam's hands was of this same general nature, for it was selected for her by Aunt Hepsy, who had charge of her education, and Aunt Hepsy was resolved to leaven the natural mind of that naughty Miriam, who cost her many a groan, with such leaven as should work out her unsaintly tendencies, and make her worthy of her precious privileges, of which she, Aunt Hepsy, was the chief.

Miriam shut the " Life of Ann Millet " with a discouraged sigh, and wondered why it was necessary to be so dull and sickly in order to be good. It was n't altogether her fault, she reasoned, if those wonderful leadings had n't come to her ; it was a matter quite out of her control, like the trouble about her hair, that would crinkle and fly out into loose locks round her face, in spite of all Aunt Hepsy could do, by brushing and combing and straining it back tighter and tighter every day.

Resigned to this conviction, she went and stood by the window where the summer breeze came lazily in, waving the white dimity curtains, and looked across the backyard, a spot of immaculate neatness, where the short grass spread out from the broad doorstone to the edge of " the bank," that is, the abrupt slope of the ground to a much lower level. Beyond, she could look over the roofs of the houses that were on the streets " under the bank," to the blue waters of the harbor, and see the Nantucket steamboat when it rounded the Point and came in to port. Although she might see it every day, she never lost the feeling of excitement with which she watched it returning from what, to her, were unknown regions, about which she had dreams. As she stood watching for the boat and dreaming her dreams, she hummed softly to herself, as she had heard her friend Pel'-tiah Groves do.

"There, there! Don't thee make that noise, Miriam," said a measured voice from the next room.

"She don't know it's *singing*," said Miriam, smiling to herself. "Now, who'd ever think that that little bit of a sound, come to call it singing, was worldly and sinful?"

Aunt Hepsy's firm, almost noiseless footstep moved on from room to room, and presently her deep voice called, "Miriam!"

Miriam, quickly obeying the summons, presented herself before Aunt Hepsy, who stood with an in-quisitorial air before a tumbler of wild flowers and grasses, that Miriam had meant to place in her own room to brighten its austere plainness, and make it look like cousin Ruth's room, but which she had imprudently left on the dining-room table.

"What's thee saving these weeds for?" Aunt Hepsy desired to know.

"I—I thought they were pretty," replied Miriam, blushing.

"Thee go give them to the cow—that's what they're for—and don't thee go bringing litter into the house again," was Aunt Hepsy's decree.

While Miriam was offering her unwilling sacrifice to the cow, she seemed to be throwing over the fence a great deal besides the flowers, and the cow, grazing on the farther side of the little piece where she was pastured, added to the bitterness of the occasion by her stupid indifference. Miriam frowned upon the cow, and was about to waste some consideration upon the old riddle, " Why don't we continue to be happy? " when she heard Jerry's footsteps and the rattle of the old chaise, and her elastic spirits seized upon happiness itself, and left the riddle unsolved, as she hurried to meet her father.

She drew back and stood in silent amazement, however, when she saw get down from the chaise, after her father, a ragged, barefooted boy, with great shocks of light hair all out of place, and no hat at all. The boy also drew back and looked at Miriam anxiously, trying to screen himself behind Obed.

" Thee go call Rosanna, Miriam," said Obed.

Miriam hastened to find Rosanna, as a possible step towards an explanation, but she was still more bewildered when Rosanna, after receiving some directions and a large parcel of things which Obed had bought, disappeared with parcel, boy, and all.

Obed then called Miriam to listen to the story of a boy whom nobody wanted, nobody loved,— whom he had found weeping because there was no place for him in the world. Tears came into Miriam's clear eyes.

" Oh, father, *I* love him, and *I* want him," she
said, and when, in course of time, Rosanna returned with the boy shining and fresh from his
bath, hair neatly cropped and brushed, with clean
linen, whole jacket and trousers, and brand-new
stockings and shoes, Miriam went to him, and
with the tears hardly dry on her lashes said, with
timid earnestness, —

" *I* love thee, and *I want thee.*"

Poor Joe stood confounded by this new wave in
the tide of peculiar circumstances in which he had
been already nearly drowned. He met Miriam's
impulsive overture with a look that was pitiful in
its bewildered helplessness. Such doings as these
were too remarkable for him to understand.

Miriam turned away, crushed and disappointed.

" He does n't love *me*," she said with quivering
lip.

" Ye - yes I do too," gasped the boy, and then
shrank into himself again, with sudden terror at
having made such a bold and hazardous venture.

" Then," said Miriam, brightening, " I shall be
very good to thee, — thou 'll see. I shall give
thee the very prettiest and best of my two new
kittens, to begin with, — the one named Solomon.
I 've lost a good many kittens," she added with a
sigh, meaning, no doubt, to imply that having had
sorrows of her own she was the better qualified to
sympathize with an unhappy boy like him. " Come
and I 'll show thee their graves."

She took the boy's hand, and drew him along

with her out of the open door, round into the prim garden at the right of the green backyard, where sage and summer savory, balm and mint, boneset, catnip, and pennyr'yal were getting the better of a few flowers, and when they reached a secluded corner in the extreme lower end, she paused and pointed to a row of little earthy protuberances, each with a shingle stuck up against it, and each decorated with one cinnamon rose.

" There they are," she said, waving her hand over them with impressive solemnity. " It's worldly to have gravestones and flowers for them, but " (in a confidential tone) "I *do* like worldly things! Aunt Hepsy says it's a sin to make such a fuss over cats, but th' sees, *she* don't know what it is to love cats very much and have 'em die. Those two are Esau and Jacob. I called them so because *this* one was always getting the messes away from *that* one. That one's Nebuchadnezzar, because he used to eat grass, and I think that's what killed him. Grass is n't good for cats, thee knows. That one I called Rosanna, because it was black, and those three are Faith, Hope, and Charity. The other two died before they had any names, and I wrote some lines — ebbytoffs I believe they call 'em — to put on their grave-stones. Thee can't read 'em, I know, they're wrote so bad. This one says : —

' Under this stone a kitten lies,
   Its mother's pride and hope ;
Before it had opened its eyes,
   It into the grave did drop.'

And the other : —

<blockquote>
' This pretty little kitten,
Of eight days old,
By death it was smitten,
Caused by a great cold.' "
</blockquote>

All this impressed Joe immensely; not so much the nine dead cats, however, as the girl, not so old as himself, who could talk so much, could read and write and make ebbytoffs, and, in short, knew about so many things of which he had never heard. He gazed, speechless, at the nine lumps of earth. Miriam was pleased. His silence seemed sympathetic. She imagined him sharing her regret, and felt her tender heart drawn to him with another impulse of affection. Reaching up on tiptoes, she kissed Joe's thin cheek, and Joe returned the caress, after a fashion.

The superabundant tenderness of Miriam's heart, which had hitherto overflowed upon kittens, rejoiced more and more in this new object; and a hundred kindly influences poured like rain and sunshine upon the object himself. The bruised plant revived and held up its head with a timid joy that was almost as pathetic as its misery had been.

The untutored mind and misused body of this poor child, who had lost his place in life, needed large amendments, and Aunt Hepsy felt that she was the one being qualified to make them. To begin with, he was no longer allowed to be Joe, but was called upon to support the reputable name of Joseph John Gurney,[1] and to complete his respectability the name of Swain was added by Obed.

Aunt Hepsy rejoiced with peculiar satisfaction in a new opportunity to train up a child in the way it should go. She considered that her most remarkable gifts lay in that direction. Being a spinster herself, she had looked to find a field for her talents in her brother Obed's family, but unfortunately for the scope of those talents, and Miriam, the field had been limited, for Elizabeth Swain had supplied her with but one case to experiment upon, and died. Miriam very reasonably felt that such powerful forces, all brought to bear upon one small child, were a good deal too much for the child.

But Aunt Hepsy devoted herself with uncommon zeal to Joseph John's education, which divided the pressure most agreeably. Miriam had a feeling of relief that was akin to liberty, — that was liberty itself compared with former things. While Joseph John was saying his lessons she could often slip out and execute some fascinating plan which had once been too difficult for accomplishment. The window of Belinda Cottle's little millinery and fancy goods store offered fruitful suggestions, and Joseph John's extremity was her opportunity.

One day, Aunt Hepsy was at her wit's end trying to demonstrate to Joseph John why it was n't

---

[1] The founder of that division of Friends called Gurneyites.

correct for him to say, "Will you let me take thy pencil?" and Miriam slipped up-stairs with an eager look which showed that this was an important moment to her. She gathered together certain things that had been previously laid away in anticipation of such an opening, and was soon absorbed in creating the expression of an ideal. She was so deeply engaged that she did not hear Aunt Hepsy's step on the stairs. Who could have heard it when she wore such abominably soft slippers? Poor Miriam started up with a flushed face, and held her hands behind her when the door slowly opened and Aunt Hepsy stood before her, the impersonation of fact.

"What's thee doing, Miriam? What is't thee's got in thy hands?" she demanded, with a dreadful calmness that was worse than a thunder clap. Her keen eyes, aquiline nose, and the high poise of her head made her look like an eagle.

Miriam knew the revelation must come, so she held forth at once — what — in the name of wonder? Her little plain bonnet with a huge bunch of cherries fastened on one side, and atop of these a fire-red bow!

This was too much for words, and it was according to Aunt Hepsy's principles to use few words at any time. Groans answered every purpose.

Miriam knew full well what was to be done. Aunt Hepsy, swelling with suppressed emotion, led the way in silence to her room, with the captured bonnet in her hand, and Miriam followed with downcast eyes.

On a shelf in that room were some books which represented the rod to Miriam, and the rod was never spared.

Whenever she committed an offense, she was required to read aloud to Aunt Hepsy for an hour from one of these. If the offense had been moderate, Aunt Hepsy handed her "No Cross, No Crown," or Barclay's "Apology," or "The Journal of Thomas Chalkley," but if it had been uncommonly heinous, "The Sinner Awakened" was the penalty. They were severe looking books, in which all the *s*'s were *f*'s, and Miriam had as much as she could do not to call sin, fin, which would have seemed very absurd, for who ever heard of a man groaning under the burden of his fins?

Aunt Hepsy took down "The Sinner Awakened," and handed it in awful silence to Miriam, who proceeded to look for the place where her last transgression had left her. It was n't really so bad as it used to be, for Joseph John was there; he would be sorry, and it is in the feminine nature to enjoy being the object of sympathy. Even if Aunt Hepsy went so far as to make her stay and meditate after "The Sinner Awakened," Joseph John would come and whisper through the keyhole and tell her what figures the hands on the clock were at, so that she could guess the time and know how much of her captivity was past. She had done him a similar favor. But Miriam had not learned all of human nature, — its capabilities and shortcomings.

In the midst of her humiliation Joseph John came and looked in at the door. Aunt Hepsy's back being turned, he looked at his leisure, and saw the little dove-colored bonnet lying on the table, with its comical decorations, and understood the whole predicament. Miriam glanced up at him, and he was laughing! actually laughing with delight, and she so mortified and troubled!

This was too much. Miriam hid her face in " The Sinner Awakened " and wept. Aunt Hepsy saw in this unusual demonstration an evidence of repentance.

" I am gratified," she said, in a measured, solemn tone, and after due reflection, " to know that thou hast seen thy error and art concerned. Take those bedizenments off th' bonnet. I shall leave thee to the silent working of the better mind."

Saying which, Aunt Hepsy went out and shut the door. Whatever Aunt Hepsy did seemed to say, " I know what's right; not only so, I also practise what I know." She was doing severely right when she imposed a penalty. She was doing severely right when she remitted the penalty. Her lenity, even, had an air of strictness which robbed it of any cheering effect. When she closed the door upon Miriam, the child was more miserable than before. In addition to all the rest, she felt guilty of having gained her reprieve upon a false supposition. She wanted to tell Aunt Hepsy that she was not crying about the bonnet, but she could not. The real cause of her tears was a matter upon which she was too keenly sensitive to make it a subject of discussion. But, after all, was n't she sorry about the bonnet? She was sure of it, especially as things had turned out.

She tore the bedizenments off her bonnet, and threw them out of the window, threw the poor bonnet, I am sorry to say, into a corner of the room, and leaning her arms on the sill of the open window, and her head on her arms, grieved that she had been born into such a disappointing world.

Joseph John, meanwhile, was impatient of the time he was obliged to wait for his playfellow. Lessons were over, and there was no computing the pleasure that was being lost. He watched the clock until the hands had gone over the ordinary space allotted to Miriam's penances, and then went softly to take another peep. He opened the door carefully. What was his surprise to find the usually wide-awake Miriam bowed down in that abject fashion.

"Miriam, why Miriam!" he said. "Why don't thee come and do something? We can take a little cruise to the mill. Come!"

Miriam shook her shoulder away from his touch, and made no response.

"What's the matter? Why it ain't the *bunnit!*" said Joseph John, in a tone which implied that he should hope she would scorn such weakness.

"It's *thou!*" said Miriam.

"*Me!*"

"Laughing, when I wanted thee to — to be sorry."

" What thee want *me* to be sorry for ? "

The old foolish feminine demand for tenderness ! The old masculine short-sighted obtuseness !

Miriam in despair and desperation got up, snatched her bonnet from the corner, ran headlong down stairs, and letting herself out at the front door, darted down the street. Away she flew, through a crooked lane, down another street, until she came to a house even more remarkable for its exceptional respectability than the Swain house itself. It actually had a projecting façade and Doric columns, and Nantucket took pride in it, though pride was a vice which its owner abhorred upon strictest principles.

Miriam disappeared between the Doric columns, through the big front door, and appeared suddenly before two persons who sat mending linen, beautiful fine snowy linen, in a room where everything seemed to belong by right of kinship to the pure linen. An angel in spotless raiment would hardly have seemed out of place there, and might have lingered long without fear of defilement.

The elder of these two persons was a woman with a sweet classic face and bands of smooth gray hair, though she looked as fresh and fair as the morning, — the morning, when it dawns in a silvery mist and gives promise of a long bright day, — for she was clad in soft and sober-hued garments, like that morning mist, but she held underneath a world of sunshine and gladness. The other was a pretty blonde girl of about nineteen.

Miriam flashed in upon them, panting and flushed, and, throwing her bonnet into one chair and herself into another, announced herself thus : —

" I 've run away, Aunt Dorcas. I 've come to stay !"

CHAPTER II.

THE LONG VOYAGE.

AUNT DORCAS and the fair young girl dropped their work and gazed upon Miriam with the puzzled look with which one accepts a joke that is n't quite plain.

"Look at that face, mother!" said the girl.

"My *dear!* Why need thee have run so, and got so heated?" asked Aunt Dorcas. "Here, take this fan and keep quiet till thee gets thy breath."

Miriam took the round feather fan with pictures on it of soft - looking Chinese ladies, incredible birds, and impossible flowers, held it off to get the full effect of the long silken tassel swinging from its carved ivory handle, and fanned herself with subdued satisfaction. The lustrous feathers, the glancing colors, and the dancing tassel offered some consolation. She surveyed them as she waved them with an air of chastened melancholy, and gradually became calm and cool.

"Now suppose thee tells me what the running away means," suggested Aunt Dorcas.

"Nothing pertickler," said Miriam, examining the fan with a scrutinizing frown, her head on one side, like a connoisseur of fans. "I only want to stay here," she added, bringing the fan up quickly, so that only a pair of earnest hazel eyes, a white forehead, and very frowsy auburn hair showed above the feathers.

"What for!" Aunt Dorcas asked.

"I need a change."

Aunt Dorcas and her daughter laughed.

"*Thee* no need to laugh, cousin Ruth," said Miriam, opening her eyes very wide, and shutting them again with a snap. "When thee wanted to go to Philadelphia, thee said everybody needs a change sometimes."

"I confess, there was another uneasy person," assented cousin Ruth.

"I should *think* so!" said Miriam, with an emphatic nod, which seemed to fix the charge of uneasiness chiefly upon cousin Ruth.

"What about father and Aunt Hepsy?" pursued Aunt Dorcas.

"Father's gone to Yearly Meeting, and I make Aunt Hepsy groan."

"There's Joseph John"—

"Aunt Dorcas, *do* let me stay," cried Miriam, dropping herself beside Aunt Dorcas. "Let me stay a week!" and she said it with her arms round Aunt Dorcas, and looked so eager, that Aunt Dorcas, who felt a compassion for the child, kissed the flushed cheek, patted the frowsy hair, and said,—

"I should like nothing better, dear, if Aunt

Hepsy is willing. I 'm going to see her directly, and I 'll speak about it."

Miriam, hopeful of success under these circumstances, for Aunt Dorcas had a way of persuading even Aunt Hepsy, gave Aunt Dorcas a cordial squeeze, privately thought she guessed Joseph John would be sorry now, and hoped much from the probable remorse that would follow his loneliness.

Leaving the future to work out its own results, she felt inclined to accept the solace of the hour, and floated about the charming room, gazing at the beautiful and curious things that always made her wonder about the strange lands from whence they came. There was a sandal-wood writing-desk — a miracle of dexterous carving; lacquered and curiously inlaid boxes, which being opened disclosed soft pictures upon rice paper, and sent forth subtle odors upon which her fancy took wing; great jars, small and large vases, cabinets full of dainty shells, and a cupboard with glass doors, where she could see the best china. The ships that had sailed from Nantucket to all the chief ports in the world, to carry oil and candles to market, had brought back such treasures as these, and the old island was rich with the products of far-away, mysterious lands.

Miriam's fancy had never roved so freely by invitation of these foreign odors and objects, and she at length resolved to take a trip to foreign lands herself. After dinner she would go on a "cruise," as Nantucket people call a walk, and play it was a voyage to China.

Aunt Dorcas had meantime folded up her snowy apron, put on her bonnet, in which her face looked like a flower within its sober calyx, and throwing a gauzy silk shawl over her handsome shoulders tripped away to see Hepsy Swain.

Miriam finished floating about, and cast anchor in a big easy chair near cousin Ruth, where she curled herself up and watched her cousin's nimble fingers weaving the fine threads in and out on the glossy snowdrop linen. They were having just a nice quiet prittle-prattle together, when suddenly, close behind Miriam's chair, there exploded such a tremendous "*Boo!*" that she jumped like a jack-in-the-box. She was obliged to go round and look on the floor behind the chair for an explanation of this unexpected attention. There, snickering and crouching, was a long, lank boy, who, when confronted, burst into a laugh that sounded like the whinny of a horse, and showed so many enormous teeth that he looked like a pitiless devourer. To substantiate this impression, he held in his hand a huge piece of gingerbread, which had several large semicircular gaps in its edge.

"It's Paul!" said Miriam, with a dismayed look, retiring into the big chair again.

Paul was Ruth's brother, but Miriam had scarcely seen him for two years, for he had been at the Yearly Meeting School at Providence, and she took care to remain at home during his vacations. This was a special and unexpected appear-ance, however, which found her wholly unprepared. Paul had suddenly graduated from the Providence school, with a distinction not in the least due to the excellence of his scholarship, although that was very great. The proprietor of a china-shop had threatened to burn the foot-ball of the Quaker boys if it bounced so near his windows again, and when it went still further and bounced into his shop, he threw it into his stove, which resulted in an explosion that blew up the stove, and made a commotion in the school as well as the china-shop. It could never be proved who was the Guy Fawkes in this gunpowder plot ; but, following a natural sequence, Paul had the credit of stuffing the ball. This was, in fact, a mistake, but Paul accepted his sentence of dismissal with the resig-nation of a boy who had deserved it many times before. He was frequently spoken of on Nan-tucket as a "regular scamp," and yet you could never hear a person say he disliked Paul.

"Th' don't seem rejoiced to see me," he said, rising to the occasion, as one might say, and tak-ing his place directly opposite Miriam, where he rapidly multiplied the gaps in his gingerbread, and stared at her with great, protruding eyes.

"Now Paul, th' knows th' has no business to bring gingerbread into the sitting-room," said cousin Ruth.

"Don't th' bother, Friend Busybody ; nobody 's got any gingerbread in the sitting-room," returned

Paul, stuffing in his last mouthful and pulling from his pocket a pair of spectacle bows destitute of lenses, which he fixed upon his long nose, and then gazed alternately through and over them at Miriam, who turned away and persisted in over-looking him altogether.

"Thee ain't very civil, now," the atrocious boy went on, pulling his chair up beside Miriam's. "I want to have a little conversation with thee. It's a long time since I had the pleasure. How's thee been since I saw thee last?"

Miriam remained dumb and looked out of the window.

"Oh, very well, if I'm to be treated in this fashion I shall go, that's all."

Seizing Miriam's bonnet and squeezing his head into it, he tied the strings in a crazy-looking knot under his chin, and with his spectacle bows wildly askew, flounced out of the room with the appearance of lofty dudgeon.

"Oh," said cousin Ruth, "he is like an angel when mother is here, but he's enough to wear out the patience of an angel when she is away."

"I'm glad he's gone!" Miriam said, with a heavy sigh.

"He'll be back again, I'll promise thee. He won't waste any time."

Miriam began to think she had jumped from the frying-pan to the fire when she ran away from Joseph John. She had a great mind to go home again. But that would mean an inglorious failure.

She must accomplish her purpose. She would stay until tea-time, at any rate. It really began to seem that by tea-time she should want to go home and see how Joseph John felt. She imagined him very sorry and wanted to comfort him.

She was roused from a vision of Joseph John's penitence and her own magnanimity by hearing the delightful motherly mew and purr of a cat, and the fine little squeal of kittens, which appeared to come from the entry. This touched Miriam's tender spot. With an eager bound she reached the entry too soon to hear cousin Ruth's warning, " Don't go — it 's only Paul ! " and rushed directly into the face of that bad boy, who stood arrayed in an astonishing costume, consisting of a large brown table cover, gathered in round his waist by a string to represent the skirt of a gown, a drab shawl pinned smoothly over his chest in the most precise and proper fashion, Miriam's bonnet and the spectacle bows as on last appearance. He marched into the sitting-room with long-drawn face, took his seat with solemnity, and after twirling his thumbs in a meditative manner for a few seconds, with an appearance of composing his mind, arose with great deliberation, and in the sing-song drawl once peculiar to the tuneful exhortations of the " rising seat,"

> " Ranging the gamut in a single word,
>   And touching every discord on the way,"

he thus held forth : —

" My — friends, — since I have been setting

here, I have been deeply impressed with this solemn truth: I ain't treated as I'd oughter be. No, my friends, though I'm much too good for this world, I ain't appreciated! The scornful nose is elevated at my approach! Let me warn you, my frivolous hearers, to turn from the error of your ways, and show me greater consideration and respect. Oh, my children, the time will come when you will wish you had let me eat gingerbread in the setting-room and been more civil and obliging every way. But it is n't too late, — now is a good time to begin. Now, to-day, this very hour, I entreat you to listen to the warning voice, and atone for your past shabbiness by allowing me to turn a few somersets in this inviting spot."

With a sudden whirl and squat he made a "cheese" with his table-cloth skirt, turned two or three somersets in the open space in the middle of the room, touching his hands but not his head, out of regard for Miriam's bonnet, and then, kissing his hand with a bow, thus revealing some slight acquaintance with the sawdust ring, he vanished once more into the entry.

Cousin Ruth had given an occasional covert glance at these scandalous performances, with a disdainful air of not stooping to notice what she could not prevent, but Miriam stared with broad unwinking amazement at those never-before-seen-or-heard-or-thought-of enormities.

"Is n't he *dreadful!*" she said, sinking with a

limp kind of helplessness into a chair when he had
gone.

"He's a shocking bad boy," assented cousin
Ruth.

"Has he come to stay?"

"Oh, yes; all summer."

Miriam remembered that not two hours before
she had announced herself as having come to stay,
but she now resolved that she would go humbly
home when night came, whatever Aunt Dorcas's
message should be, and she had scarcely come to
that conclusion when the front door opened suddenly and a sound of fierce barking and growling
came from the entry, accompanied by the scuffling
of feet, as if a desperate struggle were going on
there. Poor Miriam, who was mortally afraid of
a dog, was about to fly for refuge to the back regions of the house, but cousin Ruth held her, saying, —

"Don't thee understand?   It's only Paul."

Happily Aunt Dorcas was not long away. There
was a long interval of peace, which seemed fright-
fully ominous, and Miriam moved about uneasily
and looked out of the windows. What should she
see but Aunt Dorcas coming up the street, leaning
on the arm of that terrible boy, who was much
taller than his mother, and who bent his head to
listen to what she was saying in such a gentle way
that it was hard to believe he was the same boy
she had looked upon with dread. He shortened
his long strides to accommodate his step to his

little mother's, took a parcel she was carrying, and looked as proud and pleased as the most senti- mental lover could have done. And Aunt Dorcas appeared to be the happiest and most entirely sat- isfied of mothers.

When they came in, Paul took his mother's shawl and bonnet, handed her a fan, and perfected his wonderful transfiguration by seating himself with a book in his hands in the very chair which had lately supported him in his folly. Miriam could no longer believe she had seen him turning somersets in the middle of that serene and orderly room.

"Well, my dear," said Aunt Dorcas, "thee may stay a few days."

"I — I guess I must go home to-night," said Miriam, looking anxiously at the texture of the pocket handkerchief with which she had been wiping from her forehead the dews of the last warm, exciting hour.

Aunt Dorcas attributed this change to a feeling of diffidence in regard to Paul, who really seemed quite an imposing boy when he was behaving him- self.

"Oh, I want thee to stay and see Paul," she said, to bring Miriam into familiarity with the idea. "What does thee think of my great boy?" she added, reaching over and patting Paul's great paw.

Paul took his mother's hand in his, and smiled as he read on, but whether the smile was a re- sponse to her, or an indication that his book was a funny one, or whether he caught a mental glimpse of Miriam's opinion is altogether uncertain.

Aunt Dorcas looked up for an answer, and Miriam felt compelled to give one.

"Oh, all boys are perpost'rous," she said, "but there's a difference in *boys*."

They all laughed at the vagueness of the reply, and answered the summons to dinner.

During the moment of silent grace, Miriam, by some unlucky fascination, felt compelled to look at Paul, who met her gaze with such an alarming squint that, in utter confusion, she said she would n't have any jelly with her meat, when jelly was the particular thing she wanted.

This making the acquaintance of her cousin Paul was an experience so uncomfortable that she resolved to escape it at any price, and by the time dinner was finished she had decided how she would do it.   She would take that voyage to China.

It was growing cooler, Aunt Dorcas had gone to take a nap, Paul was swinging in a hammock behind the Doric columns, absorbed in a thrilling book, and Miriam said to cousin Ruth, "Farewell, I'm going on a voyage to China."

"Farewell," said cousin Ruth, returning the little hand-pressure with understanding, — for she was used to Miriam's dreamy make-believes, and often came down from the height of her nineteen years and made believe with her, — " farewell, and I hope thee 'll take a fast steamer, so as to be back by tea-time."

"Well, I don't know," Miriam replied. "China's the best place to take tea in, is n't it? But I 'm going home to tea. Farewell."

Miriam had a passion for wandering on the shore and sitting in the boats that lay hauled up there. She often sat for hours gazing out to sea, and watching the white sails going on and on, — wondering to where, — and it was a greater satisfaction to wonder where, and dream that they were going to touch at charmed coasts, where birds with gay plumage, like those on Aunt Dorcas's fans and boxes, nestled among golden fruits and gorgeous flowers, and all the breezes were laden with such odors as were shut up in those boxes, — it was a far greater pleasure to suppose this, than it would have been to know that these white-winged wanderers were going down to Pennsylvania after coal, or coming from Cape Cod with cargoes of salt codfish.

When Miriam shut the back gate that opened from Aunt Dorcas's trim garden into a sandy lane, she looked up and down as if considering which was the best route to China, and then turned up the lane in the direction of her favorite haunt, the North Shore. The lane brought her into a region of scattered houses, on the outskirts of the town, overlooking the open downs, and on a breezy elevation stood a weather-beaten old windmill, swinging its arms in the face of the wind and telling it to "Come on, come on," if it wanted a fight with him.

"I must stop and say farewell to Amos Tuttle, and tell *him* I'm going to China," said Miriam.

Amos Tuttle, the miller, was a great friend of Miriam's. One of her chief pleasures was to pay him a visit at the mill and hear him spin his bright-colored yarns. He was a good, honest soul, who had got what good he could out of life, philosophically and actually; had tried nearly all parts of the world, as a seafaring man, in his youth; had made a little fortune as a digger in a California gold mine, and lost it all as a proprietor in the same; had canvassed the United States with a patent washing-machine; had himself invented a remarkable combination of mop-handle, window-brush, carpet-stretcher, and garden-squirt; had lived on a cattle-ranch out on the prairies and been attacked by Indians; had come home when he was growing old as poor as he was born, and was at last rewarding an ungrateful world by grinding its corn in the old mill.

Miriam climbed up to the open mill door, and found Amos dozing over a sedative old newspaper, with his glasses slipping off his nose, and she thought it would be a capital joke for him to wake up and start with surprise at seeing her there. So she stood quietly watching the golden grains slide from the hopper to the stone, and there, losing all separate existence, pour in a blended stream into the great box below. As the meal went on pouring, the glasses went on slipping, and presently down they dropped on the newspaper, and Amos gave the start Miriam had looked for, much to her delight.

" Oho ! " said he, " here 's that little brown bird agin. Hop in and set awhile, won't ye ? I was gitting drowsy a bit; a little chat 'll rouse me up, I expect."

" Why, thee was as sound asleep as ever was," said Miriam, with her quiet little laugh.

"*Asleep?* Oh, no, I wa' n't asleep," Amos avowed, starting up and picking up his glasses with uncommon alertness; " I *never* sleep in the daytime — not I. I was a - thinking about a boy 't swum in down to Floridy after alligaters' eggs, 'n' he got a good parcel on 'em, and was a-comin' off grand with 'em, when he heered a rousin' snap close behind him. ' What 's that ? ' says he, a-lookin' round, an' there abaft on him, about s-o fur off, was a live alligater, an' that snap would a' ketched that air boy if it had n't been for a snag that the reptyle run agin."

" He did n't catch him, then ? "

" Which did n't ketch who ? "

" The alligator did n't catch the boy, did he ? "

" Not he. The boy caught the alligater. He snatched up that gun o' his'n an' shot him *smack,* and the last time I see that boy he was travelin' out West with a valise made out o' the alligater's skin, — made it himself, — an' alligater's skin 'll be the fashion for valises some day, see if 't ain't."

" He was a smart boy, was n't he ? " Miriam was thinking of Joseph John. She was very

much afraid he would be one of those same
smart boys, and place himself far beyond her
reach.

"Yes," responded Amos, "he *was* a smart boy,
but he wa' n't nigh so smart as a girl I knew."

In this way Amos would run on and tell story
after story by the hour.

"Tell me about the girl," said Miriam, taking
a long breath to be ready for another pull.

"Well," Amos began, in a very different tone,
"this girl had n't no mother, an' her father had n't
no other but her, an' he set a gret store by her.
He was a sea cap'n, an' he could n't bear to go off
'n' leave his little one to home an' not see her for
years, so he used to take her to sea with him, an'
all she knew he larned her, an' most o' that was
navigatin' an' them sort o' things, an' she took to
'em 's if she 'd been a boy, an' loved the sea an'
the ship like an old salt.   One day, when she 'd
got to be a good deal of a woman, the ship was
a-runnin' off Pernambuc', steerin' straight for
home, an' the cap'n was took sick so 't he
could n't hold up his head.   Wal, he *was* worrited, for the fust mate he 'd cut sticks 'n' cleared
when we put into Ryo, an' the second mate was
an onsartin' chap that could n't be trusted to sail
the ship nohow.   The cap'n worrited till he was
wuss by it, an' then his darter, says she, ' Why,
father, *I* can sail the ship,' says she.   ' So you *can*,
Lyddy,' says he, an' she did.   Th' wa' n't a man
aboard that dared to say she could n't, when she

come up and took command. I tell ye, that girl had her hands full, with the ship an' father, too ; but she pulled 'em both through 's if she 'd been a commydore an' a physic doctor too, an' brought 'em both to port with every timber safe 'n' sound. Ah, Lyddy ! " Amos breathed a heavy sigh, looking out over the lonely moor through the little mill window, as if that unbroken waste might represent his own desolation.

" Is she dead ? " Miriam asked, softly.

Amos shook his head slowly. " I do' know," he said, " *Life is cur'ous!* " and then turning slowly back to the present, " Well, well," he added, briskly, " the corn 's all out o' the hopper ! "

This crisis of things recalled Miriam to her purpose.

" I 'm going to China to-day," she said ; " I stopped to say farewell."

" Chiny, h-ey ?   What 'ee goin' to Chiny for ? "

" To see things," said Miriam, making ready by pulling her little scoop bonnet forward from its place on the nape of her neck to its other place over her eyelids.

" Why, you don't know nothing about Chiny," said Amos ; " what set ye out to go there ? "

" I *do* know all about China," returned Miriam. " The-empire-of-China-is-very-extensive-and-has-a-larger-population-than-any-other-country-in-the-world. — The-inhabitants-are-called-Chinese. — They-are-a-proud-vain-people-and-believe-all-other-

nations-to-be-inferior-to-themselves. — The - empe-
ror-of-China-is-called-' The-Son-of - Heaven.' — In-
China-very-small-feet-are-thought-to-be - the - chief-
beauty-of-women. — The-great-wall-and-the-grand-
canal-are-noted-works. — The-porcelain - tower - at-
Nankin-is-a-remarkable-building. — Tea-is-the-leaf-
of-a-shrub-that-grows-principally-in-this-country."

" Whew ! " whistled Amos, when Miriam had
rattled off this rigmarole, " why, ye must 'a' been
there ! "

" No," said Miriam, " not yet. I learned that
in my g'ography, and there are pictures, besides.
And Aunt Dorcas Haddon 's got a lot of things
from China. I know by them, 'specially by the
smell of them, that things are very nice in China."

" Haw, haw," laughed Amos ; " well, some is,
and some is n't ; but I 'll resk but what you 'll find
them that *is*. Wish ye good luck, an ye 'll come
round 'n' see us when ye git back 't the island,
won't ye ? "

" Of course," Miriam answered, shaking hands
with Amos, who delighted in humoring the visionary child — he a visionary child himself.

Again the little dreamer turned her face towards China. The slender figure, tall for a girl
of twelve, with its straight brown gown and its
prim bonnet, gliding over the sober moor, pausing
to gaze before at the sea, or backward with up-
lifted hand shading her eyes, made a lovely Bough-
tonish picture, in which softness and severity, setting aside their mutual contradictions, were happily united.

The wild moor stopped abruptly in face of the wilder sea, and knelt meekly before it by way of a sandy cliff, that slanted away to the shore.

When Miriam came to the brow of the cliff, she fairly chuckled with delight. There was not only the flashing sea, with its miles and miles of blandishment, and the white sand of the shore, on which she loved to lie, but there was somebody's brand-new blue and white dory. It was just near enough to the water for the waves to wet its keel as they came rolling in, and it was carelessly tied to a stake.

" Ah," said Miriam, speaking to some imaginary companion, for all her life she had been used to wandering about alone and addressing her conversation to the people of her fancy, — " ah, the ship is all ready, we must start right off ! "

She scrambled down the cliff and climbed into the dory. A coat lay in the bottom of it. Apparently somebody meant to come back soon. Seating herself in the stern of the boat with her back to the shore and her face to the sea, so that she could see nothing but sky and sea, she leaned over, watching the waves come curling in, and listened to their voices saying, " Hush, h-u-s-h, h-u-s-h," and the time slipped away unheeded. The boat began to shiver a little, then to lift itself a trifle, as the coaxing waves came farther and farther in. By and by it gave a joyful bounce, and yielding wholly, was lifted from the sand to the lap of the caressing waves. Miriam was in ecstasies.   She jumped now and then to make the boat bounce all it could.   The motion of the water gave her the sensation of really sailing out to sea. She rested her chin on her arms and gave herself up to the delight of fancying her voyage was truly begun.   On, on she seemed to go, and she had no need to bounce the boat, it bounced itself beautifully.   Oh, what a thrill she felt as she rose and dipped again.

"Right across there is Spain," she said; "Aunt Dorcas says so, and when she was a young girl, she used to own property in Spain.   I heard her tell cousin Ruth.   And cousin Ruth must have some now, for she said to Aunt Dorcas, ' Oh, when the wind is right, I can smell the grape-blooms in my vineyards over there.'   I should n't think she could.   What pleasant places vineyards must be! Nothing but grapes aud nice smells everywhere. We can stop in Spain as well as not.   And we can go by France, too, — and Italy.   Aunt Hepsy says they are wicked places, — France and Italy, — and sometimes she says the whole world's wicked, but I don't see 's 't is.   Why, I can't see the sand through the water! How dizzy I feel " —

She raised herself and turned her face towards the shore.   "Oh!   Oh!"

She brushed her hand across her eyes to dispel an illusion.   It could n't be!   It could never be that the old home she had run away from was flitting away from her.   Yet it seemed to be withdrawing itself, and between it and the little boat the sparkling waters seemed to laugh at her, as they spread themselves broader and broader, and pushed her farther and farther on. It was like a nightmare. She could not cry out nor reach out, but she knelt in the bottom of the boat, benumbed and stifled with great heart-throbs.

There was Aunt Dorcas's house, there was the mill, and she could see an end of the old drab house itself, could see the window of her own little room with its snowy curtain flapping in and out, as if waving her a farewell, while she was "sliding — sliding — sliding into the great desert, where there is no tree and no fountain."

"Oh, father, Joseph John, Aunt Hepsy! Oh, Aunt Dorcas and cousin Ruth!" she moaned. A child's moan in that infinity of space!

Yet she had fine, firm nerves and a strong little soul, and in her blood was the calmness of generations of ancestors who had kept themselves in check and made serenity their religion. The first thing a Quaker child is taught is self-command.

When the first shock was over, she shouted and waved her bonnet, watching eagerly for some one to appear, but there was no sign of life on all the shore, and the old town looked over the cliff at her with a grim and cruel unconcern.

There was no hope, then, from the shore, but there were vessels passing up and down, and Miriam began to look out for help from one of these. She could see sails, and they comforted her with

a sense of companionship and of succor that was
sure to come. Each sail was a security, — a ground
of hope. The sea, too, was very calm, and lulled
her until she was passively content to float there
for a while and wait for the friendly help of which
she felt assured. The sun came down and rested
on the waters with the little bark, then dipped
and dipped and seemed to dissolve and redden all
the sea. There were long streaks of pink in the
sky; a gull flew over her with blushing breast,
and the cheerful sails flushed into rose tints, too.
One of them was coming nearer and nearer. Miriam pulled the coat towards her and rolled it up
for a pillow. She fixed her eyes upon the approaching sail and waited very patiently. Out
of the tender sky a star looked down. A feeling of peace possessed her. The light sea-cradle
rocked her gently to and fro. By and by, in the
darkness, a schooner passed so near that it made
the little cradle rock hard. But the child slept
on.

CHAPTER III.

PICKING UP A NATIVE.

THE yacht Juno, belonging to Mr. Asterly Vinton, had borne off distinguished honors at the summer regatta in Buzzard's Bay, and was transferring its owner, with a party of guests, to Newport.

There was Mr. Asterly Vinton himself, a social idol; there was a noble Englishman, of course, and two or three indigenous specimens of fashionable manhood, who considered themselves and were considered by others to be rival idols with Mr. Vinton; there was Miss Grace, sister of Mr. Vinton, and two Newport belles, with a chaperon more fascinating than the belles; and last, but most important of all, there was Beatrice Vinton, or Betty, as she was called, Mr. Vinton's little daughter.

They had come aboard the Juno in New Bedford harbor, at five o'clock in the afternoon, had dined there in a way befitting the various sorts of excellence which they represented, and sailed out of Buzzard's Bay when the sun's rays were so horizontal that they shot under the awning of the Juno, glowed upon perishing ices, and made the lavish flowers droop that were already faint with giving.

Again and again, as they sailed gallantly down the bay, a laugh from the gay groups on the deck startled the sea-birds on placid little islands. At sight of desolate Cuttyhunk, Bartholomew Gosnold and his hardships were cheerfully called to mind, and their own luxury was enhanced by fancying the barren, hard lives of those strange people who lived upon the rough, beaten shores of the main-land. Lightly they spoke of hardship and mental destitution, of plodding and painstaking to worthless ends, for these seemed to them all that could come of living in a region where, as they believed, the utmost height of intelligence was something concerning whales. Mr. Vinton told amusing stories of those queer people, and the distinguished foreigner felt himself very far from home.

Betty Vinton listened.

"Aunt Grace," she said at length, drawing near to Miss Vinton, "what do the boys and girls do in these lonesome places?"

"I 'm sure I don't know," Miss Vinton answered. "There may be some branch of natural history that will help you. I 'm sorry to say I can't."

"I should like to take some of them to Newport or New York and let them have a good time," Betty said, looking with pitying eyes upon Mattapoisett, or Falmouth, or whatever little town they could see just then.

" I dare say they think their times are better than yours. Oh, there are worse places than these, my dear. There is Nantucket, leagues away from the main-land, just a waste of sand and dry grass, with no living creatures on it but seamen, fisher-men, and gulls, they say; and in the winter it freezes up so that people can never get to or from it, and for weeks, and I don't know but months, they know nothing except what happens on their own sands."

" But they have missions there, don't they? "

" Missions ? Why they 're not exactly hea-then. There are very excellent, respectable peo-ple among the inhabitants, I believe."

" Well, what I want to know is about the chil-dren ! I want to stop there. Do you think we can ? "

" I should hope not ! " Miss Vinton said fer-vently.

" I shall ask papa to take me there, then. I must carry some of those poor things away and let them have one good time," said Betty, in a strong gust of benevolence.

" No doubt you will if you want to," Miss Vin-ton said, raising her plump chin to that point which indicates disapproval. " At present, sup-pose you go and ask Maria to bring me a shawl, it is growing chilly; and you 'd better get a sacque yourself."

Betty swept away like a tropical bird, her black eyes full of the snap of resolution. She had unnumbered and unbounded enthusiasms, and her latest was an enthusiasm for charity. She belonged to a Child's Charitable Guild in New York, and her whole impetuous soul had been aroused by the discovery that there were suffering children in the world. She had not as yet a distinct idea of the nature of their sufferings, or the nature of real suffering at all; but having conceived a universal interest in juvenile unhappiness, she was eager for a chance to do something about it, and that something must be something large. There was nothing her mind could invent which was out of Betty's reach, however, if it were only within the bounds of human possibility. Every wish of hers her fond papa stood ready to execute, and if she had proposed to transfer Nantucket from the bosom of the Atlantic to the heart of the pond in Central Park, Mr. Vinton would n't have given up the hope of carrying out such a proposal until he had made sure there were really insuperable objections in the matters of incompetent engineers and obstinate authorities. It promised well for the poor children of Nantucket, who vainly imagined themselves to be happy, that Miss Betty Vinton was disposed to take up their cause.

Betty got on that portion of her plumage called a sacque, and went aft to take a peep at her father's cigar and see what the prospect was of having a discussion with him. She found her chance a good way off yet, and after sauntering about in an aimless way for a while, she perched herself upon a coil of rope near Captain Baxter, the captain of the yacht.

This good-natured individual, with a passive hand in his pocket and an active hand on the wheel, was taking a thoughtful survey of his native shores.

" Well, Miss Betty," he said, feeling that it was polite to say something, " what do you think of these parts ? "

" They 're *ra*-ther pretty," said Betty, with a lenient air, " but I heard somebody say a while ago that such dull places made people a prey to melancholy."

" I wanter know," said Captain Baxter, with mild dismay. " There must be some mistake about that, for I was born and brought up in these parts, and I never heard of it."

" Oh, *were* you born here ? " asked Betty, eagerly. " Then maybe you know about Nantucket."

Captain Baxter smiled a wise smile, and replied that he guessed he did, some.

" I 'm going to ask papa to stop there," Betty proceeded ; " I 've got an important plan."

Captain Baxter regarded Betty with the amused look he would have bestowed upon a gay young oriole that had proposed to bring its important plans into relation with state affairs.

" It 's a dismal place, Nantucket," Betty observed, to lead him out on the subject.

" Well," returned Captain Baxter, willing to concede something, " there *is* consid'rable mourning there, off an' on."

" Mourning ?   What about ? "

" They lose a good many friends, — the folks there."

" Lose them ?   How ? "

" Lose 'em overboard. They go to sea, you know, and fall out o' the riggin', or get swamped in a gale, or killed by whales, and there ain't a house on the island, I expect, but what 's got a mourning piece hangin' up in the front room."

Captain Baxter wavered in his opinion as to when an i-n-*g* might be properly introduced at the end of a word.

" *A mourning piece !* " exclaimed Betty.

" A picture with a black frame, you know, of a fine moniment with a large weepin' willer hangin' over it on one side, and a weepin' widder on the other, with her face in a good-sized handkerchief. It says on the moniment, ' In Memory of So-and-so — Lost at Sea.'   I 've seen lots of 'em that had a dozen names on 'em.   Fast as the youngsters get big enough, they go off to sea, and then up goes their name on the moniment, prob'ly.   Yes, I expect there ain't a place where they make a reg'lar business o' mourning more 'n they do to Nantucket."

" What ridiculous people ! " said Betty. " What do they persist in going to sea for ? "

" Why, somebody 's got to ketch whales, or else you would n't have no sticks to your umbrels, nor bones to your dresses, nor oil to grease your ingines with."

" Well," said Betty severely, " I should let the people that wanted those things get them for themselves. *I* would n't go and drown *my*self in the sea, for the sake of other people having umbrellas to keep themselves dry."

" Now that *is* a comical way of lookin' at it. If Nantucket people could come to see it in that light, they 'd go down to New York and own railroads and live on kewpons instid. That 'd be a change for 'em."

" That 's what I mean to tell them," said Betty.

" Goin' to try to enlighten 'em some, hey ? "

" Oh, I want to make the children happy, that 's all, and show them that there are nicer places than that dreadful island, where they won't have to go to sea."

" Marv'lous man ! " exclaimed Captain Baxter, " you 'll ruin the whalin' business *com*plete ! I hain't the least doubt they 'll give right in an' say '*t is* 'nough sight better to live down to New York an' sail round in a harnsome yacht in pleasant weather, than 't is to live on Nantucket, or ketch whales the year round."

" How many of them could we carry on the Juno, do you suppose ? "

" Oh, stow 'em pretty close and I guess we could carry thirty or forty, day 'n' night ; but for just a day's sail we could carry two hundred easy enough."

" I should like to carry them all. Are there more than two hundred in all ? "

"I should say there was. I ain't good at guess-in' at children's censuses. I ain't sure but they come up to thousands."

"Oh," exclaimed Betty at the expanding pros-pect, "what a big island! I shall have to get papa to help me arrange things. There he is now!" and Betty alighted suddenly from her perch and flew away chirping, — "Here, papa! I'm here!" not doubting that the person her father was looking for was her own self.

Betty attached herself more entirely to her fa-ther, and was more in his especial care, because of her mother being a chronic nervous invalid, who was almost always away from home trying some new cure, and when she was at home she was not able to endure much of Betty's society, just as she could not bear tonics.

"I want to speak to you about something very particular," said Betty, pulling Mr. Vinton aside with an air of importance.

"Well, Betsy Baker, what is it?" and Mr. Vin-ton seated himself close beside Betty. "Is it a plan to send perfumes to the children of the Lap-landers?"

"Mercy, no! You'd better not try to guess; I'll tell you," said Betty, stretching her neck so as to reach her father's ear. "I want to stop at Nantucket, and get some of the dismal boys and girls there, and take them about, to let them see what nice places there are in the world, and how many good times. They don't know anything about it."

Betty began and finished with a very coaxing pat on her father's shoulder.

Mr. Vinton's moustache curled up more and more as he listened, and his teeth shone through it in a very cheerful way.

" What ! those web-footed youngsters ? " he said. " They could n't live away from their own sand and sea-weed any more than a fish could live out of water.   They 're used to it, and they like it."

" Oh, papa! I see you don't know anything about it," said Betty, spreading herself a little upon the strength of her superior information. "*How* can they like to live in such a dreary place? If they do, I 'm sure it 's very good and patient in them, or it 's because they don't know any better. If they knew how much nicer the rest of the world was, do you think they would stay there and be frozen up every winter, and as soon as they are big enough be sent to sea and *drowned ?* "

" Why, how came my little butterfly to know so much about the Nantucketers ? "

" Captain Baxter told me, and Aunt Grace."

" And what am I expected to do about it ? "

" Well, I should like to go there and see what we *could* do.   You would n't like to stop there now, would you ?   Oh, I wish you just *would !* "

" No, my dear, but you shall go there.   We 'll run down some day, and you shall see for yourself that these little sandpipers of Nantucket are really the happiest children in the world."

Betty tried to convince herself that she should

n't be sorry to find them so, but she was loath to give up the agreeable hope of being a benefactress, and said rather dubiously, " Oh, we shall see," as she reluctantly let her father slip away again to his guests, and then she too sat and watched the silvery sails turn rosy, and the sun go down into the flushed sea, and the same star that looked from a tender sky upon the little Nantucket girl smiled upon her; the same sweet evening that brooded over the lonely sea-rocked cradle spread its soft wings and took in Betty too.   An hour later and she also slept, and dreamed she saw the Nantucket desert blossoming as the rose.

There was hardly time for a dream, though, before the short summer night had flown.   You could see the tips of its black wings disappearing in the west, while in the east the early dawn just peeped through violet bars.

The Juno had lain becalmed nearly all night, but with the morning breeze she had started on again.

Confused sounds troubled Betty's slumber.   She stirred uneasily and tried to hold on to Nantucket. Her face rose like another dawn above the silken coverlet.   There was a lively stepping round and shouting on deck, and one white-robed figure before her was asking another what could be the matter.

" We 're putting about;   something 's wrong; hope nobody 's overboard," said a third ghostly presence.   " What a shame to have to heave to and lose this wind ! "

Then Miss Vinton's voice called to Maria to get dressed and go on deck as soon as possible and see what was the trouble.

Betty by this time sat up, as wide awake and ready to soar aloft as any lark. She heard a sound that she knew. They were letting down the boat. She resolved at once to soar as high as the deck, at any rate.

She slid quickly out of her berth, put on her wrapper and slippers, and peeping out of the saloon-door she heard the voice of one of the idols shouting up the companion-way, " What is it ?"

" We 've picked up a native," Mr. Vinton's voice responded from the deck.

" Papa ! papa," Betty sung out, " may I come up ? "

" Do, Betty," said Mr. Vinton. " Get dressed and come up directly."

" Mercy sakes, Miss Betty ! " called Maria, having heard Betty's voice, and coming down the stairs with a series of bobs and lurches determined by the rolling of the yacht. " Do let 's get your twilet made and come and see the queer little thing that 's come aboard ! She 's drifted away from home all alone in a little boat, and she thinks it 's evening."

This news created a little sensation throughout the yacht. In the excitable Betty it produced such spasmodic action as made everything turn the wrong way about, and tie up where it wanted to be untied, or *vice versa.* That " twilet " of hers was a wonderful sleight-of-hand performance, but Betty came out of it looking really a work of magic, and when she flashed up like a small piece of fireworks, and appeared suddenly before the stray little native on deck, — who was, of course, no other than our little Quaker girl, — Miriam's eyes blinked with the brightness.

It was n't Betty's pretty yachting suit, on which sparks of fire seemed to slumber in dark blue ashes, nor the gay little hat beneath which Betty's hair blew about in soft clouds, nor any of Betty's dainty belongings, marvelous as they seemed to Miriam, that dazzled her, but it was Betty herself, and her airy way of swimming along, and the bright glance which she darted here and there, and finally fixed upon her.   In all her dreams Miriam had never dreamed of anything half so beautiful as Betty.

And Betty thought there never had been such a droll-looking little body as Miriam. The sober gown, nearly touching her ankles, made her look like a very small woman, but the sweet face, with its wondering eyes and tender, quivering lips, was like a baby's.

"Mahomet need n't go to the mountain ; the mountain has started to come to Mahomet," said Mr. Vinton to Betty.

"Now what does that mean, papa?" Betty paused to inquire.   "Don't give me riddles to guess!"

"Why, this little girl appears to have come all

the way from Nantucket, to save you the trouble
of making a voyage there. She finds it such a
tolerable place that she is particularly anxious to
get back at once."

"Nantucket! Oh, you dear child!" exclaimed
Betty in a motherly tone (she was perhaps half
a year older than Miriam), "I'm sorry you were
drifted away, but how glad I am *we* found you!
Were n't you frightened? Do tell me all about
it!"

Miriam told the story of her forced voyage very
simply, without seeming conscious of the danger
she had escaped. She had gone to sleep watching
the approaching sail, and when she awoke, there
it was just beside her, as she supposed. The
long sleep had seemed a little nap, and she was
amazed when they told her it was morning.

Miriam's Quaker speech sounded very odd to
Betty. Everything about her was so odd, in fact,
that Betty was greatly delighted, as if she had
discovered a new species of being from an absolutely new world.

"I 've heard about Nantucket," she said. "I
suppose it 's rather a gloomy place."

"Oh, no, not Nantucket town!"

"Are you sure you like to stay there?" persisted Betty in a very skeptical tone.

"Why, ye-s," Miriam answered slowly, considering the matter for the first time.

"Is n't it dull and sandy and perfectly awful
winters?" Betty went on, in a manner which
meant, "Now don't deny *that!*"

"It is sandy, and it is n't as nice winters as it is summers, and before Joseph John came I was lonesome sometimes, and a good many times I 've thought I 'd like to see the rest of the world," said Miriam.

"Oh, I 'll show you a good piece of it," said Betty with satisfaction. "Who 's Joseph John?"

Then Miriam told Betty about Joseph, and presently she had told her about them all; her father, and Aunt Hepsy, and Rosanna; Aunt Dorcas, and Uncle David, and cousin Ruth; touching lightly upon Paul as a subject to be avoided, and giving sketches of her "cruises" over the moors and on the shore, of Amos Tuttle and his stories and the old mill, of Pel'tiah Groves, another old friend of Miriam's, and of various other places and people and things that lay within the narrow compass of her quiet island life. Betty feared that things had not been correctly represented to her, Miriam's pictures were so cheerful. She hardly dared to tell her she had been planning an expedition to rescue her and her fellow victims from an unhappy destiny.

"Don't all the boys go to sea and get drowned?" she asked.

"No, not all. A good many do, but there are some left."

"Now, what makes them do it?" demanded Betty, as if that were the trying question, after all.

"They like it, I guess. They need n't if they did n't. They might stay at home and dig graves

like Pel'tiah Groves, or grind corn like Amos Tuttle, or sell things."

"Oh, I thought they had to go, every one of
them," said Betty, and then she yielded herself to
the conviction that there was n't much of an opening for a benefactress on Nantucket, and concluded
to make the most of this individual case. Miriam
needed her now, surely, and she presently remembered that she was not making the most of her
opportunity.

"Do come," she said, "and let Maria braid your
hair, and "— Betty hesitated, taking in Miriam's
general appearance with a speculative look. "Maria will make you nice again," she continued,
"and you shall soon have breakfast, for we 're almost home. Where 's your hat?"

"My bonnet must have blown away," said Miriam. "I could n't find it."

"And you ought to have a sacque," pursued
Betty. "It 's chilly on the water; you ought to
have worn one."

"I did n't expect to be on the water, thee
knows," said Miriam, submitting to Betty's pat-
ronage quite gracefully.

"Oh, of course not. Well, you can have my
sou'wester hat and jacket, if you don't mind wearing them," said Betty.

"Shall I get to *my* home pretty soon?" Miriam asked anxiously, the undercurrent of trouble
that had been in her mind rising to the surface.
"They 'll feel so badly when they know I 'm lost."

"Papa'll send word. He'll telegraph right away, and we'll carry you home. Papa and I'll take care of you. Now don't you worry."

Maria, meantime, had brought a shawl and a cup of something Betty called "booee-yong," which Miriam drank and thought it tasted like beef tea.

"My stars!" said Maria, "the child's chilled through. There ain't much danger of taking cold of a summer night on *salt* water, if you have n't got anything but the sky over you for a coverlet, but it's the salt that saved her. She'd 'ave got her death o' cold if the sea was fresh water. Oh, the ways of Providence is wonderful!" And this good Presbyterian, who had been Betty's nurse ever since she was born, could n't have been shaken a hair's-breadth in her belief that everything had been so minutely as well as grandly ordered for us, that the very sea, for instance, had been made salt from the foundation of the world, to the end that Miriam might not take cold.

You should have seen Miriam holding reception when all the passengers of the Juno appeared on deck, each and every one "the glass of fashion." Whoever had an eyeglass put it up and inspected the little maiden. To this day she remembers some of the questions she answered and the remarks she puzzled over. They were all kindly, or meant to be. At any rate, considering these people had understood the inhabitants of Nantucket to be web-footed, and to have scales on their backs,

the fact that they left those particulars uninvesti-
gated offers plenty of ground for saying so.

"How do you account for that unruffled manner?" asked one of the idols of one of the belles.
"She's as modest as can be, but not the least embarrassed. She can't have had any breeding to
speak of."

"Oh, it's the Quaker manner, you know," answered the belle; "they are serene from principle
and then from habit, and serenity, of course, is
the soul of a good manner."

"Pity they are dying out, then, — that sect, —
their influence is wanted in this country amazingly, to correct the national flurry," observed an
idol, whose father had earned a great deal of
money for him, so that he had been able to devote
himself to the cultivation of an Anglican manner,
and who had lived abroad so much that he was
constantly mistaking himself for a European, re-
serving nothing of his birthright but the right to
find fault with Americans to their faces. "America is painfully crude and rough," he added, with
a sensitive shiver.

"I'm not going to be put down as crude and
rough," Mrs. Payne, the charming chaperon, declared. "I protest for myself and my country.
To be sure, the wine of life in America is still in
the fermenting stage, but where will you find, in
Europe, a child brought up in obscurity that
would have such a deportment as this child's?
How beautifully she bears her terrible adventure,

the present excitement, and her contact with unusual things. I call it positive refinement and
polish," and she appealed to the eminent Englishman.

"Ah, yes," he allowed, "it is fair to say that
refinement, or something of that sort, is diffusive
and general in this country, to a fault."

"I understand," said Mrs. Payne; "the fault is
that it does n't belong exclusively to a few. For
my part I should like the world, — society, — life,
— to be like an excellent pudding, with all the
sweetness and flavor and fruit evenly distributed,
and everybody to have his choice as to whether he
would eat it with sauce or without."

Of course there was a little outcry at the would-
be radical Mrs. Payne, and it was agreed to be a
misfortune, even by Mrs. Payne herself, in a general way, for such people as were destined to
forego the sweetening and flavor and sauce to get
an accidental taste of it, because it made the rest
of their pudding distasteful to them.

"Well," said Mrs. Payne thoughtfully, "I
should like to try an experiment with a good
wholesome nature, and find it ready to return to
the plain pudding with relish. The right sort of
nature gives a flavor of its own to everything, — a
finer flavor than art can compound."

"You 'd better join Betty's expedition," said
Miss Vinton. "She proposes to gather up the
children of Nantucket, and take them into the
world to give them a taste of pudding with
sauce."

"Really! Is that Betty's last whim? No, I should n't care to make such a general experiment; but I long to try an individual case."

"If I 'm not mistaken, you 'll have an opportunity by establishing an intimacy with Betty," repeated Miss Vinton, who thought she could foresee the results of Betty's whim, followed up as it had been by this interesting case in point.

Mrs. Payne declared she meant to cultivate Betty.

Meantime the sun had come up, as usual, and only the familiar assortment of adjectives is wanted to show that he never came up with greater credit to himself. The rocky shore drew nearer and broke out here and there with houses and clusters of houses. There was the sound of surf speaking in whispers, and presently they rounded a corner and came into Narragansett Bay. There was the ruined Fort Louis, the Dumpling Rocks, and a gloomy structure that Betty said was Fort Adams, and then had to tell Miriam what a fort was. "And there 's Newport!" she added, pointing to the large gathering together of houses and spires that rose and curtesied to the bay.

"*Newport!* Why, my father 's in Newport, at the Yearly Meeting!" said Miriam, staring at Betty with eyes that looked like a double-faced town clock in a very breezy tower. Betty returned the stare, with eyes that looked like another view of the same.

"Why did n't you tell me?" she cried. "Now

he 'll find you, or you 'll find him, and *he* 'll go and carry you home, so that papa and I can't do a thing ! "

Betty was disconcerted, but Miriam was radiant with satisfaction.

" Oh, I 'm glad this is Newport ! " she said. " I shall see Newport my own self ! What will they say when I tell 'em I 've been to Yearly Meeting — especially Aunt Hepsy ! And what will father say when he sees *me !* "

Miriam visibly dilated at the prospect of astonishing so many people. But Betty was aggrieved, and told her father, with an appearance of injury, that the little Nantucket girl had got a father in Newport ! Mr. Vinton, for his part, thought that was a capital arrangement, and promised to hunt up Obed Swain directly, but Miriam was, of course, to stay with Betty until her father was discovered.

Fancy Miriam landing at Newport under Betty's wing, and in Betty's jaunty sou'wester hat and jacket ! It was so warm when they came ashore that the jacket was superfluous; but Miriam felt the contact with such a pretty thing to be so agreeable that a little extra warmth was no consideration whatever.

Having never seen anything finer than old Jerry in her father's " shay " and the two-wheeled carts of Nantucket, she was all alive to the glories of the grand equipages that waited on the wharf, flattering the morning sunshine by borrowing gleams of its brightness. There was Betty's phaeton and ponies, and Miriam was seized with awe of the resplendent tiger, and amaze at Betty, who took the red ribbons and touched up the ponies in her ready breezy way. They rolled off over the smooth road so easily that Miriam, whose experience of deep ruts and sand and cobblestone pavements had made driving a horse and driving a nail associate ideas, — each a matter of overcoming resistance, — felt her heart leap to her throat again and again at the new sensation.

It is vain, however, to undertake to tell of Miriam's sensations. She had more in the course of an hour than could be described in a week by a person of average ability.

Imagine the little Nantucket mouse set down at very short notice in a charming Newport villa, and I need n't tell you that she had all the variations of wonder and delight that a child with longings for the beautiful — a child all fresh and alive — could have.

She had n't time to recover from the outside glories of a wide deep lawn, with far glimpses of gorgeous flowers, before the beautiful house was upon her, with new bewilderments.

Not the least of these was Betty's own room, where Miriam was taken along, like some favorite cat, when Betty went to make ready for breakfast. And besides Miriam, there were Bijou and Figaro and Nip and Nabob, Betty's beloved dogs, who pranced and danced and devoured Betty, or tried to, and strained their powers to the utmost to see which could bark the loudest, partly in welcome to Betty, and partly in defiance of Miriam, until Betty gave the command, " Down ! down ! lie down ! " when each chose some favorite nook and curled himself up, watching out of the corners of his eyes to make out, if he could, what was the use of that other girl there.

Betty's lovely nest, with the gauzy cloud of white drapery hovering over it, flushed like a sunset cloud with pink, made Miriam hold her breath. " That can't be a bed ! " she said to herself, " and yet it 's got pillows." And then the pictures, and all the pink and precious and pretty things there ! Imagine a young bee with its longing instinct for the rose, settling down for the first time into a world of roses !

" Now while I 'm in the dressing-room you can be looking at my books," said Betty, pointing to some low shelves. " Do you like books ? These are the ones *I* like best, on the upper shelf. Down there are the stupid ones, all about little girls that burst into tears whatever happens, or little girls sitting at windows and saying, ' There 's a cow ! How interesting ! ' I shall be back soon. I 'm only going to have my bath."

So Betty flitted away, and Miriam took down one of the books that Betty liked best. It was Laboulaye's Fairy Book. Miriam had never had a glimpse of Fairyland before.

Now to have discovered Newport and Fairyland

in one day, — all before eight o'clock in the morning, — you would suppose was enough for one girl,
would n't you ?

But no ; before the day was over, Miriam must
needs turn out to be a discovery herself.

CHAPTER IV.

MIRIAM had gone as far as the Castle of the Chinking Guineas with Violet, the daughter of Beppo, in her search after Perlino, and was breathing long sighs of emotion over the fairy fantasy, — alas, Aunt Hepsy and Ann Millet! — and it seemed to her there was nothing too wonderful to be true.   Considering her own adventures, it was easy to believe in the story of that young girl of Paestum.   And, besides, it was all there in print. Anything in print must, of course, be true.

This point of faith and experience she had reached when Betty made her appearance again, and added ground to her faith by being the most wonderful thing yet, and as real as flesh and blood could make her.

It happened that when Betty was in process of dressing, Maria had said to her, " Miss Betty, that 's a real little lady, that child, if she is old-fashioned and queer, and had n't you ought to have asked her to have a bath and get freshed up a bit too ? "

Come to think of it, Betty was sure she ought, and she made a graceful apology to Miriam, adding

" You see, I never had any person to take care of before, and I forgot. But you'll have time," she added ; " you and I will take our breakfast on the veranda whenever we please."

Miriam had a vague hope that if she submitted to the same process that Betty had passed through, she might come out radiant too, so she accepted the offer gladly, and went with Maria. If she did n't come out quite so radiant as Betty, she came out feeling fresh and looking as sweet as a violet. Maria corrected the arrangement of her hair by braiding it loosely and letting it hang à la Marguerite, instead of straining it back and bobbing it up à la Aunt Hepsy. The end she tied with a blue ribbon, according to Betty's suggestion, who also insisted that Miriam must have a fresh linen collar and cuffs. These small touches so improved Miriam that she was noticed a second time by the glasses of fashion, when she came down-stairs with Betty, and Mrs. Payne declared she would give anything to take that girl and try a grand experiment with her. How well that Quaker foundation would uphold the structure she wanted to build.

Mrs. Payne's own children had died in infancy, and some said it was a great pity, she would have made such an uncommonly good mother; but others differed, as contrary people will, at any rate, and wondered what she would have made of her children if she could have kept them. Mrs. Payne seemed inclined to illustrate this point, for she occasionally looked upon a child as she did upon Miriam, with a wish to apply her own theories to it. She had a nephew, an orphan boy, that she had called her own since before he could remember, but fortune had never yet favored her with the right sort of a girl.

Mrs. Payne had no one to consult but herself in such matters, for Colonel Payne, her husband, was kept abroad the greater part of the time by affairs.

Mrs. Payne preferred America to cosmopolitan wanderings, and the colonel gave her the American privilege of enjoying life, liberty, and the pursuit of happiness in her own way. She liked young people about her, and she was scarcely ever without them at her house in New York. Betty Vinton was especially a frequenter there, and Mrs. Payne passed the greater part of her summers with the Vintons at Newport. She was a bright, charming woman, whose best trait was her cheerfulness. Women usually want much compassion, but Mrs. Payne, although she had had much to grieve her, never drew upon her friends for that. This trait was well illustrated by the good spirits she was able to maintain in face of all those allusions to Nantucket, for Nantucket had sad associations for her.

She came out upon the piazza and chatted with the children while breakfast was being brought on. Mr. Vinton also appeared to say that he had inquired of a prominent member of the Society of

Friends in Newport, and found that Obed Swain had gone to Providence the evening before, and would return on the following morning. He also took Aunt Hepsy's address from Miriam, in order to send a telegram that would catch the Nantucket boat and reach Nantucket that evening. Miriam fancied Aunt Hepsy getting the telegram, -- or tried to.

"Now," said Mr. Vinton, "this little girl will have a whole day in Newport, and, Miss Betty Benevolence, you may lay your own plans and make it as great a day for her as you please."

At once Betty began to arrange, and Mrs. Payne was called into council. They would take all the drives and see every remarkable thing in and around the town. These were the plans to begin with, and Betty entreated Mrs. Payne to think of something more, but Mrs. Payne said Betty had already got more on her programme than could be performed in two days.

"Oh, there 's Rol!" said Betty, as a tall, sturdy boy stepped out of a window upon the piazza, followed by a superb Irish setter. "Come, Rol, and have breakfast here."

The boy came forward and exchanged a good-morning kiss with Mrs. Payne, who said to Miriam that this was her Rollo, and made Miriam at once an object of interest to him by telling him of her adventure in the boat, and how she had been picked up by the Juno. A boy will take into his fortified regards a person who has had adventures, so, after hearing this tale, Rollo condescended to take a seat at the table with the girls, though he was rather evasive of girls, in a general way.

"And, Rollo," said Mrs. Payne, "she came from Nantucket."

Rollo gave his aunt a look of understanding, and Miriam a stare which would have been adequate if she had been announced as one of the Dyak tribe.

"Oh, was that the place?" began Betty, and then stopped, for Mrs. Payne turned away with a look which checked her.

Rollo himself did not appear to desire a continuation of the subject, but exhibited a serious interest in breakfast, which just then was announced as being ready.

He seemed rather a silent boy. Almost the only visible attention he gave Miriam was to look at her curiously from under his projecting brows, and he ventured upon few remarks beyond such concise rejoinders as "Oh, gammon!" to Betty's animated speeches. His frequently recurring glance at Miriam seemed to indicate that she was a curious specimen, and Miriam wondered what Nantucket was to him, but she would n't have asked for the world.

The boy went so far, however, as to say, as a suggestion to Betty, in making her plans for the day, that he thought bluefishing, with now and then a chance at a shark, was the jolliest fun. He had been off two days bluefishing, and they had caught two sharks. The next thing to sharking was shooting buzzards. He rather scoffed at Betty's voyage on the Juno.

" Ho," said Betty, on the other hand, " I don't believe in your sharks and your buzzards."

" No? Don't you? Wait a little. I'm going to catch whales and shoot tigers some day."

" 'That would n't be much for *you!* " Betty said, laughing.

" It would be easier than dawdling about smoking paper cigarettes and saying, 'I beg pardon!' and 'No, thanks,' every five minutes. *I'm* going to smoke a pipe, and say ' Aye, aye, sir!' "

" Ugh! how perfectly horrid! " cried Betty, and breakfast then being finished she rose from the table and said she and Miriam would go to town.

Rol whistled to Monte Cristo, his dog, and vanished. In the wonderfully short time which it takes for a pair of brisk, long legs to run over stairs, two or three at a time, there was heard from somewhere above, the sound of a violin, pouring out the overplus of exhilaration with which a boy opens his eyes upon life. How the thing was made to rejoice! It was enough to gladden the old Giant Despair, himself, to hear it. And the boy had fineness of soul, too, when he could express joy like that. It was not a rollicking, uproarious rejoicing, but the gladness of a deep, healthful nature that had not learned the meaning of dread, and it was expressed with an almost vocal clearness and explicitness, and a touch of tenderness, too, by the boy who talked in strong figures of smoking pipes and killing tigers.

Miriam stopped to listen. It was a new sound to her.

"It's Roland Weir," said Betty. "They say he has almost a genius for the violin. He does play well, don't he?"

"But how does he do it?"

"Oh, have n't you ever seen them? I'll ask Rol to play down-stairs where you can see him, when we come back from town, if we can catch him, — he's always flying off. He'll be willing, for he's very good-natured, though you would n't think it. There are three things he's perfectly devoted to, — Mrs. Payne, and his violin, and ships. Mrs. Payne is so afraid he'll be a musician that she's almost willing he should be a sailor. She thinks he'll soon be cured of his liking for the sea, but he'll always be true to his violin. *I* don't believe he'll ever be cured of anything. He's dreadfully set."

By this time they had reached Betty's room, and that impatient young lady, in a passion for experiment, pulled the ribbon off Miriam's hair, and shaking it out, let it pour over her shoulders in deep ripples of sunshine and shadow. "Oh, how nice!" said Betty. "What pretty hair! You must wear it so. And you did n't bring any trunk, you know, so you must let me lend you some things. You will, won't you?"

Miriam hesitated. She was afraid it was n't right for her to be decked out in Betty's finery, but after all, this was her old gown, and she could n't expect Betty to take her out in that. She must submit to what the circumstances required. So she said " Yes," and crept out of her old brown chrysalis and took on the glory of a butterfly.

" Why," cried Betty, when Miriam's feet were going into a delicate pair of blue silk stockings, " your feet are just like other people's ! "

" Of course," said Miriam. " What did thee suppose they were like? "

" Why, papa said Nantucket children were web-footed, — like ducks, you know."

Miriam looked astonished. " May be the boys are," said she, trying to recall the general appearance of the bare feet she had seen paddling about on the island. But either they had skipped too briskly, or had plunged too deeply in the sand, she could n't recall a distinct impression of them. She resolved to look into the matter.

" There," said Maria, standing off and looking at Miriam with her head on one side, when she had given her the last finishing touch. " What do you think, Miss Betty ? "

" I think she 's nicer than any girl I know," said Betty, wringing her hands and curveting round Miriam with satisfaction.

" Good gracious ! " cried Miss Vinton, putting up her eyeglasses and staring at the converted

Miriam, when the two girls made their appearance down-stairs. "Was ever anything equal to the way Betty Vinton is allowed to go on? That little Quaker girl, right out of the wilderness, decked out in one of her newest and most stylish costumes! I do think it's a shame!"

But Mr. Vinton laughed, and said the only use for Betty's costumes, or any of Betty's belongings, was to please Betty, and she was to get her pleasure out of them in any way she liked.

The wilder Betty's notions were, the more they amused Mr. Vinton.

The little maiden, whose longing to mix with and appropriate the brightness of the world had expressed itself in the red bow and cherries with which she had tried to cheer up her solemn old bonnet, flushed with the pleasure of being in it and of it for the moment, and to a child the moment is all.

The ponies were at the door, and Mrs. Payne, as she watched Miriam's placid manner, her tranquil movements, while a dreamy delight beamed from her eyes, said, "She certainly is my ideal of a girl."

And Miriam was almost her own ideal, as she sat beside Betty and rolled down the beautiful avenue. She felt sure that not a soul of them all at home would know her, not even the cats. She hardly knew herself. And there was that sublime youth again, sitting up behind with Maria, folding his arms in such a superior fashion, and making

Betty do all the driving. He apparently did n't know she was the same little image he had driven up from the wharf that morning, for he did n't undertake to exterminate her this time with his stare, but when she dropped her parasol, handed it to her with a touch of his hat and an " If you please, Miss."

It was wonderful to see Miriam herself, but if Aunt Hepsy could have witnessed the sight she was, with her hair and her ribbons and her long white ostrich feather all flying in the wind, it would have been more curious to see Aunt Hepsy.

Betty had shopping to do, and she must go into all the shops herself with Maria, and Miriam must go too, to be sure.

While they were in the midst of this absorbing pleasure, Betty said, —

" Now I want to get something for you to take home to help you remember me, but I can't think of anything nice. What would you like it to be ? "

" Why I shall remember thee easy enough," said Miriam. " Thee need n't buy anything for *that*," and she laughed at the idea of forgetting Betty.

" Well, people always take home what they call 'souvenirs,' you know, and I want you to have a souvenir."

" Then," said Miriam, " I 'd like a book like that one of thine I was reading."

" Is that all ! " exclaimed Betty. " Do say something besides. You won't think of me when you 're reading that."

"If I had a picture of thee"—Miriam began.

"You shall have a *nice* one," said Betty.

Betty bought Laboulaye's Fairy Book, and many other charming things, and they came out of the last shop with their hands full of parcels, and were getting into the phaeton, when some one touched Betty's arm gently, saying,—

"My child, thee 's dropped one of thy bundles."

"Oh, thank you," said Betty, taking the parcel with a sweet smile from such a kindly looking man. "There," she cried, "you 've dropped *two*, Miriam."

Miriam was climbing into the phaeton, and the kindly man at the word "Miriam" turned back. Not that he expected to see any Miriam *he* knew in that gay little equipage, but there was a little girl named Miriam who was of interest to him, and for her sake he looked back at those pretty children. He looked back,— he stopped. There was something in the soft voice and that quiet little laugh that seemed so familiar, so sweet to him, that he wanted to hear them again. So he walked back and tried to peep into the cloud of sunny hair, and get a look at the child's face, who, singularly enough, had the name and the voice and the laugh of the child he loved best in the world. Miriam tossed back her hair and her sweet face was in full sight. She also made one of her peculiar little gestures and settled herself in her own prim way, which, in spite of the airy ribbons and ruffles, was as prim as ever. At that the benign man glared under his broad brim and said to himself, " I must be dreaming ! " and just as Betty was about to touch up the ponies, he stepped up beside the phaeton and stopped her with a motion of his hand.

" I want to ask " — he began, without the faint-est idea what he was going to ask. But Miriam, before he could say another word, or make up his mind what he wanted to say, reached out her arms and cried, " Father, father ! "

Well, I do assure you, that was a staggerer to Obed Swain. Two ideas tumbled and confused each other in his mind. He could n't clearly lay hold of either. A girl in a fluffy blue dress, all laces and ruffles and a great spread of sash, with a saucy white hat and floating feather and hair running riot over everything, — a girl of this de-scription calling *him* " Father ! " that was one idea. The other was his real, true, little Quaker Miriam, there in the town of Newport, all tricked out in the aforesaid decorations. He stared at her with such a stupefied look that Miriam was frightened.

" Father, father, don't thee know me ? " she said with a trembling lip.

" *It can't be !* " said Obed, still standing aloof, and wiping the perspiration from his face with an enormous silk handkerchief.

" Oh, it *is*, father ! I was lost in a boat and Betty's father brought me to Newport, and this is Betty. They said thee 'd gone to Providence."

"My daughter," said Obed, with a shaking voice, holding Miriam's hand tightly in his own, "I can't understand this at once. I want thee to come with me. Make thy hair decent, put on th' gown an th' bonnet, and I'll come and get thee."

"But, father, I had on my old gown," said Miriam, "and I lost my bonnet, so Betty lent me some of her things."

"Yes, yes," said Obed, with the suspicion of a tear in his eye. "Thee can tell me all about it by and by. Not now, not now. I want to see and thank whoever has cared for my child. Where shall I find him?"

Betty managed to find her voice and answered, and Obed, still in bewilderment, said he would come there for Miriam directly, and the phaeton drove on, the two girls dumb, each with her own emotion, Maria remarking to herself that "the ways of Providence was wonderful," and the tiger staring just as blankly into space as ever.

Miriam's mind was divided between sorrow and gladness. Her great day in Newport had come to an untimely end, but the joy of finding her father was a compensation. Betty, however, was melancholy, pure and simple. Her very choicest plans were nipped in the bud. She was so used to girls who had seen everything and been everywhere, that it was quite a new delight to entertain one who could be so easily astonished as Miriam. Betty, in short, who had never been able to as-tonish any one very much before, was expecting a whole day of sensation, wherein she was to be a wonder herself, and furnish wonders, with the ease of a magician or fairy, to the nicest little thing that ever was. Alas, however, the end had come! Obed Swain, instead of going to Providence, and staying there, like a reasonable man, must needs lie in wait to say an " Out, brief candle ! " to all her hopes.

" Oh, it 's too bad ! " she cried, in a deeply injured tone.

" I never saw father look so before," said Miriam, who could not forget the emotion she had seen in her father's usually placid face. " He looked — well, *frightened*, I guess it was."

" I should think he would," said Betty; " I 'm sure papa would be in a great state to meet me in Nantucket, and have me tell him I 'd come nearly all the way alone in a little boat." And putting her father in Obed Swain's place, she did n't know as it would be fair not to forgive him, this time.

The little Cinderella returned to her ashes; that is to say, to her old ashen-colored gown, and in what seemed a very short time, a carriage drove up the avenue, bringing Obed Swain. Remembering Miriam's lack of a bonnet, and having noticed that even among Friends the little girls in Newport wore hats, he brought her a simple straw hat, with a plain band of brown ribbon round it, some gloves, and a sacque, so that she was quite a proper-looking child to take along on the journey home.

Obed was greatly moved, in spite of a calm exterior, by the story of his little girl's perilous voyage. He wanted to keep her hand in his continually, as if she might slide away from him into danger again, or as if to assure himself she was there, quite safe and near. He was a man of much dignity and simplicity, and Mr. Vinton felt a great respect for him and the warmth of a father's sympathy. But Obed declined all offers of hospitality, saying it was his wish to take the train which would bring them to New Bedford in time for the Nantucket boat.

There was never more honest regret than that with which Miriam and Betty parted. At the last moment Betty brought her photograph and the fairy book.

"But thee 'll have nothing to make thee remember me!" said Miriam.

"Oh, send me a picture of yourself — *do!*" Betty answered, "though I have one already" — touching her forehead — "taken when you stood on the deck of the Juno this morning. No," she added quickly, giving a second touch to the region where her warm little heart was understood to be situated, "it 's *here!*"

Miriam took this puzzle along with her and studied it out on her way.

CHAPTER V.

WHEN Miriam brought up before Aunt Hepsy, on her return from Newport, in a rather sailorish-looking hat, her hair hanging in a soft braid, the end tied by a blue ribbon, and loose locks flying on her forehead, Aunt Hepsy settled back in helpless horror, and accepted the support of her high-backed rocking chair, a weakness in which she seldom indulged.

That lofty chairback seemed never intended to support Aunt Hepsy herself, but Aunt Hepsy's dignity rather. It gave her an appropriate background, and enhanced her appearance of rectitude, but beyond that it was of no use to one who was sufficient unto herself as to back, and as to most things. The fact that she yielded herself to its long-despised overtures was proof that she was very much overcome. Not that she looked at Miriam as the lost one found, for Miriam was supposed to be visiting at Aunt Dorcas's, and as she had declared her purpose to go home to tea the day before, the supposition at Aunt Dorcas's naturally was that she had gone home. The message sent by Mr. Vinton had not yet arrived.

"Thee makes me flesh c-r-ee-p on me bones!" rumbled the voice of Aunt Hepsy. "I 've a good will to say thee sha' n't go to Dorcas Haddon's again."

"Why, I 've been to NEWPORT!" Miriam almost shouted.

This announcement burst upon the air like something long suppressed which had suddenly found vent, and was followed by a faint chuckle. It seemed to Aunt Hepsy to resound through the universe.

" *What does thee say?* " she gasped.

"I 've been to *Newport!* " repeated Miriam.

Aunt Hepsy's mind struggled to lay hold of this bold and improbable assertion, while Miriam embraced Joseph John, who made his appearance promptly at the sound of her voice.

Under the inspiration of his wide-eyed wonder and admiration, Miriam poured forth the whole story of her adventures by sea and land, and the sensation she had been longing to produce was as profound as she could have wished.

Aunt Hepsy was dumb; but her dumbness said all that mere words would have been too poor to express. She uncorked and smelled of a bottle of camphor which stood on her work-stand, and sank into the uttermost depths of her chair.

And Joseph John fairly shivered with terror and delight.

But Obed was there to corroborate the incredible tale. He wavered in and out of the " keeping room " during the recital, in a gentle, deprecating way, to give such countenance as he could to the reckless vagrant. " There, there ! " he said softly, when Miriam's key was rather high, and her style of narrative somewhat too florid for Friendly ears.

" What is 't thee 's got there ? " Aunt Hepsy demanded, indicating Miriam's precious fairy book.

Miriam clutched it tightly. " *Don't* take it away ! " she cried.

" Let me see it, my child," said Obed kindly.

Miriam placed the book in her father's hands, who opened it slowly, almost fearfully, and looked intently at the first picture disclosed ; then holding his head back, he tried another focus ; held it at arm's length and tried still another ; then took it to the window, where there was more light.

" Curious pictures ! " he muttered to himself, and turning the leaves, he fell upon such passages as these from Abdallah : —

" Whoever obeyeth God, they shall be with those unto whom God has been gracious, of the prophets, and the sincere, and the martyrs, and the righteous, and these are most excellent company."

" Acknowledge that there is but one God alone ; remain steadfast in the faith ; instruct thyself ; bridle thy tongue ; repress thy wrath ; forbear to do evil ; associate with the good ; screen the faults of thy neighbor ; relieve the poor by thine alms ; and expect thy reward in eternity."

"But the reading is excellent, most excellent," continued Obed, to himself. "I think,"—scrutinizing the curious pictures again,—"I think these must be some of the visions of the Revelation. I must see that Miriam is not deprived of this book." And he slid that budget of brilliant, delightful, Frenchy, fantastic fancies, and those good old Mahometan doctrines into his deep, safe pocket.

Meantime Aunt Hepsy had advanced to other points of attack.

"Thee come and have thy hair put up!" she said.

"Well, now," interposed Obed, "I guess we 'll leave that about as 't is. I was thinking it looked a deal more comfortable, and I noticed that Friends' children had it so at Newport."

"And *that head-gear ?*"

"Yes, yes," Obed said, in a pacifying tone; "I 'm considerable pleased with that. It keeps the sun out of her eyes."

At this probable defeat, Aunt Hepsy armed herself with her knitting work, and again renouncing her chairback, fought a silent round on her stocking. The stabbing and fencing of the needles appeared to give the necessary vent to her feelings.

"Thee go tell thy story to Joseph John," said Obed to Miriam, with the intention of clearing the field.

Miriam, well content, made a careful disposition of her rescued head-gear by holding it safely under her arm, and twining the other in Joseph John's, retreated with him to their place on the spider-legged, haircloth sofa in the south room, to show Betty's picture. This called for a long flow of eloquence on Miriam's part, and renewed and expanded admiration on the part of Joseph John.

The evening was chilly, although it was mid-summer, and Rosanna made the excuse of lighting a fire on the hearth, in order to hear this voluble narration, which had resounded to the uttermost parts of the house. .Miriam recapitulated with great willingness to a crescendo accompaniment of sobs, suppressed outcries, and ejaculations of " Oh, my king ! " " Oh, my good king ! " "Oh, marciful man ! " from Rosanna. " *Don't* go h'istin' up into de clouds so much, *don't* my lamb ! " she prayed, when Miriam had finished. " Som'n' dreffle 'll happen to yo' some day ef yo' don't take keer."

Rosanna's tenderness for Miriam was even greater than the benevolence of the Swains to-wards herself. She had been sent to the protec-tion of Obed 's father, over the " underground railway," when she was a girl, and her faithful service of nearly thirty years had been a service of love and gratitude. Miriam was the apple of her eye. She considered it her principal mission in life to watch over and defend her from real and imaginary ills.

But the present ill was several hours of fasting for the precious voyager, and Rosanna hastened to redress that as soon as possible. After the enticing biscuits, the daintily printed butter, the tall glass pitcher of milk with its richer relative, the squatty silver jug of cream, and little cakes in the forms of hearts and rounds had been shown to their places on the table, Rosanna introduced the last and most distinguished viand, — a hot corn pudding; then went up the fragrant incense of tea, and the two branches of the house were summoned to discuss matters in which they were likely to agree.

You would have admitted that to be a charming table. The old-time Quakers eschewed worldly vanities, but they had vanities of their own. Their very simplicity, originally a mark of self-denial, developed into a certain pride and a fashion more absolute than that of the world. The Quaker garb is — we may almost say was, there is so little of it now — a strict mode, and the study of its quality a nicer and more absorbing care than that which a New York belle gives to her toilettes. In drawing the line between themselves and the world, the Swains took care to include on their side the choicest of linen and the daintiest of old glass and china. The plentiful silver glittered with fastidious care, and any edible which had found its way to that table was, upon that sole evidence, the most perfect specimen of its kind.

But they were very silent people who sat about this cheerful-looking board. Hepsy Swain's was the solemn silence of a vessel freighted with so much rectitude; Obed's at this time was the reactionary pause after unaccustomed excitement, and the children were never expected to produce much table-talk upon any occasion. So the tea and the milk and the cream flowed in place of conversation, and the various dishes moved about so quietly that you could have heard the fire humming faintly on the hearth in the next room, and the light flames leaping to embrace each other, as they danced up the chimney.

At length the silence was broken by Peleg Bunker, the mail carrier, blowing his wheezy horn at the gate, and Rosanna went out to get the letters.

Peleg carried the mail to Siasconset and left letters at a few places on his way. He was always seen seated upon a bob-tailed horse, from which no person in 'Sconset had ever seen him alight, and he was looked upon there as a species of centaur.

Rosanna brought in three letters, which called for three pennies, and Obed proceeded to hunt for these. But pennies were scarce in his pockets, for he had just returned from a tour in which pennies had scattered themselves with amazing briskness. He turned over his wallet and shook it coercively over the corner of the table before he could persuade a third penny to come out. When it did come, however, it was followed by a tiny gold ring, which rolled across the table-cloth and dropped itself beside Joseph John's plate.

"Oh," he cried, as if in joyful welcome, and

" Oh, oh," Miriam cried, in accents of admiration. "Where did thee get that, father ? "

Obed looked astonished, and made the same inquiry of himself. " Why, that," said he, at length, " that is Joseph John's ring that John Dagget's wife gave me. I had forgotten about it."

" *Mine ?* " cried Joseph John.

" Thee had it on thy finger when thee was brought ashore from the wreck."

The children's heads came together, and they looked with intense curiosity at this link between the known and the unknown in Joseph John's life, — this mute suggestion of lost and forgotten things.   Joseph was allowed to keep it, and after much consideration and consultation the children carefully secreted the treasure in a very mysterious place.

Rosanna began as soon as tea was over to spread the tidings of Miriam's escape from the jaws of death.   Before the lamps were lighted, Aunt Dorcas came.   The tears were in her eyes, while she held Miriam in a long embrace, much to Miriam's amazement, for she could see nothing to cry about. She had had proud experience.   Even Amos Tuttle must allow that he had had no adventure more remarkable than hers.   And as from hour to hour and day to day a freshet of neighbors and relatives and friends poured in upon Miriam, it began to seem an undisputed fact that she was a distinguished traveler.

Even Paul treated her with marked consideration, and made her a visit of approval.

"Thee's brought some of the fashions back from China," was one of his observations upon this occasion.

Miriam looked at him dubiously.

"That pig-tail," Paul specified, nodding at the new arrangement of Miriam's hair.

"It's the way they wear it at Newport," asserted Miriam, with the air of one whose authority may be trusted in such matters.

"It's a handy thing," said Paul.

"Handy?"

"I will explain my meaning by an illustration or two," said Paul, reaching out his arm, which was like an ourang-outang's, and almost laying hold of the glossy rope.

Miriam backed up against the wall.

"We'll waive that subject, then," said Paul. "It might lead to disagreement. I suppose thee don't intend to take another voyage, at present?"

"I don't know," in a very contrary tone.

"Because, I was going to say," continued Paul, "that if thee had, perhaps, done with the boat, I hoped thee would do me the favor to return it. No particular hurry, thee knows."

"Was it *thy* boat?" cried Miriam.

"Well, it *was*, yes; thee's put it in the right tense."

"Oh," sighed Miriam, "I forgot all about the boat!"

"I won't be hard on thee," said Paul, with a

great show of magnanimity. "I 'll charge it against thee on my books, and thee can pay me when thee 's able."

"*How* can I pay thee?" pleaded Miriam.

"Well, as I have n't any boat, thee 'll have to amuse me in some other way. That 'll make it square."

Poor Miriam felt that at this cost her voyage would be a dear one.

"Come," persisted Paul, "thee might begin now. If I had a boat I should be off sailing, but I can't think what I 'm going to do. Seems to me thee might try to amuse me a little."

"Why, Paul, I 'm sure I don't know what to do."

"Well, there!" grunted Paul, throwing himself on a sofa, as if abandoning himself to his unfortunate predicament. "Here I am without any boat, my health poor, all run down with hard work, overtaxed brain, doctor says I must have recreation, — be diverted. What kind of a divert do you call this, gentleman of the jury?" he concluded, with a wave of his hand and a roll of his bulging eyes at Joseph John, who had all the while sat staring in unwinking perplexity.

"I 'll get father to take us over to Quaise and we could have a clam-bake," suggested Miriam.

Paul waved off this proposal with a sweeping gesture as something beneath consideration. Then shaking his head slowly and sadly he pressed his handkerchief to his eyes.

> " Football is all that 's left me now,
> Tears will unbidden start ! "

he muttered.

" Joseph John," said Miriam, after some deliberation, " thee might show Paul thy little ring."

Paul looked up at Joseph John with a half-resigned, half-expectant look.

" Oh, yes," the boy assented with apparent gladness, and after paying a visit to the mysterious place already mentioned, he returned with his treasure in a little pill-box.

" It 's the ring Joseph John had on his finger when he was saved from the sea," explained Miriam.

Paul gathered himself up and condescended to examine it with an appearance of interest. It was not for nothing that his eyes stuck out of his head in such a curious way. They could see the smallest mite imaginable. After holding it close to those protuberances for a moment, " What 's this ? " he said. " R-o-l-a-n-d W-e-i-r, — Roland Weir."

Miriam held her finger on her lips and stared speechlessly at the floor, as if recovering some lost idea.

" Why," she said, at length, " that 's the name of the boy at Newport ! "

CHAPTER VI.

"Here, Betsy Baker," said Mr. Vinton, "here's a parcel for you from Nantucket."

Betty attacked its coverings at once, and "Oh, how perfectly lovely!" she cried, as there came to light an exquisite ivory box, an entire piece of carving, of that miraculous fineness which is only produced by the Chinese.

"Only see, papa! Look, Mrs. Payne! Look at it, Aunt Grace! Isn't it a beauty?" cried Betty, carrying her box about with much display. She laid it in Miss Vinton's lap and raised the cover, disclosing the expected photograph and a note.

"There's Miriam!" Betty shouted, holding up the picture. "But there's a boy, too; Joseph John, I suppose."

She left the picture with her Aunt Grace, who glanced at it with feeble interest and passed it to Mrs. Payne. Mrs. Payne was always interested in everything, and she continued to gaze at the picture, appearing to derive a certain sensation from it, while Betty read her note and then followed her father, who had taken his morning papers and letters out upon the piazza.

" Grace," Mrs. Payne said, holding the photograph towards Miss Vinton, " does that boy remind you of any one? Look at the way he holds his head ! "

Miss Vinton assumed an air of interest. " Why," she said, as if considering, " do you mean — your brother Roland ? "

" Yes, he looks more like Roland than his own boy does. Rollo does n't inherit anything on our side. He may resemble his mother's ancestors. He surely is n't like her, either."

" I suppose you never really thought there was any doubt " — began Miss Vinton.

Mrs. Payne stared blankly at her friend.

" Doubt of what ? " she desired to know.

" Why, I should n't like to put any notion into your head, Anna," pursued Miss Vinton, with the cumulative readiness of one who has held her tongue for many years, " but I always thought you were easily satisfied in regard to the identity of that child."

" *Easily satisfied !* " cried Mrs. Payne, in a tone of half amazement and half resentment. " I did n't ask for more than absolute proof, of course. The man was recognized and identified by his papers as an old sailor from the Aurora, and his thorough honesty well attested. And there was the necklace that I sent the baby myself, with the mark, names and date ; and I 've never had any more doubt that Roland was my Roland's boy than I have that I am my father's daughter. What would you have done? Come."

"I? Oh, I don't know. I might possibly have gone down to the island and made some inquiries."

"What inquiries were there to make? Did it seem likely that any one could know more than one of the wrecked sailors himself, who brought the child directly to me in his own arms? Could I have asked for better testimony than that?"

"No; oh, of course not. But I always felt as if I should have wanted to see the place and know just what did come ashore. However, I am one of those persons who must ask just one question more after a story is all told."

"Well, this question is a most disagreeable one. Let us consider that it has been sufficiently discussed, and for the last time."

Mrs. Payne drew back into her chair and closed her lips tightly, to indicate her own withdrawal from the conversation, while Miss Vinton, having relieved her mind, was already tired of the subject.

The photograph stood on the table beside Mrs. Payne, and she again turned to it with a scrutinizing look, which gradually fell into an absent, undiscerning expression, while her mind went back to her girlhood, when the pride of her heart was her brother Roland. For the space of a long dream she saw him, as a boy, as a volatile youth, with spirits chiefly in *allegro*, but dropping frequently to *penseroso*, when he looked up with a peculiar sidewise droop of the head.

Sighing, she awoke from her dream, and her

eyes fixed upon Joseph John's picture again. She arose and moved quickly out upon the piazza.

Betty was in a twitter of excitement, for one of Mr. Vinton's letters was from Obed Swain. It contained some information which Mr. Vinton did not see fit to divulge at once, but it formed the ground of a suggestion, which he had just made, that Betty should carry out her plan of an expedition to Nantucket, and as Mrs. Payne came out, he also proposed that she should take command of the expedition. He could not, himself, before the last of September, and Betty was eager to embark at once. He would put them in the care of Captain Baxter.

" For we 're to go in the Juno," said Betty.

" And Betty prescribes that you are to accept the standing invitation of Mr. Swain to be his guests, whenever you do go," added Mr. Vinton.

" Of course," pleaded Betty to this charge.

" To be sure; by all means," Mrs. Payne agreed, and the whole plan was soon settled.

Just as they reached this final point, the shrill note of a very resolute whistle came upon their ears.

" We are three jolly, jolly sailor boys," was the tune which pierced the air, blown from a pair of vigorous lungs. The performer himself came presently in sight, with a rifle on his shoulder, his hat tipped back on his head, and a generally easy aspect. Behind him trotted Monte Cristo, with the settled air of a dog who is sure of his master.

The whistling ceased as the whistler came in sight of the persons on the piazza. Having planted his rifle in a corner, he took a seat beside Mrs. Payne, fanning himself with his hat, and giving expression to his feelings in an occasional " whew," for the day had grown warm, and the boy as well.

" Why, Roland," said Mrs. Payne, " you look like a ranchman, or a miner, straight from the wilderness."

" Do I ? " Roland asked, pausing for an instant in his fanning, with a look of cheerful satisfaction.

" And oh, my dear, what a sight! " continued Mrs Payne, looking with dismay at the blackness of Roland's hands, which was a combination of sunburning and, I am sorry to say, that crisis which calls for soap and water. " I really cannot endure this sort of thing. Why don't you come and read to me sometimes, or play croquet with Betty ? "

Roland sighed and looked miserable.

" Now," resumed Mrs. Payne, " I am going to ask you to let me see more of you than I have done recently. I shall expect you to go with me to Nantucket in a day or two. I wish, Roland, I could see you growing more like your father." There was a tone of despair in Mrs. Payne's voice.

Roland pushed his soiled and rumpled cuffs up under his coat sleeves, with a blush, and forgot to fan.

" What is *that ?* " Mrs. Payne asked, bending

nearer, and examining a dark blue stain on one of Roland's wrists with an inquisitive frown.

Roland uncovered his arm. It was tattooed with figures in India ink: an anchor, a constellation of stars, and the initials R. W.

Mrs. Payne stared at the disfigurement in dumb consternation. Her Roland's boy, the Weir flesh, indelibly stained with those vulgar devices!

"Roland," she said at length, in a low, cold voice, "I have always had hope of you, but I see I must give it up. It seems as if you were not my boy at all."

Roland mused over this speech, an indefinable trouble in his face.

"I wish I could be the kind of boy you like," said he, slowly and thoughtfully, pulling his hat round and round in his hands. "I do try, but I don't believe I 'm good for anything but a sailor."

"You 'd best go and wash your hands and change your cuffs," Mrs. Payne said. "Don't talk about being a sailor. You know that 's absurd. We must make the best of things."

Roland rose, hesitated, as if about to say something more, and then moved slowly away.

He was not a model boy. The very towel on which he wiped those objectionable hands, after washing them in his fashion, bore witness in distinct smooches that he was not a very tidy boy. He suspected himself of being a failure, — poor Roland, — and he often said to himself that if he could only have been blessed with the Weir features, even the Weir upper lip, or the Weir weak eyes, his other deficiencies would nave seemed more excusable. Lacking these, and so much else, he felt that he was an unsatisfactory article, which ought to be returned.

As he made the desired changes in his toilet, he glanced at two pictures that stood upon a table in his room, that were always kept before him as the *raison d'être* for everything that he was not, and finally, when he had reached the point where he considered himself unexceptionable as to neatness, he stood before them, with the intention of surveying all that which he had missed.

There they were, there they all were, those traits that he ought to have had. There were his father and mother, the ones he must be like in order to win regard in this world, and reward in that vague, inconceivable place where they had gone.

But the ones he felt himself to be absolutely like were those hardy fellows who bore bravely the perils of living, with no thought of special reward. Having visited the ships at the wharves with much frequency, he had felt himself attracted by the bronzed sailors. They had returned his regard with delightful cordiality; had spun him yarns without end, and tattooed his arm with pleasure. When he had watched them, ready to sail on their voyages, the brave ships with their top-s'ls and courses loose, their jib hanging waiting from the boom, the halyards ready to run up, and the pilot shouting " All ready? " he longed to shout back yes, he was ready, he wanted nothing but to go ; and when he heard the brisk orders, and saw the sailors jumping to obey, he could hardly hold his feet to the shore.   He looked long at his father and mother, then turned from them to his mirror and the picture there, — the picture of a broad - shouldered, overgrown boy, with a large head, crowned with a mass of short curls of an indefinite color, a brow which projected far over a pair of bluish-gray eyes, a boy's round chin and full lips, that were just then parted with a look of sorrowful, earnest inquiry.   His chief attraction, that expression of honest, simple manliness, was quite unapparent to himself.   He saw nothing but the great sunburned boy, with the anxious look on his un-Weir-like face.

" It seems to *me* so, too," he said at length.

CHAPTER VII.

NOT long after Betty's expedition landed at Nantucket, there happened the first excitement that ever broke the serenity in the old Swain house.

Mrs. Payne's first sight of Joseph John, the first accents of his voice, which had the charming peculiarity of seeming to touch a minor note, thrilled her like old associations.

Joseph John stepped into the doorway and stood gazing at her with that pensive, sidewise droop of the head which Mrs. Payne had noticed in his picture, for Obed Swain would have no head-rests, no posing, no artificial adjustments when his children were photographed, and Joseph John looked at the camera just as he looked at everything that greatly interested him, just as he looked from the doorway at Mrs. Payne, just as his father had looked at her, years ago.

Mrs. Payne started nervously.

"This is your son?" she asked of Obed, and held her hand out to the boy, who approached and gave his own in return. Mrs. Payne kept it a moment.

" He makes me credulous," she said, slowly, " of that theory of the reincarnation of souls. If my brother can have been born again into this world, I am sure he has been given to you, Mr. Swain. The soul of Roland Weir seems to look at me out of these eyes. Should you think you had seen me before ? " she asked, pursuing the fancy, and smiling down at the boy.

" Ye-yes.   I don't know," he answered.   " I often think I 've seen things before. That name is in my little ring."

" What name ? "

" Roland Weir."

" *In your ring?*   Why, what do you mean ? "

Obed had the ring in his vest pocket in anticipation of this moment. He reached it to Mrs. Payne in silence, and she, taking it to the light, examined it with an eyeglass.

" What does it mean ? How did your son find this ring, Mr. Swain? Where did he find it ? " she asked in amazement.

" The ring is his own," said Obed, " and the boy himself is only mine until he is claimed by some one who has a better right. He is a child who was rescued from the wreck of the steamer Aurora. We have only recently discovered this name in the ring he wore at the time, and I see thee has the same in thy family."

Mrs. Payne stared blankly from one boy to the other.

" Merciful Heaven! What mystery is this ? "

she said, sinking into a chair. "Let me think! Let me try to think!" She pressed her hands to her face for a long silent interval, during which Miss Vinton's words seemed to repeat themselves triumphantly, " You were very easily satisfied about the identity of that boy."

" Rollo!" she cried, looking up at length, but she did not continue, and Rollo made no response. He only sat pale and still.

Then Mrs. Payne, looking wild and half unwilling, persisting in her own mind that she could not have been so cheated all those years, took the hand of the boy with the Weir look, and drawing him to her side, gazed long into those eyes where she seemed to see the soul of Roland Weir; then, yielding to an irresistible impulse, gathered him in her arms and sobbed nervously, thinking chiefly of the one he was like, and realizing nothing so much as the improbability of the situation.

As she held the boy she had never seen before in her arms and wept over him, the boy who had been there by mistake so many times looked on with the feelings one may be supposed to have when the very end of all things has arrived, when the heavens and earth are melting away.

To Aunt Hepsy, Mrs. Payne's was an unseemly exhibition of emotion, let the case be what it would, and she motioned to Miriam to leave the room.

Miriam, although she could not fully comprehend the situation and its consequences, was full

of a vague anguish. She and Betty retreated to
the north room, and the boy who was n't a Weir,
feeling that he, especially, could be excused,
slipped out at the garden door and wandered
about among the properly restrained flowers and
the meritorious herbs, and finally sat in Miriam's
seat under the quince-tree.

Who was *he*, then, and to what must he return?

Long he sat there, bowed and lonely, suffering
the after agony of the blow that had cut him off,
and it seemed as if he were forgotten, until Mrs.
Payne, smitten with recollection and a rush of
tenderness and pity, sent for him to come to her,
when she kissed him and wept over him, too. It
was impossible for her to talk. She was overwhelmed.

There seemed to Rollo to be a terrible hush in
the house; everybody looked at him drearily, Miriam's eyes were red with weeping, and in his ears
was the constant sound of Mrs. Payne's first sobbing cry. Again he escaped; this time into the
street.

Rollo's quiet way of receiving his sudden trans-
lation from the high regions of her relationship to
the low regions of no relationship at all misled
Mrs. Payne. She did not at once guess that he
was dumb from the weight of his sorrow, and
from a half-benumbed sense of his loneliness and
destitution in surrendering all the people and
things which he had loved and appropriated, as

a matter of course, through his remembered life, to this strange boy, of whom he must feel that he had been borrowing them.

But when the hours moved on and Rollo did not make his appearance, Mrs. Payne was alarmed and went restlessly from window to door, asking again and again, " Has nobody seen Rollo? Can no one tell where he has gone ?"

He was a very punctual boy, usually. It was a part of his honesty that he gave himself always at the right time, and Mrs. Payne waited for him the more impatiently because she had been unaccustomed to wait in vain. There was much running about, calling, searching, and inquiring for Rollo, and meantime the sun did not stand still. As the day drew towards its close Mrs. Payne, with some newly awakened sense, guessed it all. Obed had already searched for the boy to the extent of all but one possibility, and he encouraged Mrs. Payne by telling her she would be almost sure to hear something of Rollo soon, for he had sent out Bela Ketchum, the town crier, to announce his disappearance. Any one who had seen the boy, or knew anything of him, would probably be reached in this way. Bela Ketchum was the advertising medium of Nantucket. He rang his bell at the street corners and shouted the various wants and losses of the people, the bargains they might find in special places, the amusements to be expected in the town hall, the times of the steamers' starting, etc. It always seemed as if the utmost possible was being done about a matter when Bela Ketchum gave his voice to it.

Mrs. Payne soon heard the far-away cry, "Lost! L-o-st!" and, more indistinctly, the description of Rollo, the time of his disappearance, etc.

All Rollo's faults vanished from her memory, and she thought of him with the solemn tenderness with which we remember our lost ones. Their kindest actions, their noblest qualities, become heroic, and their commonest words and deeds, since they are lost, lost, are invested with a sacredness which never pertains to the things we hold in sure possession. Mrs. Payne remembered Rollo's steadfast honesty, his brave manliness, the distasteful things he had sometimes struggled through for her sake.

Nearer and nearer came the town crier's clanging bell, and she could hear all he said; his description of Rollo: his eyes, his hair, the fashion of his dress, his being tall and straight, and it cut her to the heart to have this shouted upon the public street.

Fainter and fainter again grew the sound of the bell and the voice until it died away from Mrs. Payne's outward hearing, but in the deep inner silence it still reverberated like a wail.

The thought that Rollo had accepted his new destiny by removing himself in that silent way to a life of absolute loneliness was intolerable.

Lying sleepless in the darkness, that night, Mrs.

Payne could never shut out the plaintive voice which cried " L-o-st — l-o-st !" and though she had the genuine Roland Weir with the Weir look and the Weir bearing and the Weir blood safe in the next room, she turned her face to her pillow and wept.

CHAPTER VIII.

PEL'TIAH'S TWO VISITORS.

MRS. PAYNE had gone to Newport with her veritable Roland Weir and a sorrowful heart. Nothing had been heard of the lost boy. In Miriam's opinion there were two lost boys. She thought with understanding and sympathy of Violet, when the Lady of the Clinking Guineas carried off Perlino.

Let us consign to forgottenness, however, the few weeks that followed, with all the sorrow they held for the poor little maiden. "To the old, sorrow is sorrow ; to the young, it is despair." But sorrow that can be wept out upon a father's sympathetic breast is pain with the healing balm applied, and is already half assuaged. And, besides, Miriam profited by the compassionate sympathy which her friends felt for her loss and loneliness, and enjoyed unusual privileges. Life had its compensations. By her father's intervention, Aunt Hepsy's government had so many mitigations that she felt almost as free as the inmates of a certain old abbey, whose only rule was, "Do whatever you like." She was to go to school to cousin Ruth, whose acquirements were considered remark-

able, since they were obtained at a Philadelphia
school ; and she was even allowed to have Laboulaye's Fairy Book, which had been consigned to
Aunt Dorcas's protection, where it was kept as an
addition to the charm of her frequent sojourns at
Aunt Dorcas's. And at length it came to pass
that Miriam and Rosanna went to live with Aunt
Dorcas, while Obed Swain went to Trinidad, and
Aunt Hepsy was called to go and stay with an invalid sister.

Obed's worldly goods had come to him chiefly
from an ancestor who had carried on a large trade
which had seemed to Obed's father, Isaac Swain,
monstrously wrong. It consisted in bringing molasses from the West Indies to New England,
where it was made into rum. The rum was taken
to Africa and exchanged for slaves. The slaves
were brought to the West Indies and sold or exchanged for molasses again. Isaac Swain had
thought about this wrong until he felt urged to
make some personal restitution, insignificant as
an individual effort of this sort would be in view
of the thousands who had been affected. Still, he
reasoned that if he did all he could, his own contentment would be greater, however small and fu-
tile that all might be. He bought a tract of land,
therefore, in Trinidad, which he divided into comfortable farms, or plantations, and placed upon
them a little colony of negroes. In time he was
joined by others whose opinion was similar to his
own. Some kindly members of the Society of

Friends were sent there to look after the negroes
and teach them to manage with prudence and skill,
and a very thrifty community was the result.
Obed still retained an interest in what had been
his father's enterprise, and went to Trinidad occasionally to look after certain remaining interests
there. This time his stay was to be all winter.
To live with Aunt Dorcas would be Miriam's consolation.

Aunt Dorcas was the most liberal of Quakers,
and had never built a very high wall of exclusion
about herself, but had left many a chance for what
was beautiful and joyous, in that world which the
Quakers shun, to enter her own life, and still more
the lives of the dear young people about her. She
held that it was a sin to be gloomy, and encouraged only the most comfortable shadows. She
would have sunshine of all kinds. The carpets
faded, but faces kept their brightness wonderfully
within Aunt Dorcas's borders.

In spite of Aunt Dorcas's sunshine, however,
and the general agreeableness of things, in spite
of the engrossing occupation of packing away the
various sorts of knowledge that would be wanted
in the experience of protracted living, Miriam
sometimes found that the days were long, and that
there were a good many of them. She was nearly
thirteen, and was supposed to have put away childish things, if indeed there had ever been childish
things to put away. She had never had a doll,
for Aunt Hepsy's interpretation of the second

commandment was so untainted by reason that she regarded dolls as sinful creations. In the days of her earlier youth, Miriam had occasionally indulged in a very sober tea, with clam-shell dishes, in company with a little Quaker neighbor, who was now laid away to sleep in the old Quaker burying-ground, where Miriam sometimes went and sat among the mullein stalks and milkweed, and contemplated with awe, tempered to pleasing softness by the familiar sunshine, the mysterious barrier between her and her old cheerful companion. She had a feeling of continued companionship in that place, and when, as I have said, the days seemed long and many, she had sometimes brought clam shells and had tea by Rachel Gardner's quiet bedside. She had a feeling that this also contented Rachel, and she brought, besides, the innocent dreams by which she possessed the unattainable.

The prince of dreamers has said that " we have received from heaven a gift which brings all that we desire close to us, which makes it sensible and present before us, which delivers it over to us," and this gift of heaven was rich and large in Miriam.

And besides the clam-shell dishes and her dreams, there was yet something more that she brought at last when she visited Rachel Gardner. At the advanced age of nearly thirteen she had one material pleasure come to her which had been denied to her earlier years. Paul dragged Friend

Polly Hopkins down from the garret one day, and seated her in a chair in Miriam's room. Polly was cousin Ruth's old Quaker doll, which had been put away in the garret with other choice relics of the past. She had a pretty face, and was dressed from top to toe in complete Quaker garb. Well, there she continued to sit, day after day, until Miriam felt as if she were a friend and companion, and poured her little secrets, her emotions and opinions, into Polly's safe ear, and the reliable Polly always smiled sweetly, which seemed to show her responsive. Miriam was much afraid that others would not appreciate this friend as she did, and protected her from unsympathetic contact by never presenting her. But when she went to the old burying-ground, during that autumn at Aunt Dorcas's, Polly was wrapped securely from observation and taken along, still smiling cheerfully, to the loneliest spot on that lonely island, where Miriam, in sweet companionship with her two silent friends, passed hours of quiet contentment.

Polly's perpetual, complacent smile would have discouraged some girls, for Miriam sometimes had troubles to confide to her, and it did not seem appropriate to these. But she saw no ground for complaint, because she interpreted the smile to suit the different phases of her own feeling. When she was in trouble, it was an effort to console her.

One afternoon Miriam, sitting among the sere grass and weeds of the Friends' burying-ground with Polly Hopkins, drew from her pocket what appeared to be a carefully respected document, unfolded and studied its pages carefully, and at length, with a perplexed sigh, said, " It 's a nice letter ; I think he 's a beautiful writer. See, *is n't* that beautiful writing ? But he says his tutor — that 's his teacher — told him it was stiff and old-fashioned, and he must n't make his letters that way. And sometimes he tells him that things are countrified and vulgar, and he asked Friend Payne what countrified and vulgar meant, and she said, ' Not elegant or refined.' He 's trying real hard to be elegant and refined. I looked in the dictionary to see what those meant, and it says, ' Graceful, neat, pleasing to good taste ; purified, separated from what is coarse, rude, or unproper.' I wrote it all down here, so that I could try to be elegant and refined, too. Aunt Dorcas is, and cousin Ruth, for thee can see for thyself, Polly Hopkins, how neat and pure, and pleasing to good taste, and separated from what is coarse, rude, or unproper *they* are. Aunt Hepsy is n't pleasing to good taste, for when she finds out what we don't like to do she always makes us do it; and it was n't pleasing to good taste when Joseph John and I were shut up all day — Joseph John in the garret and I in the store-room — for losing Aunt Hepsy's cap, when we had n't touched it. Aunt Hepsy hung her cap on a chair back, close to the fireplace, and when she wanted it, it was n't there, and she said Joseph and I put it somewhere. But we did n't, thee knows. Rosanna found it in the plum-tree, all covered with soot, and Rosanna said the draught took it up chimney. And last Quarterly Meeting time, when we had some Philadelphia Friends coming, Aunt Hepsy had Rosanna make some Quarterly Meeting cake, some had plums in it and some was plain, and she said, ' When our Philadelphia Friends are here, thee may bring us *this* cake, Rosanna, but when we have only Nantucket Friends, thee may bring *that.*' Well, I heard Rosanna say she did n't know which cake to bring, one day, so I thought I could help her, and I went to the south room where the Friends all were, and said, ' Shall Rosanna bring the Philadelphia Friends' cake, or the Nantucket Friends' cake,' and after that she made me read ' The Sinner Awakened ' every day, and that was n't pleasing to good taste, either.

" Well, I meant to tell thee, I can't understand those things that Joseph John — Roland Weir, I mean — is learning to do. He says he goes to dancing school. I asked Aunt Dorcas what that means, and she said dancing was a pastime that worldly people had, and they had to go to school and learn it. Well, I was very much surprised to find that *David* was worldly, for he danced; and he tells people to ' Praise Him with the timbrel and dance,' so I looked in the dictionary again, to see if it would tell how they do it, and it said, ' To leap and spring; to leap and frisk about; to move up and down with measured steps, regu-

lated by *a tune sung or played upon musical instruments.*' Now just think of that, Polly Hopkins! Think of David leaping and frisking before the Lord! Think of his doing that, and singing, and *having musical instruments!* I thought
of that yesterday, in meeting, when Friend Abra'm
Coffin had so much to say about David. I wonder
if he knows. But of course he don't, if he did
he'd have David put right out of the Bible. I
wish Friend Coffin would look in the dictionary!
Hark! there's Pel'tiah Groves over in the south
burying-ground! If David frisked and had musical instruments, I guess there's no harm in his
making that noise they call whistling, and I *like*
it. If thee'd like to have a nap, Polly Hopkins,
dear, I'll step over and speak to Pel'tiah."

Polly Hopkins smiled a full consent, and Miriam wrapped her very comfortably in a small shawl,
and left her reposing peacefully side by side with
Rachel Gardner, while she took her way to the
south burying-ground. The fact that Miriam
could hear Pel'tiah's whistle was no evidence that
he was near, for Pel'tiah was whistling, —

> "I'm gla-ad Salva-ation's free!
> I'm gla-ad Salva-ation's free!
> Salva-ation's free-e for you and me-e,
> I'm gla-ad Salva-ation's free!"

And as he came out monstrous strong on all the
glads, it wouldn't have been strange if a good pair
of ears had heard him out at sea. Miriam's quick
ear caught every one of the clarion notes, and to

her mind it was glorious music. She bent her steps towards the spot where the performance was going on, but before she could see the performer the sound ceased; and she was without her clue and was wandering among the weeds and brambles that hide forgottenness in the south burying-ground, when out from the yawning iron gates of a tomb issued an old man, who looked upon her with what seemed a bland hospitality, as if he were about to ask her to " come in."

He was tall and lank, his grave, kindly eyes twinkled when he laughed, and the whole expression of his amiable face was as innocent as that of Polly Hopkins. The long white curls that hung about it increased its infantine gentleness.

This was Pel'tiah, — a sort of old Mortality, — who had the general care of all the burials and burying-grounds on the island, knew whose mortal remains each grave contained, and the history and genealogy of every separate family which had been bereaved to help fill his dreary domain. One might have felt, perhaps, in looking at him, that it would be pleasant to be laid away in the last rest by such gentle, innocent hands as his.

" Why, good-morning, little maid! Was you looking for me?" said the grave digger, leaning under the low arch as he closed and locked the door.

" I came to hear thee whistle," said Miriam. "I like it."

" Sho!" said Pel'tiah, " I can't whistle when

you 're by, — I always want to smile, and you can't do both together, you know. Try it and see."

"Why, I can't whistle at all," Miriam acknowledged regretfully. "I *have* tried, but I can't make it go. Joseph could whistle some. He can do 'most everything. He 's a very capable boy, *I* think." This with an emphasis which implied that there were opinions contrary to her own.

"Well, how 's he getting along now? Ain't he homesick any?" Pe'ltiah asked.

"N-o," Miriam answered faintly. "I don't believe he is. He 's trying to be elegant and refined. He 's very busy, I guess. He always says so. He studies very hard things, and he goes to school to learn to ride. He 's learning to dance, too." Miriam looked sharply at Pel'tiah to see how he would take that.

"Pomps and vanities! Pomps and vanities!" said Pel'tiah, shaking his head slowly, for he was a good Methodist, and objected to those sorts of things upon principle, but to his natural, innocent heart a child dancing was a very pleasing subject to contemplate.

"Does thee know what dancing is?" Miriam asked tentatively.

"I 'd ought to," said Pel'tiah. "I used to dance myself before I was converted."

"Thee *did?*" Miriam, who had been trotting briskly along to keep pace with Pel'tiah's slow strides, stopped short and stared at this dancer of the past.

Pel'tiah nodded silently, trying to think reproachfully of himself for the follies of his youth.

"Then thee can show me how they do it!" Miriam cried in a very hopeful tone.

"Oh, no," Pel'tiah responded firmly. "I've most forgot; and besides I've renounced the pomps and vanities."

"What does thee mean by that?"

"I've given up 'the sinful lusts of the flesh and all covetous desires after the same,'" said Pel'tiah, repeating the phraseology of his vow.

"Thee has n't given up whistling and singing."

"Oh, no, there 's no harm in them."

"Aunt Hepsy says there *is*. People do have so many different 'pinions about things, that *I* don't know *what* to think," said poor Miriam. "David danced. He danced before the Lord."

"That 's so," said Pel'tiah, "but I guess his dancing was kind of slow and solemn."

"Well, why can't thee dance slow and solemn, just a little, to show me how? *Do!*"

"I could show you the steps," said Pel'tiah, stopping in the middle of the walk and placing his heels close together with his toes well turned out. "One — two — three — *four!* One — two — three — *four!*" he repeated, shuffling his feet about from one position to another. "Them 's the steps."

"Is that all?" exclaimed Miriam, with manifest disappointment. "I should think a person would n't need to go to school much to learn *that!*"

"Oh, there's lots of ways to use the steps. There's the polky, and the cotillion, and the Highland Fling, and Money Musk, and the Virginyer Reel, and a hundred more far 's I know, and you have to have music to go by. You make your feet keep time to the music — so." And forgetting his years and his renunciation, Pel'tiah whistled "Buy a Broom," and waltzed down the path to Miriam's intense delight.

"That's a waltz," he said, bringing himself up beside Miriam again, a good deal out of breath. "That was a new dance I learned when I was ashore at Mauritius, in '25. I *ain't really dancing*, you know. I'm only just giving you an idee of what sort of a thing dancing would be if 't was carried out. When you come to see a hundred or two, all in fine dress, some of the men in rigimentals, and the women all colors of the rainbow, with flowers in their hair and all about 'em, and a band of music playing its best, I *tell* you," said Pel'tiah, with kindling eyes and some intensity of tone, — "I tell you — well," suddenly bethinking himself, "there's where the pomps and vanities comes in."

"I should *like* to see the pomps and vanities!" said Miriam, with a sigh, "but Aunt Dorcas says we all have to give up something, and that 's what *I* 've got to give up, I suppose. Did n't thee hate to give them up, Pel'tiah?"

"Well, no; when we give up one thing there's 'most always another comes along. You notice

and see if there is n't. When I give up the dancing, there was the meetings, and they're almost
as lively." And this happy dweller among the
tombs looked as content as he ever could have
done at the ball at Mauritius.

· By this time they had reached a mysterious,
windowless house, and Miriam sat on a stone and
watched the blithesome Pel'tiah, while he went
in and out, and greased the wheels of a hearse,
which stood awfully waiting, — a great ghoulish
thing, which flapped its black ugly wings in the
wind and seemed ready to devour her.

There is nothing so interesting as gloomy things
to those who have never known much about gloom,
and the lugubrious and the enchanting met so
nearly together on that clear autumn morning
that they mingled their light and shadow with
pleasant effect upon Miriam 's serene mind. Cheerful life, in actual possession, triumphed over the
broadest hints of death, and as if to show its su-
perabundance of power, seemed to be bringing on
new forces. There came floating upon the air the
sound of a whistle that was not Pel'tiah's. It
was a persistent, courageous whistle, which seemed
to be in spite of everything, rather than because
of anything. Miriam could catch glimpses of a
person approaching, and he soon appeared from
around the corner of the house, and there, as if
suddenly turned to stone, stood for an instant,
without motion, without even a whistle, and gazed
with a look of consternation upon Miriam.

Collecting his forces again with apparent resolution, he raised his hat to Miriam, and advancing
a little, stood on the other side of the hearse, out
of Miriam's sight, and opened a low conversation
with Pel'tiah.

"Sho, sho; I want to know!" Miriam heard
Pel'tiah say. "Well, well, there's an end to all
things, ain't ther'? But whoever'd 'a' thought
the rheumatiz, or anything else, could have got to
his heart! It's powerful searching, is the rheumatiz."

In another moment this second visitor of Pel'-
tiah's was retracing his steps, and saying to himself, "Well, she saw me. They will soon know
now where I am, and perhaps" —

But Miriam had not recognized the face which,
in a few months, had parted with many of its old
traits. The rounded lines had straightened, the
full mouth had lost its deep corners and set itself
with such resolution as we see in the faces of hard-
working people, while there is yet some hope of
winning the battle, and before they settle into
that look of stolid endurance which betokens the
mere struggle for existence. His head, uncovered,
showed the brown, curly locks had been clipped so
close as to reveal the skull, which gave his head a
gray appearance.

No, there was nothing to remind Miriam of the
rosy, easy Rollo.

CHAPTER IX.

DRIFTED UPON 'SCONSET.

THERE were lonely nooks and wastes on the sleepy old island, far from the sound of Bela Ketchum's cry and the clang of his bell. No one thought to cross those miles of desert, over which the fishermen's carts toiled slowly and seldom, to find a boy who wanted, above all things, to put to sea and explore the world. It was at length decided, on that day when he was displaced, that the boy without a name had followed where these longings would lead him.

But the truth was that he had wandered without aim, without considering what he meant to do with himself, until he came to the old mill, and looking in at the open door, finally seated himself there to think it all over.

There was nothing to disturb his meditations, for Amos was dozing, as usual. The sedative old newspaper lay upon his knees, and his spectacles held that precarious poise upon his nose which had offered such a pleasing prospect to Miriam. The boy was well furnished with the consciousness of having been a fraud, and he remembered, with such a pang as only proud, honest natures can feel, the boy who had been defrauded. to whom his very flesh and bones seemed to belong, since they had grown out of what belonged to him.

"Here's his mark printed into my skin," said Rollo, "like the owner's brand on a sheep. And at the very first, I had a chain on my neck with his name on it, like a dog with his master's collar on. But I guess," he added, with a great sigh, — "I guess he'll make me a present of myself."

His chief thought, however, was of Mrs. Payne. Her magnanimity would make her wish to be generous, yet it would trouble her to know just how to do, — just how to dispose of a superfluous boy. To slip away quietly and completely, to give no more trouble, would that not be the kindest thing he could do? To have no parting. Ah, he could not bear a parting. He lost all his bravery when he thought of that. His lip trembled and the tears fell. The parting was already past if he should not return.

Now, do not expect this boy to be reasonable, and do exactly the right thing, for (I say it again) he was not a model boy. He made a mistake. He resolved not to return.

At this point Amos nodded emphatically, as if he approved the resolution, and the glasses were launched upon his lap. He looked up with that perennial surprise which this occurrence had always produced since he adopted the custom of wearing spectacles and taking afternoon naps, and his eyes met a pair of blue-gray eyes. He started, and forgot to say he had n't been asleep.

" Where 've I seen you ? " he said. " Whose boy be you ? "

" My own boy," Rollo answered.

" Humph! that 's the way of 'em. They talk as if fathers and mothers had gone out o' use," said Amos. " I s'pose likely you must have had a mother, anyhow."

" I suppose so."

" What 's her name ? "

" I don't know."

" *Don't know?* Well, who 's your father ? "

" I don't know."

" Jericho ! Hain't you any folks ? "

" No."

Amos looked suspiciously at the boy's costly clothing, but he looked kindly at the blue-gray eyes.

" *It is cur'ous!* " he said.

" I suppose," Rollo remarked, to change the subject, — " I suppose Nantucket is a good place to go to sea from. Plenty of ships sailing from here ? "

" That 's it, hey ? " said Amos, uncrossing his legs and recrossing them the other way. " You 've run away from home to go to sea, have you ? "

" I assure you, honestly, I have no home," said Rollo. " I have been helped by kind people, but it is time I helped myself. I 'm a poor boy who must find some way to earn his living, and I want to go to sea."

"Don't go to follerin' the sea!" said Amos. "I've follered her, and I know her. I've had a good many hard pulls, but there wa'n't one on 'em ekle to follerin' of that there pesky sea."

Amos rubbed his knees slowly, as if to comfort his tired joints.

"But I'm going to try it for myself," said Rollo. "I must master something, and it may as well be the sea."

Amos uncrossed and forgot to recross. It seemed to him he had seen that same determined look in another pair of eyes.

"Well, there ain't any ships starting just now," he said.

Rollo looked out over the lonely scene before him, wondering in what direction, then, he should turn his steps. He had no money to take him off the island. He had spent the last penny of his allowance the day before for some new rigging to his boat, and if his pockets had been full, he would not have taken a dime that was no longer his. As he considered the twofold desolation before him, a shaggy head appeared over a "hummock," as the rolling undulations of the moor are called. The head was presently shown to be supported by a body equally shaggy, and the body again supported by one of the two-wheeled carts of Nantucket. The horse which propelled all this was the shaggiest part of the whole exhibition. The *tout ensemble* drew up at the mill door, and Amos stepped out to help a customer with his bags of corn. He was a hard-looking old fellow, destitute of some fingers, the result of an encounter with a shark. The remaining fingers were knotted and distorted by rheumatism and hard work. A perpetual scowl had stamped deep seams in his leathery face. He was altogether a repellant object.

"How 'r' ye, John?" said Amos.

John responded with a growl that was almost a howl. It seemed as if he had reached the very outermost bounds of discomfort and could go no farther in that direction.

The boy, as if touched with compassion for so much misery, stepped quickly down and laid hold of the sack of corn at which the knotty hands were tugging so painfully, and in a twinkling it was deposited on the mill floor. The old fellow glowered at him with no abatement of discontent, and shuffling up the steps to the mill floor seated himself with what might have been a last gasp in Amos's chair.

"Why, what be you a-going to do?" said Amos. "If ye keep on at this rate, you'll be bed-rid."

"I *won't*, I *won't!*" snarled John. "I'll keep a-goin' till I drop. When John Dagget takes to his bed, the bed'll be underground."

"Why, you must ha' laid up something of a pile by this time," continued Amos. "Why don't you have somebody to help you? You might go shares with some smart chap in the fishin' and lobsterin'."

"Where's the chap?" snapped John. "Smart ones don't swim in these waters."

"What would you want a person to do?" asked Rollo.

"What pusson?"

"If you had one to work for you, I mean."

"*Do?* Why, *work, work,* to be sure."

"Want to try me?"

"*You?*" The old bear looked at the smooth, handsomely dressed boy with contempt.

"Yes," returned the boy. "I can work. Want to try me?"

A spasm passed over the leathery, deep-lined face. It was John Dagget's laugh.

"Don't want no 'ristercrats," he said.

"But I'm not one," returned Rollo. "I need to work."

John fixed his hard eyes upon the latest New York fashion. "You'd make a dandy fisherman," he said.

"I can change my clothes, you know, and I'm as strong as a horse," said the boy, doubling his fists and making thrusts at imaginary obstacles.

"Humph!" grunted John, but he considered the matter with a faint accession of interest.

"Try me for a day or two," said Rollo.

"Wal, then, youngster, if you want to know what hard work is, I'll give you the best chance you ever see," said John.

And he had kept his word, until now there had come a day of rest for himself and his boy as well. On the evening of that day, returning from his visit to Pel'tiah, the boy, after putting up the shaggy horse and the two-wheeled cart in an old barn, whose roof, covered with tufts of grass and moss, had also a shaggy appearance, lifted the wooden door-latch of the cottage, and stood on the threshold of a room where a dying fire of drift-wood on the hearth shot out a feeble, iridescent flame, and confused still more by its wavering light the dim uncertainties of the room. The boy stopped, repelled. He had never entered there with pleasure, nor yet with such a horror before.

But no, the awful thing which had appalled him was not there. He hastened to encourage the failing fire by throwing upon it great splinters of wood from an old sea-chest, and bringing out from among the shadows a bucket from which time had almost effaced the word Aurora, he went for water to the same pump which had long ago witnessed the sorrows of Roland Weir. He was filling and hanging the tea - kettle over the fire, when the door of the front room opened and Dame Dagget, limping on crutches, and two brown old women of the neighborhood came out. One of them had a lamp in her hand, which she placed upon a table. Its dull flame, fed by fish oil, added little cheerfulness to the room.

" Nothing don't seem nat'ral," said Dame Dagget, sinking into her rocking chair, " 'specially to see him a-laying there so peaceable. Wall, he was John Dagget, and so he could n't be Elder Lovejoy. Poor old John ! "

Thus Dame Dagget unconsciously expressed a

thought of a great philosopher, that "all things are what they are because they are so constituted that they could not be otherwise; therefore we cannot be angry with our brother because he has disappointed us."

"He *was* John Dagget." That tells all that need be told of an event which had happened in the Dagget cottage.   John Dagget *was.*

The two old women lent helping hands until supper was on the board, and departed.

"Gi' me the crutches," said Dame Dagget.

Rollo picked up the crutches that had fallen to the floor, and held them while she pulled herself up.   She stood leaning upon them for a moment, looking, one might have said, wistfully at the boy.   There was something like gentleness in her face, which softened its hard lines.   This tall boy, with plenty of physical strength and courage, pleased Dame Dagget, whose own boys the sea had snatched from her long ago, and she had shown him a rude kindness ever since he came to the cottage.

"What be I to do when you 're gone!" she said. "I can't draw wood nor water, nor go to town for things.   Could n't ye make up your mind to stay, now there 's peace an' quiet?"

"Oh," said the boy, "I shall lose my chance! I 'd like to stay until you get another boy, if — if I *could.*"

"You 'd stay a spell, then," said Dame Dagget, smiling grimly, "for there ain't a boy on the

island that 'ud come and live with Ma'am Dagget."

' She laid her hard hand on the boy's shoulder.

"I 'm a'most helpless," she added. "I *must*
have you for a while. Jest you give up that there
notion o' goin', and maybe you 'll ketch fish that 'll
amount to more 'n one voyage to sea. John an'
me hain't worked an' saved for over forty year for
nothin', and many a bit worth pickin' up has
come ashore to us. Don't you make a mistake
and choose the wrong hand."

The boy looked perplexed.

Untold treasures would not have tempted him
to stay, but how could he leave this helpless old
woman alone ?

"How long will it be ?" he asked, disconso-
lately.

"Wall, I expect I sha'n't be real spry agin all
winter. Old folks's bones don't mend so fast as
young ones'."

All winter! The boy turned away dumb with
the awfulness of such a vision as a winter there
with Ma'am Dagget.

Ma'am Dagget's prime virtues were cleanliness
and thrift, and the brass lamp which dimly lighted
their repast shone almost brighter than its feeble
flame. In washing, scouring, scrubbing, polishing,
diving into dark corners with soap and water and
broom, she enjoyed the comfortable sense of being an exterminator of evil. She meant to fight
dust as long as she lived, she said, if she did turn

into it when she died.   Her broken ankle was received in one of these battles, when she scaled the outer walls of the cottage to dust the ship's figurehead, which decorated its front.   She fought upon crutches still, and her zeal burned warmer, confined within closer bounds.

It was a neat little table at which she and Rollo sat down, and in addition to the peace which had settled upon the cottage, Rollo enjoyed the equally new blessing of being able to satisfy his hunger. Ma'am Dagget — things being left to her own disposal — disposed them so as to tempt the boy to stay.   Bread and butter, stewed lobster, preserved beach plums, and gingerbread, seasoned with a vigorous appetite and this new hospitality, were very delicious to poor Rollo, and when he was permitted to go to bed without passing the evening in the back shed, mending nets and other old traps, he might, if he had been a moralizer, have feared that he was beginning to suffer the pernicious effects of prosperity again, instead of deriving all the wholesome benefits that plenty of adversity is supposed to confer.   As another luxury, he was permitted to take a light with him, instead of feeling his way in the darkness to his hard bed under the eaves.

Some neighbors came in to sit and doze through the night, according to the custom when there is death in a Nantucket house, and after many anxious charges from Ma'am Dagget to be sure not to set the house afire, not to drop any oil, and not

to scatter any sand on the floor when he took off
his shoes, but to mind and take them off on the
mat, Rollo retired to his little nook in the garret.
He placed his spark of a candle in a safe place on
the floor, and seating himself on the edge of his
clean, hard bed, adjusted his mind to reflection.
He was too good-natured to consider with indifference a project which would leave poor Ma'am
Dagget alone. Her past friendliness, and its present rich increase, made him feel obliged to her.
Her intimation that he might find it profitable to
stay with her affected him not at all as a temp-
tation. He could imagine possibilities of large
gain in much more agreeable circumstances than
those present. There were mines of gold and
plenty of treasure somewhere, and he did not
doubt but that if he once made a start he should
get at them with more or less facility. It had
taken him long to earn the money he needed to
start with, but this was Nantucket, where he expected to leave all his limitations.

At the same time, he was loath to leave Ma'am
Dagget in her helplessness. If he should gain by
such selfishness, the very gain would be hateful.
And underneath this consideration was another,
which in low whisperings and with unacknowl-
edged influence pleaded on Ma'am Dagget's side
of the question. Words could not tell what the
boy had suffered from homesickness. His affection for all he had lost was very true and tender,
for Mrs. Payne especially. It was the affection of

a son for a mother, and it was that in a rare degree. No change of relationship could change the fact or diminish the measure of it. It was a very durable compound of the natural filial attachment with admiration and gratitude, and he would gladly have suffered anything for the sake of the smallest assurance that she missed him and wished for him. The little Quaker girl had seen him. Mrs. Payne would know, presently, where he was to be found. Would she come to him? Would she send for him? Would she write to him? He lay down upon his pillow with the conviction that he could not leave Ma'am Dagget yet. He would wait.

CHAPTER X.

"WHAT'S FOR THEE, THEE 'LL HAVE."

THE winter was severe. The Nantucketers were locked in for six weeks, and the island was a lone little world by itself.

You will easily see how restricted a young life must have been when you know what was the most novel and exciting event of that winter to Miriam. It was when she was allowed to have an old sled of Paul's and coast in the back yard, over the gentlest slope that could be. It seemed, in prospect, a very headlong, ungoverned thing to do, and she wondered how she should feel in the abandoned act; and when she finally let herself go, she held her breath with as much of a sensation as any young lady ever felt at her first toboggan slide.

And it would be hardly believed by some young people that the same faces Miriam had seen framed in their sugar-scoop bonnets all her life would have afforded her pleasure when their owners came with their knitting work to pass an afternoon. But she listened with interest to the gentle, crooning gossip of those dove-like women, and sometimes went out with Aunt Dorcas to return their visits, and stayed to tea. One of these friends, whose hospitality was tempered with frugality, used to say, "Hereth quinth for them that don't like butter," which made Miriam feel that life was not without its troublesome alternatives as well as its restrictions.

And another, a phenomenon of placid contentment with adverse circumstances, which were largely the result of her easy improvidence, sat in her chimney corner sniffing her pinch of snuff, and met the sighs of her discontented husband with the unsoothing response, "What 's *for* thee, thee 'll *have*, Simeon."

Miriam frequently finished exploring the map of her fancy by making a broader and more cheerful application of these words than poor 'Kiah Hussey was able to do. She comforted herself with the charming assurance that she could not, by any chance, miss the beautiful things that were *meant* to be hers.

Among Miriam's diversions were also Aunt Dorcas's stories of when she was a little girl, and drove in the gig with her father, and cousin Ruth's riddles and puzzles. But above, and beyond, and exceeding all else, in her estimation, were Uncle David's rhyming stories and sketches of old Nantucket times, which he delighted to rehearse, as opportunity offered. Aunt Dorcas interfered with the pleasure very much indeed, though, by shaking her head in a deprecating way, and calling the verses "David 's jingles," which was dampening to self-confidence. Miriam, however, was as delighted to listen as Uncle David was to read, and with mutual satisfaction, they often stole away by themselves, and enjoyed whole evenings of poetic overflow, Miriam drinking eagerly and never seeming sated.

Those scenes were all present to Miriam, and her admiration of Uncle David's cheerfully chiming rhymes would raise his fallen confidence five, ten, fifteen per cent., until he continued more and more resonantly with his island pastorals, — which I wish there was room for on these pages, — Miriam firmly believing that even her beloved Whittier had but one rival, and that was Uncle David!

But we will not undertake to enumerate all Miriam's opportunities. Everything was an opportunity to the child, even the long First Day and Fifth Day meetings, for while the grave, elderly Friends were twirling their thumbs and waiting for inspiration, her inspiration had always arrived; her imagination was always ready; not all the bare severity of unpainted walls and benches and long-drawn countenances could chill or forbid her, and "the truest and sweetest things in life are (after all) not those which we see, but those of which we dream." When Friends Ab'ra'm Coffin or Merab Gardner had something given them to say, she drew from their innocent platitudes a conclusion of her own, in the consideration of which she found an abounding interest. Sitting demurely afterwards before the fire, as she turned her apple to roast all sides impartially, she turned those raw truisms over and over in her mind, until they also gained warmth and tenderness and sweetness.

She was sitting in this way, one evening in February, her apple hissing on the hearth, prematurely ready for supper, when Uncle David came in with the look of a victor bearing spoils, his huge overcoat pockets running over. As he stood on the hearth warming and rubbing his hands, exhaling ozone and comfortable "ahs," his round, smiling face beaming like a genial full moon, Miriam was invited to explore the contents of the pockets.

"Letters!" she cried. "Aunt Dorcas! Cousin Ruth! They've landed a mail!"

"They landed forty mails at the east side this morning, and there's been great commotion at the post-office and about town all the afternoon," said Uncle David.

And there was some commotion at David Haddon's that evening. Miriam's excitement was contagious. "There's no knowing what's happened on the continent! A good deal might be done in six weeks," she said, as she eagerly sorted the pile of letters and gave up the newspapers.

There were letters from Obed Swain, Aunt Hepsy and Paul; letters from aunts and cousins and friends; letters in abundance from Roland Weir and Betty Vinton; "And here's one from New York for *thee*, Aunt Dorcas!" said Miriam.

Aunt Dorcas took a look at the New York letter

before indulging in her boy's long pages. She glanced over it, and then at Miriam, whose eyes were big and bright over Roland Weir's communications. There was something of interest enough to make Aunt Dorcas linger long to consider it while those dearer pages were waiting in her lap. It was an urgent invitation from Mrs. Payne for Miriam to come to New York. A serious matter, indeed, and Aunt Dorcas, at first, had some doubts.

The old Quakers shook their heads and looked grave at the mention of David Haddon, and they were apt to speak of Dorcas with a smile of mingled affection and regret, and the grave look and the regret were due to that large allowance which they gave to things that were of the world. Yet Obed Swain gladly committed his child to their care, and he had given them such absolute liberty of decision for her that when Dorcas had duly considered, she felt that it was only necessary to write Obed that she had consented to let Miriam go to visit Roland Weir.

So the grave question was settled, and many a good old Quaker face grew long and troubled at the news of this liberty, nay, unlawful license, that was allowed Obed Swain's child.

Dear, innocent hearts! How they all fluttered at the thought of that wicked New York! And Miriam's, when she heard the news, outfluttered them all. She remembered what cousin Ruth had told her, that all the ropes in use in the royal

English navy have a red thread running through them from end to end, which cannot be parted from them without undoing the whole, so that the smallest piece may be recognized anywhere as belonging to the Crown. Miriam thought that Aunt Dorcas's loving-kindness made just such a bright thread in her life.

The ice in the harbor and the last doubt in Dorcas Haddon's mind gave way at about the same time, and Uncle David and Miriam set out upon their great journey. Uncle David had only been waiting for the opening of the harbor to go in that direction at any rate, for Paul was at the Quaker college at Haverford, and there was anxiety in regard to a certain trouble with his eyes, and much doubt as to whether he ought to continue his studies. Uncle David was going down to look into the matter, and have the eyes examined by an oculist in Philadelphia.

It was a great delight to him to have Miriam by his side all the day, and, like the exhibitor of a panorama, to show her a piece of the world. As they passed by town after town, and there was still no sign of towns giving out, Miriam felt, with awe, how stupendous was the world; and when, after long hours of panorama, she approached the biggest town of all, and caught glimpses of interminable streets with long rows of twinkling lights, she held Uncle David's hand fast, with a feeling of apprehension. It was only when she was seized and saluted by Roland Weir and Betty, with a vehemence that quite unsettled her bonnet, and when Mrs. Payne drew her kindly under her wing, that she felt she had arrived at a definite point in the general uncertainty; but then the check for the tiny trunk, for which she had never ceased to feel concerned, was intrusted to a strange and doubtful-looking man, Uncle David saw them all in Mrs. Payne's carriage and turned his face towards Philadelphia, leaving her to be swallowed by that dreadful monster, New York!

Miriam knew so much, from his letters, about Roland Weir's home in New York that she expected to find it quite a familiar place, and indeed, being accustomed to live in liberally furnished dreams, she accepted new realities with a kind of placid wontedness. Not the least among the objects which she found surprising, however, was Roland Weir himself. She looked upon his various sorts of improvement with the highest veneration, and not being aware how much the tailor and barber were concerned in his superior appearance, she thought it was wholly the visible result of those aspirations in regard to which she had consulted the dictionary.

Opposite Miriam, at dinner, on the evening of her arrival, was a very fair young man, with a gold-colored moustache, who was Mr. Stanley, Roland's tutor. He occasionally made remarks to the boy, which were of an edifying nature, and Miriam absorbed some particles of edification herself.

Betty, who remained to dine with Miriam, fluttered and twittered and besprinkled her with compassion on account of the dreary, frozen-up time she had been having.

"I talked with papa about sending out a ship to rescue you," she said, "like an Arctic expedition, you know, but he said there were so many tea-kettles boiling on Nantucket that you could thaw yourselves out whenever you pleased. He seemed to think you stayed frozen up on purpose."

Mrs. Payne had a weary look, and much of the bloom and brightness which she had carried down to Nantucket had disappeared. She left Mr. Stanley and Betty and Roland to do the conversational duties. Betty, for one, was by no means incompetent. She took the lead when they left the dining-room, with the air of a mother-bird leading on her fledgelings, and launched Miriam upon the drawing-room, as upon a pale blue velvet sea, with glittering chandeliers for heavenly bodies, and hundreds of strange and exquisite things for surrounding scenery. Miriam sailed along, touching timidly at various points, and finally landed upon a silken island, — or was blown ashore, with Betty for a brisk gale. And there it was announced to her that Roland Weir was to have a birthday party; and presently it was expounded that the chief occupation at parties was *dancing!*

"Ah," sighed Miriam, with intense satisfaction, for she felt that she was now to have a full elucidation of the mysteries of that life which lay all outside the territory which had been ceded to the Quakers.

"And you must let us show you how to dance *one* dance," said Betty, "for you will be the chief guest, and Roland must dance first with you."

At this Miriam gasped a little, and was about to reply, when Mrs. Payne, in passing, said, "No, no; Miriam will enjoy watching the dancing, but her father's people do not dance. She is quite content with her own simple pleasures."

"Ah, but she has n't tried *our* pleasures!" quoth Miss Betty; and Miriam sighed again.

Betty was obliged to talk a great deal in her capacity of entertainer. That was not the least of pleasures to her, however, to hear herself talk.

"There are some things you *can* do, I suppose, though you can't dance," she said. "Let me think. You will want to *see* things, of course. There's no end of the things that people from the country want to see in New York. Poor things! You'll know them, they stare so, and turn round and round as if they'd lost their way, or their wits. Oh! you're from the country! But you don't stare. The people I mean look tired and troubled. You'll see them in the Park wagons, when we're driving, with bags and umbrellas in their hands, and veils tied down over their hats, and they look at us so, we feel as if we were sights. It must be sad to have to take everything on the fly so, and feel so anxious about it. I always want to do something to help the sad people enjoy things, but I can't manage it at all.

"Papa says I'm a socialist. I don't know what he means by calling me such unpleasant names, so I can't explain. Papa needs to explain a good deal, and after he has explained, I generally ask him to explain his explanation. I told him I thought it would be kind for the people in New York to go abroad somewhere, and let the country people that want to see things come and live in their houses all winter, and look a little every day. Papa said it would be kind enough, but it would n't be convenient. So there is just how it is, you see; we can never do anything unless it is *convenient.* But think of the poor things who can't stop to wink for hours and days, for fear they shall miss seeing something! I don't call *that* convenient, do you? And it's just so at Newport, when the excursion people come. It makes me uncomfortable to see them wander round with linen covers on, looking so red and tired, and pointing at things with their umbrellas. And I wonder what their bags are for. They all have little bags. Last summer I picked up one and drove her round in my phaeton a little, and she stared so it was frightful! I did n't like to ask her what she carried in her bag, or if it was only a badge. That was a good chance to find out, but now I shall never know!"

So Betty babbled on like an easy-going little brook with no barriers. She promised a hundred delights to Miriam, — promised to bring her dearest friends to see her, and rehearsed their sayings and doings; sketched them all in such colors that they would hardly have recognized themselves.

But nothing is absolutely eternal in this world, not even Betty's chatter. There was by and by an announcement that some one had come for Miss Betty, and she vanished like a bright meteor. The train of light she left behind was that string of brilliant hopes and promises which she had offered Miriam. The child was as eager to grasp it all as were those people who had moved Betty's whimsical compassion. She could not sleep for hours, after she lay down upon her pretty, lace-curtained bed, but gazed about in an exalted trance at the reflections of the sea-coal fire, where it tremulously touched the bric-à-brac and lacquered screens, and, at length, creeping out of bed, she wandered about in the light and shadow, with wide, solemn eyes, as a little spirit might, that had lost its way between heaven and earth; wandered and wandered until she was weary, and then lay down to dream it all over again.

But before she dreamed she whispered to herself, "What's *for* thee, thee'll *have*, Miriam," and she smiled a little to think how much she was like Jonas Hooten, to whom her father, wishing to make him a little gift, had offered a choice between a beautiful new jack-knife, some prime fishing tackle, and a pair of skates. Jonas considered anxiously and long, and made his answer thus: "I needs 'em *all!*"

CHAPTER XI.

AMOS TUTTLE'S " PROTTYJEE."

THAT same evening, Rollo was sitting before a driftwood fire in the cottage at 'Sconset. He had waited, and the conviction had settled slowly and coldly into his heart, " No, she does not care to find me ! "

Ah, that long, dreary winter at 'Sconset, when society was chiefly represented by Amos Tuttle !

The thought of the boy being given over to John Dagget had haunted Amos, and his afternoon naps had been broken in upon by queries of conscience as to whether he ought not to have prevented it somehow. At length his trouble of mind came to such a pass that the moment he had peacefully seated himself over the old newspaper, he saw gazing at him a pair of eyes of a particular color and a very particular expression. Amos could not stand it, and he got Pel'tiah Groves's old horse and cart and made his way to 'Sconset. That haunting expression had so intensified in the boy's eyes when Amos saw him for the second time, that his soft old heart was moved quite out of its place, so that it gave him much inconvenience, and caused him to choke, and rub his eyes with the back of his hand repeatedly.   But poor Amos had no alternative to offer; he could only resolve to try to find one, and warn John Dagget to mind how he used that boy, for he was a " prottyjee " of his.   Having once taken that definite step, and having made Rol his *protégé* by declaration, he repeated his visits to 'Sconset with Per'tiah's horse and cart, from time to time, and each time returned with a more and more important sense of having a boy to look after, which produced the agreeable effect of paternity upon Amos's mind; and before very long his kind, but hitherto vacant heart — vacant except for some dreamy memories — was filled to the brim and running over with fondness and solicitude for a boy who perpetually ruffled the surface of his memory with little breezes that blew from far-away shores which he would never sight again, and seemed at times to restore his lost youth.   It became the delight of his life to anticipate and perpetrate those trips to 'Sconset, and during all the winter he had never failed to sit by Ma'am Dagget's fire two evenings in the week. Rol was always delighted to see him, for Amos was an inexhaustible *raconteur*, and as Ma'am Dagget always went to bed with the hens, or at the same time that they did, Amos's glowing face and still more glowing stories lightened the tedious hours most agreeably.   And whenever Rollo went to town he stopped to pay Amos a visit, so they came to be intimate friends ; really, you might say bosom friends, for their friendliness often came quite within the bounds of sacred confidence. For instance, Rol had wondered how Amos came to take such a kindly interest in him, and Amos had confessed that there was something about him that reminded him, and so on, — the whole story of his old captain, and Lydia his daughter, the girl who commanded the ship and accomplished other wonders, among which need not be counted the eternal subjugation of poor Amos, that being, apparently, the effect of beauty and spirit upon a gentle, impressionable, and faithful nature.

"But, Lord!" said Amos, when he had finished his story, "she wa' n't but eighteen and I was a'most forty. I wa' n't noways fit to look at her."

"I 'd rather hear her opinion as to that," Rol declared, with the intention of building up Amos's self-esteem a little.

"Well, nat'rally, it was the same," said Amos, "though I scurcely ever spoke to her. She was the cap'n's daughter, and proud he was on her, as well he might be. Lord! to see that slim thing stand on the quarter deck 'n' give orders, so quiet like, you 'd ha' said she was fit for a king, and every man, from cabin to forecas'le, was ready to fall down and wo'ship her. I wa' n't the only one, be sure o' that. But don't you misunderstand me to say 't I ever had an idee 't I was fit to marry her. I wa' n't never so consaited as that. I only used to like to think that mebby I *might* have, if I 'd been younger, and everyways different."

The next time Amos came to 'Sconset, he brought something to show Rol, something never looked upon by other eyes than his own during all the years he had possessed it. He drew it from his pocket with the manner of performing a religious rite, and slowly opening an outside pasteboard box, disclosed an inner box of sandal-wood. The opening of this revealed a wrapping of soft paper, and this being removed, there came to light an embossed case, closed with two tiny brass hooks. This he opened and laid before Rol without a word, and without a word Rol gazed upon the old daguerreotype. That tribute of silence duly paid, Amos explained that he had watched a good deal with the captain when he was delirious with fever, — he had a knack with sick folks, and there wasn't any other aboard that seemed to understand such things, — and he had asked for the picture instead of the pecuniary reward offered him.

"The cap'n would ruther have given me a hundred dollars," said Amos, "but I'd have scorned two hundred."

"I wish we knew where she was now," said Rollo, deeply impressed by the spirited face of the heroine, whose story seemed to him a romance of the splendid sea.

It was a face that must have been clear and brown, with deep color in the cheeks and lips; a courageous face, saved from an excess of daring by a second intention in the lines of the mouth, whose lips curled back proudly and then fell into a soft, drooping line, that sank deep at the corners and gave sweetness to the whole expression.

"I sometimes think," said Amos, "that mebby you're a relation of hers."

"*I!*" cried Rollo. "What impossible things you can imagine, Amos! You ought to have made romance your profession."

"But there's something about you that's like her," said Amos. "I don't mean to say it's probable you *be* a relation of hers, but I like to think *mebby* you be. It ain't *likely*, of course, but lor, we can't half on us tell who we raley do belong to. I've seen a man born in Norway, that never was out o' Norway, nor any of his folks neither, that was so like a man born at Valp'raiso, that was never away from there, nor any of his folks neither, that you couldn't have told which was which. And I've seen them that was born on the same spot, from the same fathers and mothers, that was more unlike than cats an' dogs. They didn't belong together, an' couldn't be made to, no more 'n ile 'n' water. 'T ain't flesh an' blood altogether that settles belongings; but when folks have something you can't point at, an' can't describe, an' can't explain, that every time you notice it in one makes you think of t' other, I can't help sayin' *mebby* they belong to each other *some way*."

"How proud a fellow might be to belong to some one like this, Amos," said Rol, turning to the daguerreotype again. "To look at this picture, now, and say, 'It was my mother!'"

"Oh, good Lord! Think of it!" said Amos, and the thought made them both silent again.

"Tell me the last thing you remember about her, Amos," said Rollo, presently. "What became of her, as far as you know?"

"Well, the cap'n began to think it wa'n't right to keep the girl on the seas all her life, but *he* could n't live on land himself, so he laid out for Lyddy to have a home ashore, an' teachers, an' things, like other girls. He bought a little place in England, near Cowes, an' used to run short tradin' trips from Cowes to Calais, and other places, an' get home often. But Lyddy wa'n't quite happy, they said. She was homesick for the sea, an' missed her father, an' when he died sudden, at Bordoo — Lord! We won't talk about that. 'T was awful. But d'rectly a Mr. Allen, cap'n of a steamer in the Red Cross line, from S'thampton to New York, — a young feller that had a way of carryin' all before him, — come acrosst Lyddy, an' mercy sakes! what could you expect? He carried *her* before him, like a gale o' wind. Away she went, an' I hain't never heered anything about her sence. She was the lonesomest thing, after her father died, that I ever see, for while Cap'n Macy was livin' on the sea, an' Lyddy, too, their relations died off an' scattered, an' the girl had n't a friend to go to when her father died. He was always worried about that, an' always meant to come back to Nantucket an' hunt up some of his folks, for Lyddy's sake; but he sailed from New

York an' never 'd been back to the island but once sence his wife died, an' could n't bear to. ' Next time, next time ! ' he always said, an' then hurried an' got off to sea agin as soon 's possible. Well, after Cap'n Macy was gone, I quit the seas. It wa' n't raley the sea that I 'd been follerin', but Cap'n Macy himself, for he was a grand man, kind o' Quakerish, as he 'd been brought up. He stuck to the Quaker language, and them still ways they have, and his principles was sech that he never was known to blaze up an' swear when he was mad ; but he had a man for fust mate that was celebrated for the way he 'd rip an' tear at the smallest kind of a tax on his temper. They said he could lay the roughest sea down flat an' smooth. The cap'n could n't do nothin' to stop him.

" Well, I remember," Amos continued, with a smile at the reminiscence, — " I remember when we was walkin' in to the dock at Valp'raiso one mornin', a schooner was layin' right acrosst our bows an' did n't offer to stir an' give us the way. Cap'n Macy he expostylated with the skipper in his kind of a way, — demanded his rights, you know, several times, but the skipper never took a mite o' notice, an' Cap'n Macy begun to be con- sid'rable riled. So he steps to the hatchway an' sings out to the fust mate : ' Hiram,' says he, ' thee 'll have to come up here an' give this fellow some o' thy language ! ' An' Hiram he come up fast enough, an' poured out right 'n' left on the skipper, an' I tell ye, he cut an' cleared as if he was good 'n' ready.

" Well, where was I ? Oh, I was about to say
that the steamer Lyddy's husband was cap'n of
was that there Aurory that was lost off here fourteen year ago, come spring. But I never could
find out what become of Lyddy, though I tried.
She wa'n't aboard the Aurory. I looked the list
o' passengers over ; I look it over frequent. She
wa'n't there. I've a few papers that I do look
over now 'n' agin ; the one that tells about Lyddy
Macy bringin' the ship home, the one that tells
about the cap'n dyin' at Bordoo, what a good
square man he'd been, an' so on, an' the one about
the wreck o' the Aurory. I hain't much int'rest in
the new ones — they tell about things I ain't con-
sarned in, but I'm never tired lookin' over them
old ones."

Amos was more charmed to visit 'Sconset than
ever, since he could talk to some one there of the
dear old times, and of Lyddy. He never neglected
his opportunity, and Rollo welcomed the subject.
In his turn he told Amos his own story, and the
bonds of confidence and sympathy were strong
between this seemingly incongruous couple.

That same evening, as I have said, when Miriam and Betty and Roland Weir were discussing
the pleasures of life in Mrs. Payne's drawing-room,
Rollo sat at Ma'am Dagget's fireside wondering if
Amos would come.

The cruel sea thundered upon the beach, and
the spray fell frozen upon the cottage roof. The
wind ran round and round the house, shaking the

doors and windows, as if praying to come in, and Rollo leaned towards the fire and shivered. But Amos seldom stopped for wind or weather, so Rollo listened hopefully, and half expectantly, and presently heard the sound of wheels crushing through the sand, and Amos was at the door. He came in with uncommon gravity, and remained quite silent after seating himself by the fire.

"Why, what ails you, Amos?" asked Rol. "Have n't you any remarks to offer this evening?"

"Well, yes, I have; more 'n common," Amos answered.

"Fire away, then. I 'm uncommon ready for them."

"I 've seen a man from off, to-day," began Amos, with an impressive manner, "an old mate o' mine, who asked me nine an' forty questions about the boy at John Dagget's. I pinned him down so tight he could n't stir, an' asked him what business it was o' his'n. Well, to come to the p'int, he told me there was a man at the Sailor's Snug Harbor that knew all about you two boys, — both on ye, — a man that 's been lost up in the Ar'tic regions an' hain't long to live. He would n't tell me any more, said he could n't; but he wrote some directions on this here bit o' paper, and said if you 's a mind to go an' find him, you 'd git the whole story. He 's repented of his sins now he 's like to die, an' he wants to confess 'em. If you want your share, you 'd better go quick. There ain't a minute to lose."

"You don't suppose I 'm *his*, do you?" asked Rol, looking aghast.

Amos shook his head. "I don't know," he said gloomily. "We can't tell till we find out."

"Because I could n't stand it to be the son of a sneaking, cowardly cheat!" said Rol, his chest heaving.

"But could n't ye feel to forgive him, some-how?" asked Amos.

"*No!*" Rol almost shouted. "I can answer that fast enough. *No*, I could n't!"

Amos left that question as settled. "Well, you 'll go down an' see what he 's got to say, I s'pose?"

"I don't know. I guess I 'd better leave things where they are. It 's better never to know *what* you are, than to make sure you 've got such poor stuff in you," said Rol.

"Come, come; we 've all of us got poor stuff in us," said Amos, looking compassionately at Rol, who sat frowning at the floor.

They did not talk much that evening. When they had both stared at the sputtering fire in si-lence until it seemed to Rol he had lived through a long, solemn age with that man who was slip-ping away into eternal silence, who might tell him all, "Did you ever think," he asked, "that I have n't any name, Amos? I should n't have any to give if I were asked for one."

"Well here, take mine!" said Amos quickly, as if he were offering Rol the use of his umbrella.

" I 've never had a chance to give it to anybody before. If it suits you, you 're as welcome to it as can be."

" Thank you," said Rol. " It 's an honest one, you good old Amos ! " He patted Amos's bony hand, and Amos drew a deep breath of satisfaction. " If I should ever know my name, I won't take it unless it 's an honest one. I 'd rather have yours, though, to tell the truth, it is n't a very pretty one."

" No," said Amos, " It 's hombly, but such as 't is you 're welcome to it."

" Thank you, thank you, Amos, but I shall always keep Rollo. It is all that seems to belong to me. It 's what my — what they called me when I was a little fellow, and it seems to be quite my own. It is n't *Roland* — it is n't *his* name, you know."

Amos seemed satisfied with giving his surname, and by and by when he had returned to his coat and mittens and was ready to go, he cleared his throat several times, with an appearance of hesitation and embarrassment, and presently, with a resolute effort, discharged his parting salutation, " Well, good-night, *Mr. Tuttle !* "

" Good-night, good-night, godfather," returned Rol, with an appearance of cheerfulness. He promised to stop on his way to town, if he should go to New York on the morrow, for that question was left unsettled.

When Amos had gone, Rollo threw himself into

his chair with a smothered moan. He was proud of his courage. He wanted a heroic career, and felt contempt of danger, but he shrank from that dying man at the Sailor's Snug Harbor. To be charged with being kin to such as he would be an injury that he could not fight about. He settled himself to consider what he would do, but found it impossible to be quiet. He wanted space to move about in, so fetching his hat and his pea-jacket from a peg, he went out under the sky, and pushed on furiously, seeming to beat against his fate as he beat against the gale. The wind-blown clouds were trailing down the southern sky, the moon was setting, and a few stars looked down upon him with the expression of calm eyes from a clear space overhead. He had a sensitive soul, that manly boy, and he felt the influence of things great and high. That look which the stars gave him was a reproach, and the grandeur of the sea hushed him, and presently there arose from among the miscellaneous accumulations of his memory this : —

> " Resolve to be thyself ; and know that he
> Who finds himself loses his misery ! "

He had not the faintest idea where it came from, where he had learned it, — but there it was, at just the right moment. He stopped and repeated it slowly.

" After all," he said, " is it anything to me, really, the sort of creature somebody else was? Why can't I be just *myself*, at any rate ? "

It was the outgrowth of this thought that gave him courage, and an hour afterwards, when he turned back to the cottage, there was tranquillity underneath his determination, and both were born of a new kind of heroism, without which mere physical courage is a poor thing. To be ready to fight was nothing. He was ready not to fight. He alone could give origin to his future self. What had that man at the Sailor's Snug Harbor to do with it? What had anybody? It was for him to build up any sort of self he pleased.

He went to bed with that consolation, and the resolution to go to New York, and his sleep was profoundly peaceful.

It was a day of great excitement to Ma'am Dagget, to say nothing of the boy himself, when he started for New York. The dame suffered the dread that he would never come back, and Amos, when he stopped to say good-by to him, watched the light craft shooting away with the same look of being docile under compulsion with which the old hulks hauled up on the strand seem to watch their smart successors sail on to ports where they will never touch again.

When Rol awoke on board the boat at its pier in New York, on the morning after his start, the object before him seemed dreary and distasteful. The enthusiasm with which he had resolved to be himself, undisturbed by what had ever been, cooled away for the time, and left him like a locomotive with the fire gone out. But he had a motive, and

an unwavering will to pursue it, and he was soon
mixing in the increasing flow of life in the great
city, — mixing, and at the same time realizing
how entirely separate he was, what an irrelated
atom in that great tissue of relations.

He established temporary relations with things
by taking a car up town to where he remembered
a nice little baker's shop with a tidy restaurant,
where he had peeped at the jelly tarts in the windows when he was a little fellow, walking with
Rosa, his nurse, who had seemed to have frequent
affairs to settle with the baker's assistant. He
found the baker's assistant still on duty, and while
Rol took his hot muffins and coffee in the restaurant, thinking of some people who were just awakening in a certain house up Fifth Avenue, who
should come into the shop, through a glass door in
the rear, but Rosa herself, his old nurse, with a fat
baby in her arms, which she carried with an accustomed air that she had perhaps acquired in
ministrations to him.

The degree of comfort Rol felt in being near
those humble people was the measure of his loneliness. The old association seemed delightful to
him, and he went out of the shop with a craving
for old associations, and resolved to pass the time
which must elapse before he could visit the Sailor's
Snug Harbor in being as near and getting as much
of his old home as he could from the outside.

Yet how to insure himself against a painful encounter with those who might not consider asso-

ciations, as connected with him, quite so pleasant? He hated miserable disguises. He had determined to be honestly himself, everywhere and always; he would never take a false part willingly, but he must have one look at the one who had always been dearest to him. He could not come to New York and go away without seeing her.

While he was considering the matter, there was in his mind a sub-consciousness of some place in Broadway where he had bought appurtenances for private theatricals, and without any definite motive, he took the direction of Broadway. In doing so, he passed a man at a wayside stand, upon which were displayed every sort of eyeglass, — colored glasses of all shades of blue, green, and London smoke, glasses for old eyes, and glasses for defective young eyes. Rol scarcely looked at the useless things, in passing, but suddenly possessed of an idea, he ran back and bought a pair of blue glasses, which he tucked away in his pocket.

Upon reaching the establishment of *A. Guizot, Costumier,* he paused upon the sidewalk doubtfully, then slowly mounting the stairs, entered those gorgeous rooms. They were vacant at that early hour, except for the presence of a young man, who was dusting, arranging, and taking the covers off of forms, upon which were displayed the representative portions of military generals, kings, queens, Roman emperors, dancing girls, flower girls, fairies, and demons. In the glass cases, disposed upon all sides, were wigs of every hue, beards, moustaches, eyebrows, eyelashes, everything required to make up a human or inhuman countenance, — even noses and ears, of such infinite variety, it seemed that every hideous possibility of fancy in respect to ears and noses had found expression. There were the ears of fauns, of asses, of rabbits, and enormous human ears that would have answered for sails; there were the feet of satyrs, and the cloven feet of that equivocal gentleman who never shows his feet at all in good society. There was a glitter of false jewels, tiaras, diadems, flowers, laces, everything, *everything* that could be wanted to make up any kind of a creature, ancient or modern, and there was a terrible impression that all races of men, all demons and divinities, had been shattered and scattered and their recoverable atoms carefully collected by Mons. Adolphe Guizot, who offered every man a chance to be any other man he chose to be from Adam down to Napoleon III.

Rol looked upon these things with sickening and disgust. To be without affectation or disguise seemed to him the most precious of privileges, but he resolved to exchange this privilege for another for a few hours, and he fancied he could do so without giving up too much of himself. Long moustaches would make him older, and he was really so thin and dark that he looked like a strange boy, even to himself. His glasses would hide his eyes, that were persistently the same under any circumstances, and he could wander fearlessly among the old haunts.

He bought the moustaches, and the young man in attendance fastened them upon his smooth young lip.

You have twenty-five year, monsieur?" he exclaimed, stepping backward and looking at Rol with an appearance of astonishment.

"Ah," said Rol with a little sigh, "j'en ai cinquante!" and he drew his blue glasses from his pocket, placed them upon his nose, and looked at himself in a long mirror.

"Juste ciel!" pursued the young man. "Personne ne le connaissait jamais!"

And Rol made a great impression upon himself, as he surveyed his reflection in the mirror. It was incredible what an entirely different person he had become. His closely cut hair made a great difference, to begin with, for it changed his curly locks to straightness, and his thin face seemed of an entirely different cast from that of the old, jolly Rol. His unusual height and his moustaches really did give him the appearance of being twenty-five. He could go fearlessly anywhere, for he didn't even know himself.

When he regained the street, he marched up town with a quick step. You would have said he was hurrying home to a joyous welcome. But he caught a glimpse of something in the window of an establishment where the most unwished-for things are to be bought, and abruptly checked his pace. What might not have happened? He began to have fears, and approached that most accustomed spot on earth with dread. The face he longed to see might have vanished altogether and forever. His heart beat hard and heavily when he could look up the avenue and fix his eyes upon the very walls of his old home. Yes, there appeared to be some change. There was a wagon before the door, and men at work. Rol stopped on the corner opposite and below. He saw that they were putting up a covered way from the door to the curbstone. There was no grief there. They were in preparation for a party. No one would be thinking of him. He could be still bolder. He crossed over, and walked up past what seemed his own door. It stood wide open, and Matthews was taking in the morning paper, indulging in one of his prerogatives, a first glance at the news. He took no notice of Rol whatever, who walked slowly and tantalized himself with a sight of the familiar objects within. There was the tall, hand-some, Dutch clock, — Grandpapa's clock, he had called it, and he shivered at the thought of the proud old man who had held him on his knee, shivered again at the thought of the man at the Sailor's Snug Harbor. There was the old suit of armor against the wall, and the bronze cast of the knight without fear and without reproach. But Rol did not see what was coming up from the base-ment door. He was interrupted in his furtive con-templations by a pounce upon his arm. He felt himself seized upon, arrested, held fast, and his violent recoil did not loosen the retaining grasp, it only brought him face to face with the exultant, triumphant Monte Cristo, who, shivering and whimpering with a joy which he found the dog language utterly incapable to express, held his runaway master as inflexibly as if he had been a rigid member of the police force.

Rol felt like a convicted outlaw, and looked about him as a thief might have done for some place of refuge. He thankfully perceived that Matthews, with his eyes fastened upon the newspaper, was turning slowly and unconcernedly about and closing the door. He thrust his faithful dog aside with difficulty, though he had never seemed such a precious old fellow as at that moment, and hurried on. But the dog hurried as fast as he did, to be sure, and was much too excited to heed Rollo's commands to him to go home. He had n't been searching all those months for a boy, to turn about and leave him to lose himself again. Rol longed to give the poor fellow a friendly word, but he knew it would make matters ultimately worse, so he plunged along with no aim but to escape from the very thing he longed for, — an old friend. A church door stood open. Rol darted inside and closed it, whereupon Monte Cristo laid siege, and if scratching and howling were the appliances for conquest, he might have taken the city.

The dog would never be the one to give up, Rol was sure of that, so discreetly, and only half reluctantly, he opened the door and received the

wild caresses of his trusty old follower (which soon
knocked off the moustaches and the blue glasses),
with a hungry, almost happy heart, returning
them, on his own part, with equal warmth. He
knelt there in the porch of the Church of the
Heavenly Rest, and let out the pent-up tenderness
of his heart on Monte Cristo's neck.

This precious indulgence could not last long,
however, for the early Lenten worshipers began
to come, and to frown upon the dog. The porch
of the sanctuary was no place for him, for " Without are dogs," it is written.

" Now, sir, go home! " said Rol, with an effort
to be severe.

The dog crouched at his feet, looking up into
his face with such pleading eyes that Rol turned
and walked half way up the gallery stairs. How
he longed to take the dear fellow with him!

" Go home! " he repeated, turning upon the
animal, who crept nearer, whimpering and shivering.

Rol went up and sat in the dark place at the
top of the stairs. Why might he not have his old
companion? His heart warmed and lightened at
the thought. Monte stole up and put his nose
on the boy's knee. The dear, faithful, familiar,
half-human friend! Why not take him away?
The dog had been his own, expressly his own, a
Christmas present from Colonel Payne. *His own?*
Would the kin of the man at the Sailor's Snug
Harbor have had that high-bred, costly dog as a

gift? Never! Monte Cristo was one of those things to which he had never had any right.

He arose and descended the gallery stairs with an air of determination, paused in the porch below to consider, then went out with the happy dog following, and looked about for a policeman. He found one at Madison Square, whom he remembered, an honest, kindly fellow, and left the astonished Monte Cristo in his keeping. It was Rol's own hands that fastened the leash, and he will never forget the sorrow and reproach that were in the petrified dog's look when his master turned away and again forsook him.

CHAPTER XII.

THAT evening, when Rol returned from Staten Island, it was with a vague, undefined heaviness, an ever-recurring wish that the dead man at the Sailor's Snug Harbor might have spoken, a haunting, uninvited suspicion of loss.

Whatever else he may or may not have lost, however, he lost the Fall River boat, upon which he had expected to return to Nantucket.

He remembered a place where he could go for the night, with his moderate means, a tidy little German hotel on Fourth Avenue. It was another resort of Rosa's, which Rol had visited with her in other days. Its privileges were offered to the world by a rosy, smiling, globular relative of her's, and everything about the little establishment smiled, and bloomed, and shone and expanded itself, even as he did. Its brick walls were painted a rich cream color, to match his unctuous complexion, and the blinds a cheerful green. There, however, the simile fails, — the eyes of the house were at fault, — for there was nothing green in Peter Klaus's eye, nor anything blind, either.

As Rol entered the gayly lighted hall, he caught

a faint and grateful insinuation of dinner, in which the rampant onion insinuated most, and triumphed over the assiduous efforts of a circle of smokers, in the room designated on the door as "*Das Amt*," to which Rol promptly repaired, and formally enrolled himself among the guests of the house. During the time which it took to accomplish this, he listened to an animated conversation among the smokers, something like this : —

First Pipe. " Vat goot schiff vas dat ? "

Second Pipe. " *Vat goot schiff vas dat?* "

First. " Ja."

Second. " *Ja ?* "

First. " Ja."

Second. " Die Gute Frau."

First. " *Die Gute Frau?* "

Second. " Ja."

First. " *Ja?* "

Second. " Ja."

First. " Vrom vere comes dat goot schiff ? "

Second. " *Vrom vere comes dat goot schiff?* "

First. " Ja."

Second. " *Ja ?* "

First. " Ja."

Second. " Vrom Amsterdam."

First. " *Vrom Amsterdam?* "

Second. " Ja."

First. " *Ja ?* "

Second. " Ja."

First. " Vat is de goot news vrom Amsterdam ? "

Second. "*Vat is de goot news vrom Amster-dam ?*"

First. " Ja."

Second. "*Ja ?* "

First. " Ja."

Second. " Hans Schmidt is dead."

First. " *Hans Schmidt is dead ?* "

Second. " Ja."

First. " *Ja ?* "

Second. " Ja."

Between each query and response there was a long, grave pause, during which the pipes made up for time lost in speaking by more diligent puffing, so that the conversation, short as it appears, occupied all the ten minutes during which Rol waited and confabulated with good Peter Klaus himself. As he had no baggage, nor any visible evidence of honest designs, except his honest face, this confabulation consisted, chiefly, of a polite request, on the one hand, and a ready consent, on the other, to pay for his dinner and night's lodging in advance. His feeling of independence was therefore complete when he seated himself at table.

In the steam of his cabbagy, oniony soup, there floated visions of home, and in the aggregate of feeling accumulated during the day was a very strong deposit of sadness, and a rather doubtful joy that he was still near the only place he could think of as home.

His companions at table were three men of three diversities of age, and one striking coincidence of infirmity, — they every one wore spectacles; and between their gulps of Rhein wein and lager bier, they each deplored the lack of Wilhelm. Rol thought they might be partaking of funeral baked meats, but it presently appeared that Wilhelm had been suddenly called to Hoboken by some calamity, when they were in such need of him as to furnish another calamity in New York.

Rol had had German nurses and governesses, and had pulled away at his German, both at home and abroad, so that he was able to understand their conversation, and he felt that it would have been both pleasant and profitable to look upon a person of the importance of Wilhelm.

The three men finished their repast and departed. Directly Rol heard the tuning of strings, and gave a start of pleasure. By and by there followed a dash from some overture that he had played himself. His interest in dinner became divided with his interest in the parlor orchestra, and he at length finished hastily, and went to attend the rehearsal in progress. The instruments were a harp, a violoncello, and violin. A second violin lay unused in its case upon the piano. Rol seated himself in a corner to listen. His fingers twitched with longing to touch one of the violins. They were playing dancing music, that would have had no difficulties for him, when he was in practice. At every pause, the eldest of the men, who played the violoncello, who appeared to be the leader, and who was called Herr Amschell, settled back in his chair with a great sigh and said it was " Schwach, schwach, sehr schwach ! "

" The piano would help," one of the men suggested. No, Herr Amschell replied, they wanted only strings ; they paid much, and they must be suited. There ought to be four pieces, at least. Where could he find a substitute for Wilhelm ? He scratched his bald head and stamped his foot, and his trouble seemed to culminate in despair. It was late, everybody was engaged for the evening. He had tried Johann and Karl and Felix and Franz and Gustav. They were all impossible.

Rol started, arose, then seated himself again, but hearing Herr Amschell choose a waltz that he knew especially well, made a plunge, and confronting the unhappy man said in German, " I wish you would let me try one of the violins."

Herr Amschell started to his feet. " Ach, guten Himmel ! " he cried. " Have you dropped from the skies ? "

Rol explained that he had been out of practice for a while, but that most of their selections were familiar to him, and if they had a little time and patience, he thought he could easily bring himself up to the mark.

One of the men drew the idle violin from its case and passed it to Rol, who took it with a sort of loving look, and when he raised it to his shoulder touched his cheek to it as if caressing it. It seemed like another old friend.

. Herr Amschell placed some music on the vacant rack, and asked Rol to play it to him. He went through the part very well, with scarcely a false note. "Once more," said Herr Amschell. Rol repeated, without a fault, and Herr Amschell looked delighted. "Now, together." They took the waltz together, and Rollo's hand was in. They rehearsed piece after piece, and he gained credit with each.

" You shall have five dollars to go with us and play for dancing this evening," said Herr Amschell.

Rol gladly agreed.

They allowed him to select such pieces as he could play best, and in looking over the repertoire he had come upon one which he studied pensively, as one might re-read an old letter from a dead friend. It was an air from the Magic Flute, that Mrs. Payne had liked to play with him. In rehearsing that Rol played exquisitely, though at times he could hardly see the score, for the mist in his eyes.

" Ach ! You play well !" said Herr Amschell. " We shall have no trouble with *you.* On the contrary. Come, it is a quarter to eight o'clock. We must be off."

" But he must wear the dress of Wilhelm," said one of the violinists. " He cannot go in a pea-jacket."

" Recht, recht," responded Herr Amschell. "That was forgotten. Eilen Sie sich !" and Rol was rushed up-stairs and put into the claw-hammer coat and white vest of Wilhelm, which were a pretty good fit. Evidently he was foreordained to be Wilhelm's substitute.

" Wait a moment," said Rol, when at last all seemed ready. He pulled from the pocket of his pea-jacket his moustaches, and blue glasses, and fixed them on in a twinkling.

" Mein Gott ! It *is* Wilhelm ! " cried all three musicians in a breath, when Rol appeared in the parlor below.

They took a Fourth Avenue car, and Rol neither thought nor cared where he was going until he found himself leaving it at the corner of Madison Avenue and the very street that went through to his old home. A sudden " *what if* " flashed upon him, but he answered it with " Pshaw ! impossible." Now, you may learn this with Rollo, my friend. *Nothing* is impossible. When they came out upon Fifth Avenue, there was *the* house blazing with lights, and Herr Amschell crossed straight over to it and turned up the covered steps. Rol followed so far as to stand under the arch that spanned the sidewalk, where he stopped and looked up the tunneled stairway with a stupefied stare.

" Was fehlt ihnen ? " asked the harpist, who brought up the rear.

" Es fehlt mir Nichts ! " responded Rol, with an abrupt resolution, and in a moment he reëntered the doorway, from which he had gone out so carelessly eight months before, with his heart swelling and throbbing until he was stifled.

But there was nothing to fear, — not even Monte Cristo, who was invariably banished to remote regions on festive occasions, because he howled at the music.   Yet Rol would hardly have trembled more, or been more nearly overcome by universal trepidation, in face of a den of tigers.

His tumult had not had time to subside, after he had taken his place in the hall, behind the plants, which made a bower for the musicians just between the drawing-room and music - room, when there were footsteps on the stairs, the rustling and soft hissing of lightly brushed silk, and there she came!   In a moment she was sweeping past him, her long skirts almost brushing his feet.   He snatched off the blue glasses to look at her, and his heart leaped to his mouth again, — then sank with misgiving and alarm, for she looked quite pale and ill, and did not glance about her with the bright, interested smile which he had always seen her wear, but kept her eyes fixed upon the floor as she walked, with a grave, absent look, although close behind her followed that boy who was every inch a Weir, with the excited Weir blood flushing his thin cheeks, and — sun, moon, and stars! was that the little Quaker girl from Nantucket with Betty Vinton?   What times those were, when you could n't tell for a minute what would come to anybody!   Mrs. Payne paced slowly up and down in the drawing-room, while Roland Weir and Miriam stood upon the fair surface of creamy white, and turned round and round and round to look at the banks and pyramids and festoons of flowers. Rollo could see them all. The dear little Quaker girl had looked almost frightened at herself when she came down-stairs, but she appeared to forget herself altogether in those broad, sweet, bright spaces, and Roland Weir held up his handsome head and swept his eyes about the horizon like a newly landed discoverer taking possession.

Betty never ceased to twitter and flit. She flitted across the hall, where only Matthews stood like a wooden image by the door, and the musicians were arranging their music. Miriam came slowly after, while Roland Weir paused midway in the hall, by the bower of tall plants, to look back at his aunt.

"I wonder," he said confidentially to Betty, — "I wonder what's the matter with Aunt Anna. I may have done something to trouble her. She never looked like that before."

"I don't believe it's *you*," returned Betty.

"What then?"

"I think it's Rol," Betty answered in a loud whisper. "The last time we kept this day it was for him. Everything was just as it is now except — there was *Rol* instead of *you*, you know."

A string of one of the violins broke with a jarring twang, there was a roll of carriages, Matthews swung the door wide open, Roland Weir took his place beside Mrs. Payne and received Rol's old friends, while Rol himself, poor fellow, had all he could do to receive the strange sensations which crowded upon him.

CHAPTER XIII.

ROLAND WEIR looked dizzy when he had welcomed his two hundred guests, and the little Quakeress was in a pleasant delirium, and seemed bewildered, as she watched what she fancied to be the bits of a shivered rainbow lightly blown about her by the wind.

Mrs. Payne enjoyed the satisfaction of feeling that she had produced the example of something perfect in the way of a young girl, something as fresh and modest as an orchid on the margin of a Nantucket meadow, and quite unexceptionable in the world's eye, too. She considered that there was no danger of erring in the matter of richness and choiceness of material, in the pretty toilet she had given Miriam, for who was more exacting about those things than a Quakeress? Had she not seen them, — rigid as to the proper plain cut of their garments, while they attracted every eye by the sumptuous richness and delicacy of their texture? A simple white gown of exquisite quality and a rich, heavy sash would be perfectly suitable, then (so it seemed to Mrs. Payne), and Miriam would give all the color and adornment herself. Waking or sleeping, that soft white gown and shining sash had floated in the child's fancy for a week. She would have liked some bright colors, like Betty, and more ruffly, fluttery things, but the fact that she was denied them made her believe that she was really within safe and proper bounds. The truth was that the plainness of her dress seemed like a distinguished style, and there was not a more charming girl at the party. Roland and Betty were proud of her.

Since she could not dance, Mrs. Payne had Roland, with Miriam, lead the procession of his guests through a long march. To Miriam those moments were sublime. Her face wore a look of earnest gravity, for she felt that nothing more grand or important could ever happen.

Most of the young people knew that Miriam was the little Quaker girl of Nantucket, who had drifted out to sea and been rescued by Betty Vinton (so Betty told the tale), and who was connected with the story of Roland Weir. Roland was a live hero of romance. He had been a small lion ever since he came to New York. His history, much to Mrs. Payne's annoyance, had found its way even into the newspapers, and nothing could exceed the regard in which he was held by the boys and girls of his acquaintance, or the immense curiosity and interest of far-away ones who were not of his acquaintance, and who only had the privilege of seeing him pass on the street.

After the first dance, then, they gathered about

Miriam to have a few words with a real native of that romantic desert island upon which Roland Weir had been cast away. They were disappointed to see her so much like other girls.

"I wish she had worn her uniform," said one.

"What uniform?"

"Why, the Quaker uniform. I expected she would look like those Quaker dolls they have at fairs, with walnuts for heads."

They asked absurd questions about Nantucket, and when Miriam had begun to talk, they asked anything, to keep her talking, it was so funny to hear her, and so pleasant. She told them she had never seen any one dance before she came to New York, except Pel'tiah Groves. Who was Pel'tiah? He was the gravedigger. He dug all the graves and buried all the people that died on Nantucket. Oh, a gravedigger dancing! Where did he dance? Among the graves in the moonlight, or on dark nights with pale blue lights flickering about him? Miriam felt called upon to clearly represent her friend Pel'tiah, that there might be no mistaken impression left upon the mind of any person. She explained with earnestness that he had given up the pomps and vanities, but that he was a beautiful whistler. When he was greasing the wheels of the hearse he whistled a nice tune, "Away with Melancholy," he called it. One boy remarked that Pel'tiah must be a philosopher, but Miriam said no, he was a Methodist.

All the while the music was calling, but very

few were dancing. The novel entertainment of hearing such uncommon things from such a new kind of girl was not to be lost for the more ordinary pastime, and because they had been so amused, some of the more thoughtful and courteous ones proposed that they should do something which would give Miriam a chance to accompany them. It seemed rude to leave her to watch the dancing alone.

"What would you like to do?" they said. "Do you know any game we could play? Do teach us some of your games."

Miriam shook her head. "I never played a game," she said. "If everybody would like it, I should be glad to march once more, when you 've done dancing. Please don't stop."

The boy who had called Pel'tiah a philosopher seated himself beside Miriam, and said he did n't think much of dancing.

"I wonder to hear thee say that," said Miriam.

"Why, should you like to dance?"

Miriam drew a heavy sigh. "Yes, but I can't," she said. "Friends don't dance."

"Why, *my* friends do," said the boy. "I should like to dance with you. You 'll march with me, then, won't you? This quadrille, now, is n't much different from marching. See? They only walk about. I should think you might do that."

"I think I *could*," said Miriam eagerly. "There, now they 're all going to walk round and shake hands with everybody, first with one hand and then with the other. I should n't think it could be wrong."

" *Wrong?* Why of course it is n't ! "

" David danced, thee knows."

" David who ? "

" Why, King David."

" Oh, yes."

" But perhaps that 's why he worried so much about his sins.   Thee knows he keeps saying what a sinner he is."

" That was when he had n't danced as much as he ought to, probably."

" I don't know ! " said poor Miriam.   " Is n't it queer about opinions ? "

" It 's queer what they want of so many," said the boy.   " I should think *two* would be enough to give contrary people a chance to dispute."

" But is n't it hard to understand things ? " continued Miriam.   " When we want to do right, and want to be happy, too, is n't it hard to tell *what* to do ? "

" Now here 's a chance to do the right thing and be happy, too," said Miriam's chatty friend, as the quadrille was finished, " for we 're going to have our march.   You 're to march with me, but just excuse me a minute, please."

He stepped down the room and spoke to the director, and then Miriam was led to a place in the line of marchers.

They marched and countermarched. They took now a serpentine and now a diagonal course;

they parted with their partners at one end of the room and met them again at the other. Their lines intertwined and intertwisted, united and separated, intervolved and dispersed. They paired and dispaired again and again, and when there seemed to be only confusion and breaking up, everything came back straight and simple just as it had been at first. It was exhilarating to the little girl of simple senses. She was never allowed to go wrong, for when things became very bewildering a kind hand was laid upon her shoulder and she was guided aright. Presently the couples formed into squares — it seemed only a continuation of the marching figures — and Miriam's partner said, " Now we just want to go forward a little and come back."

While the side couples were doing the same, Miriam was directed to give her right hand to the girl opposite. The girl turned her about, and her partner then caught her left hand, turned her about also, and brought her standing in her place again. There had been so much turning about that Miriam's head was completely turned, and she went on with grave absorption, feeling perfectly innocent, through figure after figure of a quadrille.

Her attention never for a moment wandered, until it seemed some magnetism drew her eyes to the hall door, near which she was placed, and there stood Uncle David and *Paul !*

Uncle David had an astounded, stupefied look.

He had apparently been arrested in the way through which Matthews was leading him, by the sight of his little Quaker niece, arrayed in *what* garments! and treading the mazes of a dance!

Miriam in her turn was arrested by that look of Uncle David. It reduced her dream to reality. She remembered who she was, and realized her unfit position. Unheeding the urgent prompting of her partner, unconscious that she was breaking up everything, she hurried straight to Uncle David.

"My dear," said he, "is it really thou? I don't understand. Was thee *dancing?*"

"I—I'm afraid I was," Miriam answered. "We were marching, and we went right along."

This explanation did not clearly enlighten Uncle David. He was an easy-going, charitable, innocent-hearted man—a very liberal Hicksite; but Obed Swain was orthodox. His trouble was to put himself in Obed's place and conduct these conditions to the right issue.

"Thee better not. Thee better keep quiet," he said, with all the severity of which he was capable.

Great discomfort entered Miriam's soul, and to add to it, Paul appeared to be practicing some of his absurd tricks, for he wore a pair of eyeglasses and gave Miriam the same alarming stare which had frequently transfixed her before. As she gave her hand to him, in rather a perfunctory manner, he adjusted his glasses and held his head back stiffly, so as to look straight through the middle of them at her, as Aunt Hepsy was wont to do, and he also gave a faint groan after the manner of Aunt Hepsy.

" Why does Paul wear those spectacles ? " Miriam asked.

" The world is a different place to him since the doctor ordered those," Uncle David replied. " He finds he has never really seen things before."

" I see *remarkable* things now," said Paul, with a long survey of Miriam.

Miriam fancied he saw her as she had seen an ant under Dr. Mayhew's microscope, — an ant, that looked a tiny, innocent atom to the naked eye, but which, under the glass, was a hideous thing as large as a lobster. She wondered uneasily what sort of a creature she was under Paul's revealing glasses.

" Ah," said Mrs. Payne's gracious voice, at that moment, as Mrs. Payne herself came to them through the hall, reaching out a cordial hand to Uncle David. " I hope you 've brought us a reprieve."

" I 'm sorry to say I 've come to execute the sentence," returned Uncle David. " This is my son Paul. I have come back a little sooner than I expected, and it occurred to my mind that Miriam ought to know we were going by to-morrow's boat, so I ventured to call, though I saw thee had company."

" And must we give up Miriam so soon ? "

" Well, her Aunt Hepsy 's at home now, and is

very particular to have the child back again directly."

Miriam started as if Aunt Hepsy had suddenly materialized before her. Joy yielded to its natural enemy and died without a struggle. The brightness of that charmed hour had furnished her with something more to be given up, with new desires to be denied; and, to emphasize the pain of denial and renunciation, Roland Weir, glowing with the pleasure of his career, came sailing towards her in one direction, and careless, contented Betty in another, attracted by the group in the doorway.

To Roland, the sight of Paul Haddon was the promise of extraordinary things. He had never lacked sensations himself when that pleasantly perplexing youth had appeared, and he was charmed to be able to present such a remarkable person to his new friends.

Though Mrs. Payne could not prevail upon Uncle David to desert his plain quarters at Friend Eunice Gray's, in Sixteenth Street, and stay at her house, she easily persuaded him to take a seat by the library fire and look at the newspapers until after the supper, and Paul was borne away and exhibited as another native of Nantucket. His eyeglasses made him look so wise, and his rather grave manner gave the young New Yorkers such an impression of awful rectitude and overwhelming example, that they politely withdrew from the discouragements these seemed to offer. Betty, however, was not so easily discouraged. The most illustrious virtues could not intimidate her. She took a fixed position near Paul, and seemed to wish to avail herself of such advantages as his superior society offered. They were very near Miriam, who sat looking upon everything pensively, as one does for the last time. But upon Betty Vinton and Paul she looked as for the first time. Betty chattering to Paul, not the least embarrassed by the way he fixed his eyes upon her through those glasses, and Paul answering Betty with considerable deference !

"I'm sure it's a great misfortune," Miriam heard Betty say, alluding, probably, to Paul's trouble with his eyes, on account of which he was returning to his home.

"But my misfortune is nothing compared with that of a friend of mine, at Haverford, — at least he *was* there," returned Paul.

His solemnity seemed to indicate that his friend had been removed by death, at least, and it was reflected in Betty's grave eyes.

"What was the matter with him?" she asked gently.

"It is hard for me to dwell upon the subject," Paul replied, gazing fixedly, with drooping head, at the toe of his boot.

"It's no matter, then," Betty quickly responded.

"Still," resumed Paul, "I should like to show how a small misfortune, like mine, for instance, might have saved this young person from something much worse."

" Oh," murmured Betty.

" The love of home," continued Paul, " as the copy book says, is inherent in the human breast."

Betty listened with parted lips.

"This boy I am speaking of had it stronger than any one I ever saw. He wanted to go home, and he had no appetite for rye pudding. In fact, he used to groan and wish for home and a rye famine in the same breath. He suffered so, poor fellow, that once in his desperation, he was heard to say, — no, I won't tell thee what he said. It was *awful*. If he had only had bad eyes, now, he might have gone home on account of them, as well as not. But he had n't a thing ailing him, — not so much as a headache or a toothache. All his sufferings from homesickness and rye pudding did n't count. Every day he grew worse and worse, and I felt as if I ought to watch him. There was no guessing what he might do. One evening, we were strolling out together, and this unhappy boy stopped and rested his elbows on the top rail of a fence, which inclosed a fine, tall field of rye. No, it was the *rye* that was tall, come to think of it, instead of the field. I thought he was admiring the sunset, but I soon perceived it was the rye he was looking at, — and he looked disgusted. Presently he laughed, — a dreadful laugh. I said to myself, Alas, his reason has departed ! 'Paul,' said he, ' I 'm going home on Fourth

Day,' — this was Second Day, — 'but I'm going to do you all a favor first, and give you something pleasant to remember me by.' Then he laughed again. I slipped my arm through his and led him to his room, where I tried to divert his mind from his sorrows. But it was all in vain. A few hours later I missed him, and hurrying wildly about in search of him, I at last thought I saw him going across lots leading Dolly, the gray mare. There was a little moon just setting, and I could see very well. I crept along by the wall, intending to meet him when he came out upon the road, and if he undertook to mount Dolly and trot away home, I meant to go too, — just to see that he was safe, thee knows. I felt that the sooner he went home, the better. When he reached the road, I was puzzled to know what he *was* going to do. He held something in his hand which looked like a large tin coffee-pot, and pulling a string from his pocket, he tied it to the end of the mare's tail. 'That is a convenient way of carrying a little refreshment,' I said to myself. He must have made the coffee-pot uncommonly secure, for he was a long time about it, and then he led Dolly across to the rye-field, and letting down the bars gave her a smart slap and told her to 'get up.' I never did see anything get up as Dolly did. I could hear the coffee-pot thumping against her legs and the lid flapping up and down as she went round and round the rye-field. The next morning there was n't rye enough standing to make one small pudding. It was all trampled into the earth."

Betty's stare had gradually changed into a broad smile, which went off suddenly into a laugh. This ridiculous event, in place of the awful fatality she had expected, was amusing by contrast. But presently Betty drew a long, slow breath and looked at the matter from another point of view.

"That was an abominable boy!" she said. "He had no business to do such a thing. It was dishonest."

"I see the reasonableness of thy position," said Paul, pinching his sharp chin with his long thumb and finger, and thoughtfully considering his boot-toe again. "And that is the melancholy part of it. His father made him go without things until he had paid for the rye; but he said even humble pie was easy to swallow, after rye pudding. Anything for a change."

"Did he go home?"

"He *did*, without fail. His home is here in New York. I'm going to see him to-morrow."

"What's his name?" asked Betty, but Paul was prevented from answering by great surprise at feeling the tip of his ear seized by an invisible thumb and finger. He tried to turn upon his assailant, but his head became fixed in a vise.

"Oh, come," said Paul, "who is it?"

"I am thy pardner's ghost," responded a sepulchral voice, "doomed for a certain time to walk the earth."

" Then what ? "

" And then to take to the water, about the first of July."

This time the voice was the natural voice of the boy who had led Miriam into dancing.

" Perez Howard ! " exclaimed Paul, wrenching his head away.

The two boys grasped each other's hands — both hands — with the cordiality of congenial spirits.

Betty Vinton regretted the fate that forced her to leave such an interesting scene and be led away to the dancing.

" I did n't know you with those goggles," said Perez Howard. " You 'd put an owl out of countenance. Do you come to us as a — a missionary ? Have n't you a few tracts in your pocket ? "

" I 've come to fetch my cousin home," said Paul, looking straight at Miriam, and speaking for her to hear. " She has fallen into bad ways. Her aunt and I are much afflicted about her. We expect to have to labor with her all summer. But there 's a book on a shelf somewhere that will have a good effect upon her."

" Oh, now," said Perez, lowering his tone, "don't bother such a nice girl as that ! I knew she was your cousin, but I did n't let on for fear she might have heard of those little et ceterys, and I want to start fair with people. If they 've got an opinion about you, to begin with, you have to do so much tacking and beating about to get on with them."

" Well, I don't know," said Paul, " my cousin

has an opinion of me, but I get on with her first rate."

"Are you staying in New York without letting me know? That is n't the way to get on with me."

"I meant to try to see thee before I went. I only came to-day, and I 'm going to-morrow."

"To-morrow? No!"

"Yes, that 's the decree."

"Did you come up for this party? I 'm afraid you 're getting worldly."

"I 'm on my way home."

"What have you done now?"

"*I* done? Humph!"

"Oh, maybe it 's the eyes again."

Paul nodded.

"Was that your father I saw in the hall?"

"Yes."

"Won't he leave you with me a few days?"

"Come and see father," said Paul, moving on in the direction of the library. "He 'll be glad to see thee for the sake of thy father; he often speaks of him and the old times at Haverford."

When they reached the library door Paul was shocked to see his father sitting staring into vacancy, with a pale, drawn face.

"Father, father, what is the matter?" Paul said, stepping quickly to his father's side.

The newspaper which David Haddon held shook as if blown by a draught of air. He spread it out with nerveless hands, and pointed to the telegraphic news. Paul glanced over the paragraphs and dropped the sheet.

"It can't be!" he said. "These dispatches are often wrong. Don't let us believe it until we're obliged to, father. I'll run and get thee a glass of water. Excuse us, Perez, we've had bad news. I'll see thee again by and by."

"Don't say anything to Miriam," said David Haddon.

As Miriam sat ruefully considering what Paul had said about the book of judgment that awaited her, she saw Mrs. Payne passing through the room, looking anxiously from side to side, with a strange, overwhelmed look, and an agitated manner, that was in remarkable contrast to her usual calmness. When her eyes fell upon Miriam, her effort to repress her emotion was so apparent that the child perceived it.

"My dear," she said, "your uncle has determined to start for home to-night. You will have to leave us in less than an hour. Come up-stairs with me."

Miriam followed passively, without asking a question, except the one she asked herself, "Does she hate to have me go so much as that?"

On reaching her room she found a maid packing her little box, and in strange, silent haste the pretty gown and its dainty accompaniments were removed, and the grave, brown gown received the little Quakeress again.

Even the haste seemed hardly to explain the

solemn silence. Roland Weir and Betty, who had
followed protesting loudly, were so impressed by
the strangeness, the stillness, the suddenness, that
stillness fell upon them, too.

The carriage which had taken Uncle David to
Sixteenth Street after his belongings returned and
waited at the door. Miriam's box was brought
down. It looked like a small coffin, and held the
remains of her departed pleasures, — the lovely
white gown and the shining sash. All adieus
were said. Roland Weir's guests crowded into
the hall to see the departure of the natives. Perez
Howard ran down to the carriage with them,
while Roland Weir stood shivering in the doorway
with nervous foreboding. He felt an impression
of calamity which was not to be accounted for by
Miriam's premature departure.

When they turned from the door, after the carriage had rolled away, the musicians were playing
the air from the "Magic Flute." Mrs. Payne
stepped quickly across the hall, her hand raised in
protest. "Don't play that!" she said. "Don't!"

She remembered afterwards how suddenly one
of the violinists had dropped his instrument, how
unreasonably sensitive and troubled he had looked.

The birthday party was ending sadly for those
who had been most joyous at its beginning, but
the second violin hardly knew what to call the
emotion with which he passed those last moments.

The refreshments for the musicians were spread
in a basement room that had been Rollo's school-

room, play-room, gymnasium, graduating from one
use to another, but always the use was Rollo's. It
had come to be the servants' dining-room, but the
old pictures had never been removed from the
walls, and in many respects it still had the look of
his beloved den.   While the other musicians re-
galed themselves, he forgot the tempting refection,
and went back to the days when all the world
seemed his own.   He lingered to give a long look
behind, in returning to play for the last dance, and
then, with a parting look at everything, went out,
and the door closed fast again upon it all.

CHAPTER XIV.

STRANGENESS IN THE OLD HOME.

IT was a dreary journey back to the old home, and long before it was over Miriam would have been glad to be harassed by Paul for the sake of having things seem natural once more. But to crown the strangeness of everything, Paul's manner had a touch of gentleness and kindness. It was marvelous. And cheery, chatty Uncle David only sighed and was silent.

It was a blessed sight, at last, as they drew near the end of the journey, to see Rosanna in the front dooryard chasing a vagrant bit of litter. Having captured it, she paused to get her breath again, and watch the clattering old carriage that was coming up the street.

"Lors bress my ole eyes, if it ain't my sweet lamb!" she cried, swinging the gate wide. The door of the carriage swung wide at about the same time, and Miriam alighted in Rosanna's arms. Uncle David inquired for Aunt Hepsy.

"She isn't come back from meetin'," Rosanna said.

"Is there any news?"

"I ain't hear of any," was Rosanna's cheerful response.

" Rosanna, what is it ? What does thee suppose is the matter ? " Miriam begged to know, when Uncle David had moved on. " We had to hurry and get ready in a few minutes, and come in the night cars, and Roland Weir was having his birthday company. Uncle David and Paul seem very strange."

" Thar, never mind, my pretty sparrer ! It 's on'y a way the men folks has," said Rosanna, bustling along after Miriam like an old black hen with one soft little brown chicken.

" It is n't a way Paul has, — very often," said Miriam dubiously.

Everything looked very small and sparse as she glanced at the familiar old things. Even the south front room, their very best room, looked exceedingly bare, like an immaculate receptacle of unfulfilled design.

Rosanna fairly coruscated with delight as she helped Miriam off with her things, but Miriam, tossing them on a chair when she had come out of them, turned and leaned against her old black friend with a sigh.

" Thee dear old Rosanna," she said, " I wish I was n't so big, and thee could take me in thy arms and rock me, as thee used."

" *Big*, my robin ! You is n't a mite too big. You 's all wore out with so many goin's-on. Come set in Rosanna's cheer in the kitchen. But 't ain't goin' do to leave them things thar, honey. Miss Hepsy 'll be yere in a minute."

Miriam gathered up her cloak and bonnet and went to hang them in the closet under the front stairs. As she opened the door her heart lifted and lightened with a cheerful bound, for there hung her father's old drab overcoat and hat. She could almost see his gentle eyes looking at her from under the broad brim, as she took it down from its peg and stroked its nap gently, leaning her cheek against the coat with a foretaste of the peace she should feel when she could lean upon her father himself. She would confess all to him, even the wicked secret wish that had crept into her heart, that he would cast such homely things aside, and belong to the world, like Mr. Vinton.

Then, with a better courage, she went with Rosanna into the kitchen, where the long, open grate, with its heap of bright coals, was not the only cheerful thing to behold. There was the glitter of clean glass in the windows, the shine of bright brasses and tins on the shelves, and there were fowls roasting in the tin kitchen before the fire, and savory vegetables in the bubbling kettles that swung from the crane.

"Have a bite o' something, honey," said Rosanna.

"No, Rosanna, I want thee to hold me a little before Aunt Hepsy comes," Miriam answered, and Rosanna drew the child into her lap, where, leaning against the clean white kerchief that neatly crossed upon the ample bosom which had been her pillow since the day she was born, she accepted gratefully the comfort that had soothed her childish woes, and was rocked and patted and crooned over until, after trying to chat about Roland Weir and her great experiences in New York, she dropped away with the words scarcely gone from her lips, and slept the sound sleep of a child exhausted with excitement and fatigue.

Rosanna carried her gently in her strong arms to the sofa in the keeping-room, trotted away for a shawl to cover her, and then stood and watched her, so entirely at peace. "Yas," she muttered to herself presently, as she shuffled softly back to the kitchen, "but thar 's always the wakin' up, an' it 's a onsartin worl' they comes back to."

That perfect peace lasted long. The sound of footsteps, the murmuring of voices, even a deep, agonized moan, that sounded strangely in the serene old house, were all shut out by the comforting wing that wrapped the child closely.

From the deep sleep she was lifted into dreams. She moved and moaned, and called " Father! father!" and her own cry woke her. Aunt Dorcas was bending over her weeping, and Uncle David was disappearing with great haste through the entry door, while Aunt Hepsy —

But ah, how can I show you the faces of the bereaved! How should I tell, with light, ineffectual pen, the heaviness of sorrow!

"Another steamer lost!" we say, turning the evening journal carelessly, as we sit by our cheerful firesides, from which not one dear face is missing, and the sheet is passed on, perhaps with the remark that there is n't much in it. But to those who had dearest hopes and dearest lives embarked upon that lost steamer, the world itself seems over-charged with the woe that is in those words, "Lost off Cape Hatteras, and every soul on board perished."

There were no loud cries in the old house where Obed Swain had been expected. Deep, impressive silence denoted the presence of a great anguish, for sorrow and joy are alike repressed by those quiet people, to whom the expression of strong emotion is an unseemly thing, and indulgence in wild grief, especially, a sinful outbreak against that divine will which both gives and takes away in mercy and wisdom.

From time to time the door softly opened, and quiet, sober figures glided in with sympathetic faces, and, after holding in a long clasp the hands of the sorrowing ones, sat down by them in silence. Occasionally, one would have words of comfort given him to speak, in measured chanting tones, but, for the most part, they brought only the blessed balm of silent sympathy, and departed as noiselessly as they came.

To hide her agony, that would not be stifled, that could not be permitted to break upon that solemn silence, Miriam crept away to the closet under the stairs, and there, in the darkness, clasped with trembling, clinging arms, the empty coat, and buried her face, sobbing, against the still void where her father's loving heart had been. The old drab coat and hat! This, then, was her terrible judgment for wishing to abolish all such plain, ugly things from her life!

Her vaguest temptations rose before her in the guise of actually accomplished sins, and every one was a wrong against her father, who was never, never to return, — never to hear her sorrowing confession, never to bestow the comfort of his forgiveness! It was like physical suffering, it racked her poor little breast with such cruel pangs. She thought she could not live to bear it, and that thought was welcome, for the locked door might open, then. She would possibly come to some place where she might speak across a gulf to her father, as Dives did to Lazarus.

Rosanna had also sought a hiding place where she could do her weeping after her own fashion. Her African blood and her Free-Will Baptist faith consented to no restraint. She exercised her free-will to the last degree, sitting on the back stairs in the wash-room, from whence, if any sound reached the other inmates of the house, it was very uncertain, and as likely to be the bleating of the sheep on the bank as anything.

Everybody disregarded or forgot the physical need for a time, but Aunt Hepsy's strict care for the common duties of life returned to her at length, and she rose with something like her old rigid manner, and started to go to the kitchen to see that the domestic machinery was not allowed to stand still. She took a few unsteady steps, stumbled, and fell.

"I was dizzy," she said, when Aunt Dorcas hurried to help her to her chair again. "I must have tripped against the rug."

The idea of Hepsy Swain tripping against anything!

"Thee let me see to everything to-day, Hepsy, do!" said Aunt Dorcas.

Strange to say, Aunt Hepsy complied, and when the tea was ready, she even accepted Uncle David's arm to go to the table. Miriam came in just in time to see her weakly leaning upon an arm of flesh like any other woman. It seemed past belief. She even allowed Dorcas Haddon to take her place at table, while she sat aside and was served like a guest. And after tea, or after the rigid, empty form of sitting at table had been observed, she returned to her chair and was passively tolerant of other people's doings, not even proposing to do anything herself. She leaned and drooped heavily. The whole expression of her face and figure was unusual.

Dorcas Haddon followed David as he went out.

"I'm afraid it's a stroke," she said. "Thee go ask Dr. Mayhew to step over here."

Dr. Mayhew came, and advised Aunt Hepsy to go to bed. He helped her up-stairs, and she made no objection, as the stable, resolved, self-sufficient Hepsy Swain would have done. She was that Hepsy Swain no longer.

Miriam, as she watched her, feebly submitting to be led, felt all her old dread melt into compas-

sion and tenderness. The eagle that fixes its keen
eye upon us from among the rocks is no object
for tenderness, but when it falls wounded, whoever is capable of compassion will feel a tenderer
compassion for it because it was an eagle.

When the doctor came again that evening, he
said Aunt Hepsy would always be partially par-
alyzed, if she arose at all from the shock. Miriam
meditated long over this announcement, and the
result of her meditations was something hardly to
be expected. She went with a look of calm resolve to the kitchen, where Rosanna was filling
some large bottles with hot water to put to Aunt
Hepsy's feet.

" Rosanna," she said, " I must learn to take care
of Aunt Hepsy."

" Bressed kingdom !" cried Rosanna. " Why,
my chile, you hol's yo' head 'zac'ly like Miss Hepsy
herse'f. What ails yo', honey ? Susan G.'s a-comin'
to take keer o' Miss Hepsy."

" Susan G. won't stay always, Rosanna. Dr.
Mayhew said Aunt Hepsy might live twenty
years ; she is only sixty, and the Swains live to be
very old. I can do these things myself. I must by
and by, so I'd better begin to learn right away.
And, Rosanna, I think thee'd better not talk to
me as if I was a baby any more. I'm almost
thirteen, and I'm very tall, and if thee pleases, I
wish thee'd treat me as if I was a woman."

Rosanna looked at her baby, standing there so
straight, with her hands clasped precisely before

her, and that strange look of dignity on her young face. Some latent quality, never needed before, got from the determined old ancestor who had chosen that almost desert island and a hard life, in order to carry out a righteous purpose, had risen in Miriam, and armed her to carry out a righteous purpose of her own, and accept a life which seemed as hard and barren to her as, perhaps, the desert island did to him.

Rosanna's inclination to laugh suddenly departed. She sat down, covered her face with her two great hands, and wept aloud.

" Rosanna," said Miriam, " I wish thee 'd be quiet and get the bottles ready. I 'm waiting to carry them up."

" Don't, darlin', don't ! " sobbed Rosanna; " I hate to see yo' so, my lamb. Ef yo' want to take up yo' mind orderin' things an' havin' yer own way, honey, yo' can jes' do it. Do anything yo' likes, dear, but *don't* look that 'r' way, *don't !* "

Miriam was unused to Rosanna's tears, and they produced the effect of bringing her to embrace and coax her old friend, until a more comfortable understanding ensued, and Rosanna wiped her eyes and finished filling and wrapping the bottles with only a few more sniffs.

" Is yo' sho yo' can take them heavy things up, darlin' ? Don't they burn yo' ? Yere, let Rosanna take 'em to the top o' the sta'rs for yer."

" No," said Miriam, " Give them to me," and clasping the burden in her arms she mounted the stairs without bending an inch.

When she reached Aunt Hepsy's room, there was no one in attendance for the moment. She raised the coverings at the side of the bed, and placed the bottles near the cold feet, then seated herself in the chintz-covered rocking-chair by the Franklin fireplace. In the great brass balls on the top she could see a diminished reflection of the solemn-looking room and her far-away, lonesome self in the heart of it. It seemed like a magic mirror, in which she could look at her future. There was nothing for her any more but what was there. There she should sit day after day, and year after year, with Aunt Hepsy, and the years seem eternal to youth.

She listened to the clock in the entry slowly ticking away the hours. How many wearisome ticks in a minute; how slowly the minutes grew into hours; how the hours stretched on and on through day and night and week and month and year; and all — it seemed to the girl just coming to her thirteenth summer — all filled full of grief for her father, and duty to Aunt Hepsy! The tears did not fall, as they had done. They were frozen by the cold awe which filled her, at that appalling view. Her heart ached with a sore agony, which involuntarily sought relief in long, quivering breaths that sounded like repressed sobs; but the tears, — they belonged with the indulgences of past days, those days which had appeared sometimes hard and unlovely.

Aunt Hepsy slept on for hours, and the first

thing her eyes rested upon when they opened was the sharp nose of Susan G. projected above her pillow, in an investigating attitude. There was not the faintest trace of pleasure or welcome in the stare with which her patient responded. Susan G. was indifferent to that, however. She stalked across the room, her highly starched dress and apron speaking for her general inflexibility with a loud rattle, and taking a cup from the top of the fire-frame, stirred it vigorously, poured some of its liquid into another cup with a spout to it, and returning, presented the spout to Aunt Hepsy, inviting her to drink the uncertain contents. Aunt Hepsy ignored the spout and the invitation.

" You must take this nourishment, Miss Swain, before you go to sleep again," said Susan G.

When had Aunt Hepsy been told what she *must* do?

It was like opening the slide in a dark lantern when she opened her eyes. Susan G. felt the flash in her face.

" Thee can take thy nourishment away, — and thyself also," she said, very slowly and distinctly.

Aunt Hepsy accepted few people, and Susan G. was not one of her elect. Absolute, irresistible laws, like those of natural selection and the survival of the fittest, determined these matters, and they determined that Susan G. should perish from the narrow sphere of Aunt Hepsy's favor. It was Greek and Greek, and all night the contest waged, but early in the morning, before the sun had fairly shown his face, there stole into Aunt Hepsy's room, upon tiptoe, a quiet little figure, which stood at the foot of the bed with a sad, calm face, in which the roses were pale and the sweet eyes heavy.

When Aunt Hepsy saw the sight, the expression of her own face softened, and she raised her well hand with an appealing gesture, reached out for Miriam's hand, and held it, while a mist arose in her eyes. They did not kiss each other, those lonely companions in affliction. Aunt Hepsy could never have been guilty of such folly, and the clasped hands said enough.

"I 'm going to learn to do everything for thee, Aunt Hepsy," said Miriam. "I 'm going to take care of thee always, and I shall never leave thee — never."

Aunt Hepsy, whose waking hours all through the night had been filled with the horror of life-long contention with Susan G., looked up with glad surprise. The dawning of something like a humble feeling crept into her hitherto self-confi-dent heart at the sight of the one she had meant to correct with severe discipline looking down upon her so compassionately. She did not speak, but something rolled out of the corner of her eye and fell upon her pillow which startled Miriam. It was the first tear she had ever seen in Aunt Hepsy's eyes. The weakness of the strong is ter-rible. Miriam instinctively felt that she must not notice it. She was trying to think of something she could do to comfort Aunt Hepsy physically, she did not dare offer to console her otherwise, when Susan G. came in with the appurtenances for Aunt Hepsy's toilet.

"Set the things on the stand, Susan G.," said Aunt Hepsy, quite tolerantly, for she was inoculated with gentleness for the moment. " Miriam will attend to me while thee brings up the breakfast."

Susan G., accustomed to be in command herself, stared at her refractory patient.

" I see you 've got a nuss," she said, "and you only want me for help.   There 's them that needs me so as they don't know how to get along without me, and it 's lucky for 'em I need n't stay here another minute."

"No, no, Susan G.," said Miriam, "thee won't go away until I 've learned to do everything for Aunt Hepsy myself.   I 'll be the helper, and thee will teach me what to do, won't thee ? "

Susan G. looked down into the pathetic face of the child.

" Wal, I hain't no objections to that arrängement," she said ; " but I 'm a-going to manage my patients my own way, or I 'm a-going to give up nussing — one or tother."

" Well, shall I bathe Aunt Hepsy's face and hands and make her ready by the time thee wants her to have her breakfast ?   Would that help thee a little ? "

" I 'm sure I don't care," said Susan G., rattling out of the room.

So Miriam furnished a cushion that prevented any dangerous clashing between Aunt Hepsy and Susan G. What Aunt Hepsy dreaded to accept from Susan, Miriam managed to do for her herself, so that Aunt Hepsy was brought to tolerate the unwelcome services.

Susan G. was by no means unaware of her exceptional worth, and she considered it only a suitable and natural provision that she should have an assistant, and the assistant often found her office rather more arduous than that of the principal. Besides the many steps she was allowed to take, she felt an anxious care from which Susan G. was blissfully free. When Susan G. spoke to Aunt Hepsy during her ministrations through the night, Miriam, in her own room across the entry, would waken and go to see if there was need of a mediator between the opposing powers; not with the appearance of a mediator, however, but with a question as to whether she could n't do something, and she always found she could soothe Aunt Hepsy by staying with her for a while, and the sleepy, weary child would sit in the chair by the bed for hours with her head braced back so that it need not nod, and always left peace and comfort behind her when she returned to her fitful rest. Sometimes when Aunt Hepsy called, Susan G. was only too glad to have some one else respond, so that she might continue her nap, and Miriam would rise and go to give Aunt Hepsy the glass of water or the beef tea, or lift the tiresome weight of the helpless arm and gently rub and soothe it into ease again.   Aunt Hepsy was always glad it was Miriam instead of Susan G., and if she thought of it as being hard for the child, she also remembered that her own cares had begun early, and what wholesome discipline had done for her it might do for Miriam.   Aunt Hepsy's voice was still for discipline as a necessity of the human nature.

CHAPTER XV.

THE GHOST OF OBED SWAIN.

BUT what was wholesome medicine for Aunt Hepsy disagreed with Miriam exceedingly. Her sorrow and her self-imposed burden were enough to crush her, yet not even Rosanna knew of the weary night-watches, and the daily offices which Miriam was so willing to undertake she seemed to ask for as indulgences, so that before any one was aware of it the young body and spirit were sadly broken, and the serene child came to have nerves, an affliction of which she had perhaps never heard, and which she could not understand. The spring grew sweeter every day, and she felt it glow and breathe upon her through the open windows, but those lovely things that grow upon the moors, in the meadows, and down by the margin of the pond seemed very far beyond her reach.

The days and weeks, which took so much from Miriam, gave help to Aunt Hepsy, so that she was at first able to sit up in her bed and manage her repasts for herself, with Miriam to supply the place of her withered right hand. It was Miriam always, and Miriam only, who did that. At length

Aunt Hepsy could sit in her chair, with Miriam beside her to minister to her in the hundred little ways that a helpless person can suffer best from a hand that is, after all, their own. And finally, Aunt Hepsy was able to move about with a crutch, or the support of a kind arm or shoulder, and the arm or shoulder were almost always Miriam's. Aunt Hepsy would wait long rather than have any other. The little, round, solid shoulder had grown slight, and the arm very thin, and people said it was because she grew so fast, for on her thirteenth birthday Miriam was nearly as tall as Aunt Hepsy.

In all the slow time, she had borne whatever was to be borne in silence and in secret, excepting once.

Once Rosanna had wakened in the night with the impression that there was some one in her room, and found at her bedside a little shivering figure that moaned.

"Oh, Rosanna," it said, "I'm afraid — I'm *afraid* I can't bear it! But if I could only see father *once*, I could. I *think* I could."

"There, now, my lamb," said Rosanna, holding Miriam's little trembling hands in one of her great black fists, while she patted and stroked the heaving shoulders, "'t ain't onpossible, honey, but you may see him yet. Folks have seen 'em. Lors, my precious, it's 'nough ter draw him right down ter have you takin' on so. Don't darlin', don't!"

"I don't see how I *could* see him when — when"

— sobbed Miriam, unable to put into words the mournful mystery of her thought.

"'T ain't no matter ef we don't see *how* things happens, they goes on a-happenin' jes' the same," said Rosanna.

"Did thee ever see — any?"

"I specs I has."

"Tell me about it!" pleaded Miriam, clinging to Rosanna's arm with quivering eagerness. "Tell me if thee thinks I can see my father!"

"I ain't sho as it's best to talk much about them things," said Rosanna, with a reserve which depended somewhat upon the hour of the night, the melancholy darkness, and even more melancholy light of the room.

"Yes," urged Miriam, "thee must tell me, Rosanna. I shall feel better if I know they do come again, if thee says thee has seen them."

Keeping her eyes averted from the uncertain far corners, Rosanna, to comfort the child, whispered : —

"I seen ole missus."

"*Did* thee, Rosanna?" Miriam cried in a tone that sounded like the gladness of hope. "Oh, then, don't thee think I might be permitted to see father?"

"My sweet lamb!" said Rosanna, "'t would n't 'stonish me none ef you was let to stan' an' look right into Heab'n's do'!" and stimulated by Miriam's eagerness, she told tales that had circulated among the negroes in the days of her bondage.

Miriam listened with eyes strained wide upon the darkness, and with palpitating breath, that prolonged itself into sighs. When Rosanna had finished, her own teeth were chattering with a ghostly terror, but Miriam was exalted by a great hope. She could hardly speak, her little heart was so full. At length she said : —

"I 'm better now, dear old Rosanna, and I think I can bear it. Good-night."

"Lor' bress ye, honey ! Don't ye want Rosanna to come an' lay on de flo' by yo' ? "

"No, thank thee," and Miriam turned away to enjoy this new, great hope in silence and alone.

After that, a person who had watched her might have perceived that she had an expectant look. She turned, when the door opened, with eager eyes, and looked as if she were ready to smile, then her eyes drooped, and the promise of a smile faded into the old, submissive gravity again, as if the one she expected had, after all, not arrived.

Thus a few weeks went by, and there seemed, at last, to be a trace of anxiety and disappointment on her patient face, until, one night, Rosanna was awakened by feeling a grasp upon her arm, and starting up with a frightened outcry, she saw standing in the pale light of a low, waning moon a tall white figure, — it looked very tall to Rosanna.

"For d' Lord's sake, who *is* you ? " gasped Rosanna.

"I 've seen him ! I 've seen him, Rosanna ! " returned a low, exultant voice.

"Oh, my bressed chile! Is that yo'? Sho! How yer skeered me! Who has yo' seed, honey?"

"Father. I've seen my father," said Miriam, solemnly.

"Whar, darlin'? When did yo' see him? Lor', yo' makes my skin creep."

"Rosanna"—

"What, honey? Oh, my king!"

"Rosanna, I must go and find him. I saw him go by in the street. I was sitting at my window in the moonlight and I *saw* him! I tried to call, but I could n't speak. Oh, I hope he won't go away before I speak to him! Come, Rosanna, thee get up and go with me!"

Rosanna's teeth chattered audibly, and the bed shook under her.

"No, my chile, don't ye do it! *Don't ye do it!*" (in a tone of solemn warning.) "They don't like bein' follered. Jes' yo' stay quiet. Go git right into bed, an' Rosanna 'll come an' lay on de flo' side of yo'."

Rosanna slipped on her gown and lighted a candle with shaking hands. Then she arranged a mattress on the floor in Miriam's room, as she had often done when Miriam was a little child, and lay down beside her. Miriam submitted to Rosanna without words, but she watched with almost un-winking vigilance. All was silent except the clock in the hall. Rosanna left the candle burning on account of what might make its appearance. She preferred cheerful candlelight to ghostly moonlight, and she lay shivering with superstitious dread.

The only apparition, however, which presented itself was that of Susan G. in her green wrapper, with the aureole of her nightcap upon her head. She should admire to know what was the matter, she said, and Rosanna answered that Miriam was rather feverous or on the voyage of it, and Susan G. rejoined that she made a puffect baby of that great girl, and disappeared. That was all. But the sight of the matter-of-fact Susan, and the sound of her moving about, had the effect to dissipate a good deal of Rosanna's dread. Miriam seemed quiet, so she presently sank into undisturbed repose, which lasted until the morning had fairly dawned. But Miriam had not slept. She had watched the candle flicker and go out, and then her eyes had wandered about in the morning dusk with eager restlessness. She had listened with supersensitive ear to every suggestion of sound. The faint crackling of expansion or contraction in the old woodwork of the room, the nestling of a sleepy swallow in the chimney, had thrilled her over-wrought nerves. When the white dimity curtains shivered, it seemed to be because of something strange, something more than a gentle draught of air.

Suddenly Miriam sat straight up in her bed. What was it she heard? Something approaching softly. It was at the gate outside. No ordinary sense could have caught that small, almost inaudible clicking of the latch. A quiet sleeper would never have noticed that faint footfall on the edge of the grass in the yard.

"Rosanna!" softly called a voice that Miriam would not have heard if she had not been unnaturally alert, it was so far away in the backyard, under Rosanna's window.

Miriam sprang to the floor and Rosanna bounced up with a cry of terror.

"Oh, for d' Lord's sake, honey, did yo' see it agin?" she groaned. But Miriam, in one instant, had darted through the back entry into Rosanna's room, and taken a peep out of her window.

"It's father! It *is* father!" she cried, in a gasping, husky voice. "He's calling *thee*, Rosanna!"

At that moment Rosanna herself distinctly heard the voice which called.

"Oh, good Lord, he's come for me!" she shrieked, bumping down upon her knees. "Oh, Lord, I ain't perpared. Oh, my bressed Mas'er, I ain't ready! I 's a pore mis'able sinner! Gi' me time! Gi' me mo' time!"

This outcry brought Susan G. Even Aunt Hepsy roused up and reached out for her crutch, as if she, too, must try to do something, whatever this dreadful matter might be.

While Susan G. was dealing with Rosanna, whom she supposed to be suddenly lunatic, Miriam flew away down-stairs, like a ray of white light, through the house to the kitchen door, all the way grasping her throat, panting and choking, as if in pain. Her trembling hands struggled long with the lock, and then the door flew open, and still gasping and speechless, she was gathered into the arms of Obed Swain.

"My child! Have I frightened thee? What have I done to thee?" he said, in a beseeching tone, gazing with alarm at the pale, wild face of the child, distorted by a vain effort to speak.

This appearance of Obed Swain had hollow eyes, and the pallid, shrunken look that a ghost should have, but I must honestly confess that it was no ghost at all, but the worn and wasted substance of the living Obed Swain. He tried to lift his child and carry her back to her room, but he seemed not to have sufficient strength, and seating her in Rosanna's rocking-chair in the kitchen, he bent over her, trembling as much as she did, while two great tears rolled down upon her hair.

" There, my daughter," he said, " let us be calm and thankful. There, there, my little one ! " and he stroked her cheek and her hair and kissed the child again and again, but she did not speak. Then Obed knelt beside her, saying, " Speak to me, Miriam ! Speak to father ! " But Miriam only buried her face on the breast of the drab coat, kissing that, but still saying never a word, only choking and weeping and laughing in a helpless, piteous way ; and her sobs had a tone of joy, but her laugh was like a mournful wail.

Obed Swain was more and more frightened. He

stepped into the front entry, where he heard the voice of Rosanna praying in a faint and failing tone. Rosanna was probably ill, then. Perhaps the faithful creature was dying. But some one must come to his child. He would call Hepsy Swain. Nothing could ruffle or discompose that strong soul. She would accept his sudden return with the same equanimity which had marked every event of her life. Obed climbed the stairs. The door of his sister's room stood open. He tapped on the wall to give warning of his approach, and called gently, " Hepsy, it is I. It is Obed."

And directly, in the doorway before Aunt Hepsy, stood what, as I have already said, seemed but the ghost of Obed Swain.

CHAPTER XVI.

THE BLOSSOMS.

THOSE quiet ones who came softly to offer sympathy to the bereaved came in almost the same hushed and solemn manner to rejoice when the dead was alive again and the lost found. The old home was very still. Miriam lay upon her bed overwhelmed and nerveless, while Aunt Hepsy, smitten by joy more severely than she had been by sorrow, — what shall we say? Was it life or death they looked upon who stood beside her? Down-stairs in the keeping-room Obed Swain sat with head bowed and hands dropped at his sides. It was Obed, and it was not. No one disputed his identity, but where was the cheery Obed of past days?

Up-stairs in the sombre " spare room," which, in its snowy whiteness, broken only by the blackness of old mahogany, seemed appropriate to solemn occasions, Ruth Haddon was seated in an attenuated rocking-chair, rocking and weeping, and giving her whole heart to it, apparently. On the bed lay something straight and still, wrapped in a linen sheet, like some shrouded thing. It was the lovely white gown that Rosanna had prepared to lay away in its eternal rest when she had unpacked the little trunk, but which had lain there embalmed in sorrow and forgotten ever since.

Presently Aunt Dorcas peeped in at the half-open door.

" Ruth! I 'm sorry for this, daughter," she said. " I need thee to stay with Miriam."

"Oh, mother! It is just that that breaks me down; to see the poor little thing lie there so helpless and strange, and she has n't spoken a word yet. What can be the reason? "

" It is probably hysterical. There, now, don't thee get hysterical thyself."

" Well, Uncle Obed has ridden his hobby into the ground, and the whole family with it, almost. How could he call that wild notion of going into those out - of - the - way regions of the Southern States to help the freedmen a *leading*, — he, a Quaker Abolitionist, and such bitter feeling still remaining there? Has he said what was the reason he did n't let us know before he went on this fool's — this foolish errand ? "

" Ruth, my daughter, think what thee 's saying ! They sent letters home by the City of Havana, to let us know their change of plan, and did not hear of the loss of the steamer. Of course, in their imprisonment, they could neither send nor receive messages. The supply ship that they were put on board at Charleston transferred them to a Nantucket packet just before they reached Boston, and they got in here at midnight.

Poor Uncle Obed longed so to get home that he left the packet and came and wandered about the house. When he thought Rosanna was up, he went to the kitchen door and spoke to her. He did n't expect to be taken for a dead man."

"Does thee think he showed good judgment, mother, dropping down so — like a bomb?"

"My dear, whatever Uncle Obed's virtues may be in other respects, I can't say he was ever remarkable for good judgment."

"No, mother; and I 'm afraid he won't be easy until he goes back South and gets himself persecuted again in the Freedmen's cause. The sight of a Quaker coat and hat are as exasperating to those Southerners as a piece of red cloth to a bull. Poor little Miriam! And what does Dr. Mayhew say about Aunt Hepsy? Is she to live on, if we can call it living?"

"Perhaps so."

"What an awful house, mother! What an atmosphere for that child, who needs happiness so much!"

"*Happiness*, dear? Is that what we 're here for? It is our duty to be happy if possible, but is n't there a higher and better than happiness? Remember, ' we can do without happiness and instead thereof find blessedness.' "

"But that does n't apply to a little girl of thirteen. We surely ought to be happy in childhood."

"*Ought*, my dear? *Ought?* Who is to say when the training of the soul is to begin? Thee go bathe thy eyes and look more cheerful, and don't expect to see the end of things yet. If thee has any courage or comfort to offer, now is the time; there 's need enough of it. Try to comfort Uncle Obed. See how the poor man is suffering over the result of his imprudence."

For many a long, hot summer day, there were in the old Swain house only two relations, that of the ones who needed help and comfort, and that of those who ministered to the need.

Miriam seemed not to care to ask how things were, nor why they were. She heard new voices in the house, but they awoke no curiosity in her. She missed one feeble voice and the soft thumping of a crutch upon the floor, yet she asked for no explanation, said no word at all, but looked upon whatever passed before her as a marble image might have looked, except that she smiled upon her father and shook her head with a look of surprise and something like reproach when questioned or urged to speak. The doctor explained that the entire prostration of nervous force extended to the will; she had no strength of will, which was all that was needed to enable her to speak.

At length, one day, to the joy of everybody, she made a sign for pencil and paper and wrote very scrawly and feebly, "Who is John Nye?" "John Nye!" repeated cousin Ruth, looking doubtfully from Miriam to Rosanna, who was Miriam's nurse. "What can thee mean, dear? We don't know a person of that name."

The pencil dropped from Miriam's fingers, and she sat quietly indifferent again, in the great easy chair. By and by, however, she took the pencil again, and after a very long, slow, trembling operation, produced the following : —

"I keep hearing somebody say, 'John Nye thinks so,' 'John Nye's going to do it.' I thought he must be somebody important."

Just then a great, soft, unctuous, motherly voice came from somewhere down below, in response to Aunt Dorcas, " Yes 'm, it's all right. John Nye's done it."

Miriam pointed towards the open door and nodded.

"Oh, I see, I see!" cried cousin Ruth, laughing. "It's Mrs. Blossom. She means *John and I*, but she says John 'n' I. John is her son. They came from Barnstable. Mrs. Blossom is going to stay here and keep house, but she and John are one, thee perceives, and she could n't come unless he did; so he helps Simon Pewer do the work out of doors and helps his mother in-doors, too. The two always think alike, and feel alike, and do alike, and I think Mrs. Blossom could hardly speak of herself alone. It is always 'John 'n' I.' 'John 'n' I thinks it's going to rain,' 'John 'n' I ain't feeling very smart to-day.' And John has the same peculiarity, *of course.* What one has, the other has, really, even to the toothache. I'm not exaggerating."

"Laws no, dear, she ain't, Miss Ruth ain't,"

said Rosanna, chuckling with a complex delight, made up of her appreciative attitude towards John 'n' I, and her satisfaction in regard to Miriam's new interest in things. "Miss Ruth hain't tole yo' haff, for I seen 'em bof setting in the kitchen takin' ginger tea, an' Mis' Blossom say, 'John 'n' I's got a cramp in the stomick,' 's if they on'y has one stomick a-tween 'em."

Miriam smiled faintly, but showed no further interest in John 'n' I.

One charming morning when the clear, cooler atmosphere of September made the blood quicken, and the weak nerves react in a pleasant way, and take all they could of balm and strength from the salt air mellowed with sunshine and aromatic with the exhalations of sweet, ripe things, Miriam was dressed, and sat trembling a little at the exciting thought that she was to be taken out for a drive. It seemed to her too much to dare to do, and she looked forward to it with a touch of dread.

Presently there was a step in the entry outside, — it sounded like one, — and Rosanna, opening the door of the room, disclosed two jocund-looking figures, tall and plump and everything that could denote a prosperous and satisfactory sufficiency. It was John 'n' I. John was smiling, and so was his mother. John possessed what one might call a draughty countenance, — and you could plainly see it was taken from his mother, — his mouth being singularly broad and a good deal ajar, his nos-

trils uncommonly expanded, and his ears of a very
open and wide-spread order, all of which offered a
cool and pleasant effect for sultry weather, but it
gave an impression of terrible exposure on a raw,
cold, windy day.

Mrs. Blossom produced the same impression,
cheerfully enhanced by a very broad expanse of
clean calico, and the biggest and glossiest white
apron ever before seen, while, however, the ears
which added so much to John's expressiveness
were covered by a cap, from either side of which
a pink ribbon streamer rested upon Mrs. Blossom's
shoulder.   She was a very gladdening creature to
behold, and her voice poured slowly and smoothly
forth like oil.

"Well, now, there ain't so much of you as there 'd
ought to be, by half, nor so much as there will be
come Thanskgivin' Day.   I s'pose I ought to say
Quarterly Meeting Day.   I'm a-going to have
plenty of flesh put right on to them little bones,
and you must let John 'n' I take you down-stairs
and weigh you, so 's we can tell what we hed to begin with.   Shall we ? "

The very sight of Mrs. Blossom made Miriam
feel stronger and more courageous, and she thought
it would be a relief and a blessing to be lifted and
carried by those fresh, strong, capable-looking people, — or that was what her manner and the expression of her face said, as she leaned forward in
her chair a little, and nodded and smiled pleasantly
upon John 'n' I.

This unified duality clasped hands in such a fashion as to form a chair, while Rosanna lifted Miriam and seated her upon it, and away she went down-stairs, and through the house, actually looking about her with an air of faint, awakening interest.

Obed Swain lifted his eyes from the keeping-room floor, where they had been fixed in grave abstraction, when he saw them coming, and followed on behind, smiling, quite like the Obed Swain of former days, and Rosanna kept up a succession of triumphant chuckles all the way, as she brought up the rear.

The scales stood in the middle of the kitchen floor, with a little flag-bottomed chair upon them, John 'n' I having made the preliminary arrangements. They placed Miriam in the little chair, and John managed the weights while his mother fixed her eye upon the figures to announce the result.

" Seventy-five pound," said she, " takin' out five for the chair," and extracting a piece of chalk from her apron pocket she chalked it up on the bottle-green surface of the wash-room door.

" There!" she said, " that 's where we start from."

Rosanna placed Miriam in the old kitchen rocking-chair for a moment, where she had always liked to sit since the time when she was so little that she could not climb into it without help, and where she had watched Rosanna's performances with an attention as concentrated and an admiration as profound as a zealous play-goer might give to the greatest actress of the age. Obed stood beside his child, stroking her hair with the dreamy, doubtful look which he had worn ever since his look of anguish had subsided.

"Stop a bit," said Mrs. Blossom, stepping upon the platform of the scales; "there's some of us needs to have some took off. Two hundred weight is all sufficient for folks that only measure five feet ten.   How much is it?"

"Two hundred 'n' ten," replied John.

"Ten pound too much.   Nantucket air is fattenin'," said Mrs. Blossom.

"John ain't weighed hisse'f," remarked Rosanna, as the young man was about to take away the scales.

"Oh, I don't need to be weighed," returned John, "I *know* how much I weigh."

"Has yer been a-heftin' of yerse'f some o' dese yer odd times?" asked Rosanna.

"N-o," John answered, with a look of grave sincerity, as he slowly piled the weights and placed them on the shelf. "*I always weigh just the same's mother does.*"

"For d' land's sake!   Does yo' *weigh* alike?" cried Rosanna.   "Yo' does n't differ 'bout nothing, does yo'?"

It was John who brought Jerry to the door, and what Jerry brought was nothing less, I do assure you, than a shining, new, light carriage with an easy step, and two seats, so that Miriam could have other company besides her driver. The only real wish she had appeared to retain during all those weeks of illness was to have her father near her, or where she could see him, and in this first drive he was seated beside her. Rosanna, who would n't have let the child out of her sight for all Nantucket Island, took her place beside John on the front seat.

They had hoped the new carriage would surprise Miriam into speaking, but she only smiled and looked at her father gratefully, before she settled into her cushions and pillows.

The morning had an opal softness with all its brightness. They drove to the south side, past the thickets of scrub oak and dwarf pines, and Miriam looked exactly the same at all things: at the pond with its border of pickerel weed and arrow-head; at the sweet-scented clethra, which she was always before so eager to possess; at the scarlet pimpernels, the lavish gerardia, the blazing star, and flaming heads of butterfly weed that seemed almost to expect her, she had been so sure to come to seek them. Rosanna got down and filled her hands full of sweet, bright things, and laid them upon Miriam's lap, who looked upon them pensively.

At the place where the ways divide, and go in one direction to the South shore and in another to 'Sconset, Miriam really indicated a preference for the 'Sconset road, to the joy of those who wished always that she would choose something. She liked the long beach, with the light-house in the distance, and the row of fishermen's cottages, and even the town pump. There was a group of old women that morning, their caps nodding at each other, and their petticoats flapping in the breeze, and a collection of brown-faced children digging in the sand with clam shells. Leaning on a feeble-looking fence, four or five men fixed four or five pairs of vacant eyes on the horizon, and mixed their meditation with occasional dialogue. Their red and blue shirts made a pleasant bit of color among the neutral tones of sand and dry grass, and on a bush in a dooryard some gay calicoes were spread out to dry.

The Dagget cottage looked gone to sleep. It was fast closed and the windows darkened. Life had departed from it. Miriam sat up and looked at it, which was enough to awaken an interest in Obed Swain. He stopped the carriage, and would have rehearsed once more the scene of the boy and the town pump. But one of the women, feeling called upon to do the honors of the village, inter-fered with that inclination. A shining new car-riage was a new thing indeed in 'Sconset, but Obed's was a well known face to everybody on the island. The fact that he had been considered dead and was alive again made him a person of peculiar interest, and it was with great alacrity that one of the old busybodies presented herself beside the carriage with a profusion of nods and smiles, while her con-sœurs gathered what they could from their more retired position.

"Lonesome lookin', ain't it?" said the self-commissioned delegate, sliding her leather-colored hands back and forth from wrist to elbow on her folded arms. "They're all gone now, — boy 'n' all."

"What boy does thee speak of, friend?" asked Obed.

"Why, Ma'am Dagget's boy, that stayed with her all winter. 'T ain't possible you hain't heered about him, an' the will!"

"What will does thee allude to? Is n't friend Dagget living?"

"Oh, no, sir! Why, you hain't heered that neither! She died last spring. She was in such a hurry to clean, after she got spry agin, — that's after her broken ankle got well, — that she went at it in cold weather. She was up aloft some-w'er's, a scourin' the chimleys, an' she catched the pneumony. That boy she sot so much by was gone away. I can't tell nothing about what he went for, and I do' know who ken, but so 't was that when he come home, — I was there and seed it and heered it all myself, for 's I took care of Ma'am Dagget to the last, — when he come home she says to him to go after Squire Coffin quick, an' he went, an' Squire Coffin come right over from town that night, an' she told him she wanted to give everything to the boy, for he'd been good to her; an' Squire Coffin he writ it all down, how that Ma'am Dagget was in her right mind, an' she give an' bequeathed to the boy the house an' furnitoor an' money, — everything, old hoss an' all, — an' the next day she died; an' 't wa' n't long afore the boy he shut up house an' locked it an' off he went, an' he hain't never come back sence. There 's them that says John Dagget had a chist of money stowed away somew'er's. I ain't a-going to say as I b'lieve it, nor as I don't, but there was one as did, an' was so besot to git a pocketfull of it, that he broke into the house an' was a rummagin' of it when some o' the men that come in late from the fishin' saw the light, an' went an' caught him, an' hed him shut up at the town farm. He 's there now, an' he 'll stay a spell. There wa' n't nobody 't ever sot foot in 'Sconset that was liked better 'n Ma'am Dagget's boy. We 'll stand by him an' pertect his property till he comes back to do it for himself, an' ef he needs any help then we 'll give it to him, I can tell ye."

"He must have been a worthy lad to make such good friends."

"Yes, sir; he deserved all he got, however much 't is, an' his chist is as safe here as 't would be in the Centre Street Meeting-House, and he a-setting on it."

"Wal, that ain't any of it what I was a-going to say," resumed the gossip. "What I *was* thinkin' to remark was, that we 're all glad you 're alive agin, sir, to do good to them that needs it, as ever, and to enjy life yourself. How 's the little girl? Poor Miss Swain, she 's" —

" We 're as well as can be expected, thank thee," said Obed quickly and nervously, with the manner of shrinking from the subject, and after a few kind words of inquiry about 'Sconset people he directed John to drive home. " Or would thee like to go farther, my child ? " he asked Miriam.

But Miriam seemed indifferent, and Jerry settled the question, at any rate, by turning about and starting for home with an air of great decision.

CHAPTER XVII.

AN END.

WHEN Miriam awoke from the long nap which followed her drive, a letter lay upon the candle stand beside her bed. She gazed upon it long before resolving to take it. Everything she did was preceded by a fit of indecision. At length she slowly reached for it and held it, looking at the address and the postmark. The former was in Roland Weir's handwriting, which had reformed from the standard of Aunt Hepsy to that of Mr. Stanley.

When she had determined to open the letter, it offered her tidings of Roland's progress across the continent of Europe, with Mr. Stanley ever at hand to dip and plunge and steep and soak him in knowledge, to cover and adorn him with coat upon coat of improvement. As Mr. Stanley was a very erudite and accomplished young man, and as all the accumulated advantages of Europe were waiting to be absorbed, there seemed little doubt that Roland would come out drenched and dripping with knowledge, — thoroughly gilded and garnished with improvement.

At the time of the writing of this letter, however, he had only been dipped just enough to leave him in a state of gasping bewilderment.

"I ought to tell you more about these places," he said, "but I can't. I see so much, and Mr. Stanley tells me so many things that I must be *sure* not to forget, that you might as well try to find each separate corn when it has been ground and mixed up in Amos Tuttle's meal-box as to find anything particular in my head. We're to stay in Germany, and I 'm to have other teachers besides Mr. Stanley. I shall send some pictures of these places, and it will be almost the same as if you saw them, and then I won't have to describe them. Mr. Stanley says my powers of description are — well, he meant *bad*, you know. When he uses a word I don't understand, I 'm to ask what it means, and get it explained. I knew well enough what *that* ought to mean, so I did n't ask. He says so many of those words that he 's quite incomprehensible at times. *That 's* one of his words! but he did n't catch me there. Aunt Hepsy nailed *that* into me. *He* don't find anything incomprehensible, except some of the things I learned at Nantucket. He understands all the *rest*, I can tell you."

Roland's experience of Europe being, in the main, extremely like that of other travelers, his letter need not be offered in full. It finished concisely, in these words: —

"Betty Vinton is coming here in October. There 'll be no pleasure in life, then, for she has a way of making a fellow feel so *useless.*

" Now, Miriam, when shall you be well enough to write to me?   They always say you are better. When will you tell me yourself that you are well?

" *Do write as soon as you can!* "

This prayer of Roland's was answered, after some weeks, as follows: —

" I have tried to write.   I began.   There have been a good many beginnings, and there has been an end, too, Roland, and I knew nothing about it. There was a long time that I could not think about things.   A little piece of a thought would come, and then fly away again, and I could not remember what it was.

" Some very nice people came to live with us. They are Blossoms, — Betsy Blossom and John Blossom.   It makes me feel better to look at them. Betsy Blossom said to me often, ' You hain't got nothing to think of nor to do but to set there and get well and grow fat.   I 'll see to the *how*.' That 's the way they talk.   One day when she said that, it seemed as if somebody else said to me, ' *Has n't* thee got anything else to do?   What about thy Aunt Hepsy?   There 's that promise, thee knows.'   I was left alone in the south cham- ber.   I thought I must go to Aunt Hepsy right away.   I got up and held on to the chair back, it made me shake so to stand up alone.   Then I walked along zigzag — kind of dizzy — till I came to Aunt Hepsy's door.   It was so still in her room that I thought she might be having a nap, so I opened the door very softly, and looked in.   Aunt

Hepsy was not there. The bed was all made up
as smooth as ice — not a wrinkle in it. It was a
chilly day, but there was not a spark of fire, nor
any ashes. The fireplace looked as if it had been
swept and washed out clean. Nothing of Aunt
Hepsy's was lying anywhere. There were no bottles nor glasses nor spoons. Even 'The Sinner
Awakened' and Barclay's 'Apology' and 'No
Cross, No Crown' and 'Thomas Chalkley's Journal' were gone. Everything was gone but the
furniture, and that was so still! It sat up stiff and
awful and looked at me. I was so surprised that
I sat down in the chair by the door and looked at
the bed, and the chair where I used to sit. The
chair had a new chintz cover. Everything looked
as if Aunt Hepsy had gone. 'Gone where?' I
wondered. While I was sitting and wondering,
I heard Betsy Blossom coming. When she saw
me, she did not say anything, only made a queer
noise, and took me right up like a baby and carried me back to my room. I spoke right out.
'Where's Aunt Hepsy?' I said. I did not know
I was going to speak. It came right out.

"I shall have to tell thee that I could not speak
after father came back. I had not said a word for
— they said it was six months. I see they have
n't told thee. I have thought many times, 'Roland Weir will never hear my voice again.' I
had been struck dumb, like Zachariah, because I
was discontented and worldly-minded. My father
was given back to me, and my speech was taken

away instead, because I could bear that, and the Divine Wisdom saw that I could not bear the other. Now it is all forgiven, and I have my father and my speech both, for ever since I said, 'Where 's Aunt Hepsy?' without knowing it, I have gone on saying things every day.

"Just as I asked the question, father came to the door, and Betsy Blossom, instead of answering me, kept saying,'She 's spoke! She 's spoke! Bless the Lord! She 's spoke!'

"'*Where 's Aunt Hepsy?*' I said again. Now thee knows my father always answers people right out plain. That is his way, and it is the right way. He came and took me up in his arms,— I'm very light though I 'm so tall, — and kissed me and seemed glad, but he said, 'Thy Aunt Hepsy has gone where we shall all go, my daughter. She has finished this life.'

"'Father! Is Aunt Hepsy *dead?*' I went on asking.

"'Yes, daughter,' father answered me.

"Then I could not say any more. I sat there thinking of Aunt Hepsy *dead*. But I could not see her *that* way. I could only see her walking round in heaven and looking at everybody right through the middle of her spectacles, to see if they had any business there. And then I thought of a time when she was on her bed — so feeble — and we held each other's hands, and a tear rolled out of her eye. Then the tears came to my eyes, and dropped down, a great many of them, on father's best coat, for he had just come home from meeting. Just to think, Roland, that there will be no Aunt Hepsy any more! Those strange places can't seem much stranger to thee than my own home does to me. Tell me more about them. But I 'm glad to have thee tell more about thyself. Father desires his respects to Friend Payne, and we both love thee, the same as ever. Farewell.

" MIRIAM."

CHAPTER XVIII.

WHAT PAUL HAD TO TELL.

AGAIN the winter held Nantucket in a five months' grip, and again relented and let the waters ripple in the harbor. The sea-birds made their nests in the long grass and sand on the cliff-side and along the lonely shore. The singing birds returned, and the moors recovered the pensive smile with which they listened to the pacified sea. All the gentle things took courage and came forth; the young dove from the cote in the gable of the barn, to take its first look at the sky, the luxuriant Nantucket arbutus from under the sod, and the Quaker girl herself from under the cloud. She bloomed and was strong again. In that flush of life there was a strange new sense of freedom. She seemed almost to lay hold of the bright impossibilities which had haunted her dreams. She did lay hold of one with a daring hand. She bought a blue ribbon to tie at her throat.

"Ah, I *do* love worldly things!" she said again with the old sigh, but with such a smile.

And her own sorrow had opened her heart to compassion, too, so that she not only loved worldly things, but she pitied the sorrows of the world.

And in the month of March, that year, had occurred a terrible gale, which strewed the sea with wrecks, and there were 'Sconset fishermen who went out to their work and never returned. Many hearts in the cottages suffered that grief which Miriam had tasted, and the distracted families of the lost fishermen will never forget the sweet presence which came to them when they too were saying, " I cannot bear it ! "

One day when she was returning from a visit to 'Sconset, one of the little ones wept at the parting and Miriam offered to take her home with her. The poor mother thankfully let one of her seven go, and as Miriam rode over the moor with little Sally Martin hugged up to her side, peacefully sucking her thumb, she felt as if Polly Hopkins had come to life. Ah, that was a happy day !

Sally Martin did not go back to 'Sconset, except as she went to and from with Miriam and Polly Hopkins during the summer. Again and again being taken to her mother she returned to nestle into the place she had taken in the old Swain house ; so Miriam's summer was devoted to her 'Sconset people, especially Sally. By autumn there was a question as to where Sally really did belong. The question, however, was not with Sally herself. Anywhere Miriam might be was the place for her, in her own opinion. She made no exception of Aunt Dorcas's lovely sitting-room, for there she sat in the middle of the sofa, with Polly Hopkins on one side of her and Whisker, the cat, on the other, one afternoon in the October following her vagrant summer. Aunt Dorcas, cousin Ruth, and Miriam were surrounded by small mountains of heavy cotton cloth and flannel, portions of which were cut into garments, and busy fingers stitched and stitched, while placid voices discussed the comparative needs and measurements of the poor people at 'Sconset. A lazy fire flickered on the hearth, while the bland, sedative air, that had come from over the sea and over the heathy moors, had free access at the open window, for the warm weather lingered and returned with wavering intention. From the kitchen came far-away tinkling sounds of the dishes and tins that were being washed and put away, and in the library — so called because there were a couple of secretaries there with high book cases upon them — there was the occasional crackling of a newspaper which Uncle David turned over and resumed between successive naps. All the sounds were gentle. There were never any harsh noises in Aunt Dorcas's house, never any slamming and banging, any shouting and bemoaning. Ah, what a place for nerves, especially as Paul was away! That uncertain person had gone on a vacation voyage with Perez Howard. When Perez had said he was to take to the sea about the first of July, he alluded to a privilege he had enjoyed for two or three summers. His grandfather owned ships, and one of them went to Madeira after fruit and wine, stopping at the Azores, and her captain, a delightfully good-natured man, had been intrusted with the guardianship of Perez for the space of a voyage, with the understanding that he was to apply the strict and wholesome discipline which he seemed to his tutors and governors to stand in need of very much indeed. This was soon after his escapade with the rye at Haverford. But Perez had found the treatment so agreeable that it had ever since been his chosen diversion in vacation. This summer he had invited Paul Haddon to take the voyage with him. It was now time they should return, and every day Aunt Dorcas sat by the window with her sewing, after the arrival of the boat, to watch for Paul. This afternoon, as before, she glanced out of the window frequently and up at the clock. "No," she said, "he has n't come."

The door which opened into the little dim entry that would take you to the kitchen was lightly clattering and swinging as if moved by a draught of air. Miriam got up to stop the small annoyance. As she reached out to latch the door, it opened about six inches, and in the space Miriam saw two round, shiny things, that glittered in the light from the sitting-room windows.

"Oh!" she said, stepping back. Aunt Dorcas and cousin Ruth looked up.

"'It is the ancient mariner, and he stoppeth one of three!'" said a sepulchral voice, and a long, brown, bony hand was thrust through the opening of the door, which Miriam was far from ready to clasp.

"'I fear thee, ancient mariner! I fear thy skinny hand!'" continued the voice.

Aunt Dorcas dropped her work and hurried across the room, saying, "Paul, Paul!" and a form that was "long, and lank, and brown," stepped into the room and was folded in Aunt Dorcas's arms. "My dear boy," Aunt Dorcas said, "I've been watching for thee, this hour. I did n't see thee come. How did thee get in?"

"I made a detour of the lane, fell upon the rear of the castle by the back gate; the garrison surrendered without a struggle, and only one small squeal. Officers all asleep, or at their revels," returned Paul, while he moved on, kissing cousin Ruth, and even Miriam, for ever since she had suffered, Paul had been very kind to his cousin.

"What, *Paul?*" said Uncle David, rousing himself, hearing Paul's last words and emerging from the library. He grasped Paul's hand, gave him a bear's hug, and said they could easily take care of one marauder.

"Ah-ha!" said Paul, in that funny, croaking voice that had been growing upon him during a year. "Perhaps thou hast never seen one of my kind, with teeth well sharpened up, that have n't had a good bite for seven hours," and he snapped all his great incisors, cuspids, bicuspids, and molars together in such a way that it was really dreadful.

"Well, come, my son," said Aunt Dorcas, "there was dinner saved for thee in case thee should arrive. I'll go see about it myself. Thee must be famished."

" Why, what 's this ? " cried Paul, catching sight of Sally Martin on the sofa. " Here 's a bite, handy by. Is it a h-apple? La, no, it 's only a 'uckleberry ! " and he made a feint of tossing Sally into his mouth.

But Sally, who had witnessed the clashing of those terrible teeth with terror, when she found that she, her own self, was the object to be devoured, set up such a piercing howl as to make herself a terror in return.

" By this din we conquer ! " cried Paul. " Oh, *don't !* " he groaned. " I fly, leaving cannon and flags on the field," and stuffing his fingers in his ears he followed his mother. Uncle David and cousin Ruth followed him, and Miriam remained to reassure and console Sally Martin.

She wanted to hear Paul tell about his voyage. Since she had grown old, fourteen, and Paul so kind, she no longer dreaded him as she used. After Sally was hushed, she heard the voices in the dining-room — Paul's slow drawl, Aunt Dorcas's and cousin Ruth's quiet exclamations, and Uncle David's laugh. She was afraid she must go home with Sally, and not hear anything at all ; but Sally, after weeping abundantly, fell fast asleep, and by and by they all came back from the dining-room.

" No," Paul was saying, " we couldn't walk about Funchal much, the streets are so steep, and the pebble pavements are so slippery from the

carros sliding over them all the time, and the
grease they throw on to make them slide. We
broke our noses trying to get up " —

" Thee try to be more accurate," said Aunt
Dorcas, patting Paul's arm.

" Well, mother, I 'll admit that I may be mistaken about Perez's and the captain's and Ole
Bull's noses, but look at mine ! Don't it seem to
thee a little askew ? "

" I had n't observed it," replied Aunt Dorcas,
looking at Paul's long, drooping nose with no apparent concern.

" Oh, very well," said Paul, with a toss of his
head, " if it 's improving, so much the better. I
have heard of a man who got quite a handsome
nose, at last, by falling on it now and then."

" This subject of noses is supposed to be a very
droll one — I don't know why," said cousin Ruth.
" For my own part, I think it 's very silly and flat.
I 'd rather hear what thee promised to tell us
about that Ole Bull, as thee calls him."

" Well, he was a young fellow, a common sailor,
who brought a fiddle aboard, and played it first
rate, so the people said who know about those
things, and that is why they called him Ole Bull.
Ole Bull is a great fiddler. The captain used to
have this young man or boy — I believe he 's only
sixteen — come aft to play for us evenings. The
first mate played a flute, and we called them the
band. We had some fine moonlight nights, and
sometimes Perez and the other passengers danced.

Of course I disapproved of that, and used to turn
my back round and look at the moon and think
about very improving things."

" No doubt, but we 'd rather hear what this remarkable young man was doing than what thee
was thinking about," said Ruth.

" Why, I said he was playing his fiddle."

" But at other times. How did one of the crew
of the ship come to be running about with the
captain and passengers on shore? "

" Thee has n't waited for me to finish my story,"
said Paul. " The captain was interested in him
to begin with, and then he turned out to be such a
brave fellow that we all liked him. We had a tremendous thunder storm and gale, a sudden squall,
just before we got to the Azores, and the fellow, a perfectly green hand, was aloft on the yards
ahead of the old sailors. He was always ahead —
none of your miserable ones that have to beat
their way an inch at a time. The captain said the
closer he watched him the better he liked him.
Big things or little things, he was always ready
for whatever there was to do. He passed for a
poor boy, but he seemed to know a good many
things that poor people don't get a chance to
know, and Perez and I believed he was a rich
man's son who had run away from home, but the
captain said no, he had quite a different account
of him. The captain's clerk left him at Madeira,
and he put Ole Bull in his place to try him, and
he did remarkably well. So you see it was as

captain's clerk that he was running about with us at Funchal. We were great pals after that, Perez and he and I."

"Great what?" asked Aunt Dorcas.

"Why, good friends, I suppose thee would say, mother," answered Paul. "Excuse the foreign words we use when we first return from abroad."

"Does that end the story of Ole Bull?" asked Uncle David.

"Well, no, I think not," Paul answered. "I may as well say 'to be continued in our next.' There's sure to be more to tell when I come back next year."

"Next year, indeed!" said Uncle David. "Thee seems to have thy plans all settled."

"I only mean to say that I'm invited to go again next year, father. We all said when we parted, 'Adios, till next summer.' The captain is going to take Ole with him as clerk again next voyage and teach him navigation. He says he'll be able to take his place in a few years, when he drops anchor for good. The captain is getting rather old to follow the seas. Won't it be uncommonly good times when we set sail with Ole for captain? I should like to have something to do with the cargo. I could never make a sailor, but I might be a merchant. What does thee say, father?"

"I was about to say," said Uncle David, "that thee must be ready to go back to Haverford next Second Day, and I guess that is as far as we will look forward at present."

CHAPTER XIX.

BUT we may look forward and step forward a little over a time which was occupied with matters not connected with this little history.

After the hindrances had all been removed which were in Obed Swain's way when he undertook to befriend the freedmen, his time and thoughts were chiefly occupied with them and Trinidad, and he went on his way, at length, with the joy of a successful Abolitionist beaming in his face. At sixteen Miriam was quite the mistress of the old home and her own life. During more than half the year she was left to dispose of both as she pleased.

It was when Miriam was nearly eighteen that such a terrible and sudden cold - weather wave swept over the North Atlantic in the month of February. It had seemed as if spring had come, the weather had been so mild. The harbor was open, and everybody was rejoicing that winter's backbone was broken, when that awful, last, cruel clutch was felt, especially at sea. Vessels put in at Nantucket with men on board who had feet and fingers to be amputated, and innumerable sufferings to be alleviated as best they might be.

"Why, Miriam," said Dr. Mayhew, "they are very badly off, some of them, and they are rough sailors; it is n't at all suitable to bring them here."

"Bring those here who are the worst off, doctor," Miriam answered. "They can be taken better care of here than at the town farm. Come and see what rooms we have, and bring as many as they will accommodate. Use the house as if it were a hospital. Don't think of us at all."

So there they were brought, five of those poor creatures, and as they were borne in, one after another, Miriam was pale and trembled, they were indeed such hard and sorrowful-looking men.

But the doctor never had a better assistant. The brave determination that was in that first Nantucket ancestor, the steel that was in Aunt Hepsy, were preserved in unadulterated strength in the tall, slim girl. She was ready with bandages; she could move more quickly than any other with the warm water and towels. When even stout John Blossom was faint and sick with the smell of ether and the sight of blood, she took the place at the doctor's side. She, too, was faint and sick, and there were fierce questions between mind and body as to which should yield, but, naturally, it was the stronger that won.

Although they almost hated to, one after another the poor fellows recovered and went away, with memories that helped them ever after. They all went but one, poor fellow, and he — how could he go? He had no feet to go on. He could not even hobble upon crutches, but sat all day in piteous consideration of the problem, What is to become of an old sailor without feet? It had often been proposed to take him to the town farm, but Miriam had not the heart to send him away, he seemed so very forlorn. She often sat by him and let him talk to her. There is nothing so cheering to people as the sound of their own voices. No words you can offer them are half so consoling as the words you allow them to offer you. Miriam, too, was frequently interested in the old sailor's stories of his adventurous life.

" Well, what has thee to say for thyself, to-day, Benjamin? " was sufficient to open the way for Benjamin Booth to deliver himself of a chapter of his autobiography.

" Why, Miss, I 'm a-coasting off the Newfoundland Banks jest now;" or, " Thank you, ma'am, we was a-putting in to Australy," were the simple beginnings of long and tedious, or long and thrilling experiences, as the case might be.

One warm afternoon in June, Benjamin's chair had been rolled out upon the grass in the backyard, and he sat in the shadow of the house dozing, and starting at the shrill voices of children playing under the bank. Every afternoon he was placed in that position to watch for the boat to round the point and come into the harbor. It was a sweet and peaceful spot. On the slope of the bank the carefully pruned and trained grapevines were in bloom, and their delicate odor came and went with the stirring air, as heavenly suggestions come and go in our wavering, worldly minds. The pigeons cooed on the roof, or fluttered down to drink at the wooden trough under the pump spout. On the right was the old garden where Miriam's cats were buried, but the mint and balm, the sage, summer savory, and pennyroyal, that had once prevailed, had been put under restraint, and forced to keep within bounds; while from the time the first crocuses peeped out until the last dahlias were frozen, the little garden blushed and blazed with flowers. Miriam's old passion for brightness reveled there, and as she came to the open door at the moment of which I am speaking, and stood brushing loose threads from the skirt of her gown, she wore a rose where the soft ruching closed at her throat.

Before returning she paused to consider the scene before her, especially Benjamin Booth, at the same time smoothing the rather worldly fashioned gown with an agreeable, placid air of satisfaction. From her point of view, Benjamin's bent head and drooping figure had a pathetic air. She turned away, but soon came back with some knitting work and a chair, and placing herself near Benjamin set the needles flying. This arrangement was no sooner made than Miss Sally Martin, similarly equipped with some supposititious knitting work and a small chair, planted herself beside Miriam. Her ringing voice roused Benjamin, who, seeing Miriam before him, straightened himself up, and raising his thumb and finger to the place where his hat brim would have been, if he had been graced with a hat, made what he considered a deferential motion, and prepared himself for the usual question, " What has thee to tell me to-day, Benjamin ? "

Benjamin scratched his weather-faded beard and then his bushy head, when the question had been proposed. " Well, ma'am," he said, " every time you 've asked me that, I 've had a good mind to tell you a story that I 've been a-thinkin' on ever sence I fetched up at this island."

A doubtful pause, and then : —

" I s'pose you can't rec'lect the Aurory's comin' ashore here, can ye ? Me and Ezry Hodges and a baby was the only ones that come off alive."

Miriam dropped her knitting, and gave all her attention to Benjamin.

" I vowed I 'd stick to sailing vessels after that," he continued. " When the capting was gone, I had no more use for steam-vessels, though I 'd have gone to sea on a'most anything with Capting Allen. He was the best man and the best sailor that ever put to sea. It was him that put the baby in a champagne basket, and strapped a piece o' tarpaulin round it, and sent it ashore. He was fond o' that baby, for he had one about like it. He kerried it in his arms a good deal all the voyage. The little feller was sleeping sound when he laid him in the basket, and the capting kissed him, and fairly cried. He did. *George !* ' There 's just one chance in a hundred for ye, little one,' says he.

"Wal; me 'n' Ezry must ha' been the only tough ones on the ship, for all the rest had the breath o' life beat and washed out of 'em, and we wa' n't fur from it, when we struck the Nantucket shore. But we was on our keels agin the next day and started for New York.

" On the way, I see Ezry take so'thing out of his pocket and look at it close. Dum'd if 't wa' n't that thing the baby used to wear on his neck! 'Why, where 'd you git that, Ezry?' says I. 'Wal, when I was a-holding of the baby for the capting to fish up the basket from the cabin,' says he, ' I thought 't was a pity to let that go to the bottom, when some on us might want it to help us along, having lost our chists, and I 'd had a forerunner that I was a-going to git safe to shore, someways,' says he, ' so I jest put the trinket in my pocket aginst a time o' need, and Lord! I forgot to give it back to the baby!'

" The next day, after we got to New York, when we 'd been to the company's office, and settled our accounts, and gi'n the partic'lars and bought us some clo's, Ezry says, says he, ' We 'd ought to go and see the capting's wife to offer our sarvices. She 'll want to see the men that was with the capting to the last.'

" Ezry knew where she lived, for he was a favoryte with the capting, and had been sent up to the house on arrands often. He come from Cowes, near by where the capting found his wife, and he surmised she had n't no relations and 'ud be pretty much alone in the world now the capting was gone. So we went and asked for Capting Allen's wife. 'She 's dead,' they says. 'She died of her heart, when they told her the capting was lost. Won't you come in ?' We did n't know what else to do, so we went in, and the woman of the house she come and asked us, 'Be you Mis' Allen's friends?' says she. 'We *be*,' says Ezry. 'Well, I 'm glad to hear that,' says the woman, 'for there ain't any friends made their appearance, so fur, and I don't know what to do with the baby.'

"' Don't fret, ma'am,' says Ezry, 'for I 've come to fetch the baby myself.'

" Wal, if I 'd seen Ezry swaller the woman, right off, at one gulp, I should n't ha' been more dumb-founded, and I looked at him with all my eyes to see what he meant. He seemed to know what he was about, so I let him alone, and if we did n't walk out o' that house, shortly, Ezry carrying Cap-ting Allen's baby wrapped up in his arms, as handy as you please. 'If you 'll hev his things packed up, ma'am,' says he, 'I 'll come agin by 'n' by and fetch *them*.' I kept alongside of Ezry a good while before I could muster my speakin' faculties on deck. Then I says, 'Wal, Ezry Hodges,' says I, ' where be you a-going of with that baby?' 'I ain't quite made up my mind yet,' says he. The little feller did n't cry, but he looked kind o' trou-bled and puzzled like, and kept a-sayin' ' Mamma!

mamma!'   We went on as fur as Washin'ton Square, and there we set down.   While Ezry was a-thinking what to do next, a boy come along with newspapers to sell, a-hollering 'More partic'lars o' the loss o' the Aurory!'   I took one to see what kind of yarns they had to tell.   As I was a-reading the names of the passengers, 'Roland Weir, wife and child,' says I, and then I read that Mr. Roland Weir was brother of Mrs. Colonel Payne, of New York, and while I was a-doing of it Ezry pulled the trinket out of his pocket and looked at it.   'Yes,' says he, 'that's it.'   In half a minute he fastened the thing round the neck of the capting's baby.   'Now, why ain't he the Weir baby?' says he.   'Hey?' I says, for I couldn't take the sense of his observation.   'No matter,' says he; 'you jest step over there to the 'pothecary's, and look in the directory, and find out where Colonel R. A. Payne lives, will ye?'   Well, over I went, and when I come back and told Ezry that he lived at No.—— Fifth Avenoo, 'Then *there's* where I'm a-going to take the capting's baby,' says he. 'How so?' says I.   'What for?'   'He'd be well off there,' says Ezry.   'There ain't much difference in the looks of babies, and this thing on his neck has got the name on it, and it'll make 'em think he's the Weir baby.   Don't you see?' 'No,' says I, for I wa'n't nigh so smart as Ezry. Then Ezry had to tell me, word by word, that he was a-going to take the capting's baby to Colonel Payne's and pass him off for the Weir baby.   'By

the great guns !' says I, ' you ain't a-going to do
no such a thing, Ezry,' says I. ' 'T ain't right,
and you 'll be found out.' ' I 'd do anything for
the capting's baby,' says he, ' found out or not.
He was very good to me, was the capting.' ' Yes,
but what about the Weir baby?' says I. ' Oh,
he 's well enough for a while,' says Ezry. ' They
'll find him out fast enough, but they 'll git so fond
o' the capting's baby by that time that they won't
want to let him go, and he 'll have a nice, soft
place, the fine little feller!' he says, a-patting of
the baby's cheek. ' Why, Lord save us!' he
went on a-saying, ' you need n't look so! I shall
tell 'em myself before long that there 's been some
mistake, and that the baby down to Nantucket is
the right one ; but there 'll be the capting's baby,
anchored in a safe harbor, only jest for the cost of
that other one's waiting a bit with them good people down to the island.' ' Wal,' says I, ' the capting was good to me, too. I 'd like to have his
baby well off, and if that 's all we 've got to do to
fetch it about, I sha' n't say no more agin it.' So
Ezry took the baby to the place on Fifth Avenoo,
and that 's the last I ever knew about it, for I 've
never seen Ezry nor set foot in these parts sence.
Now I should like to know whether Ezry put that
matter to rights. Do you happen to know, ma'am,
anything about the little one that was left here on
the Island?"

CHAPTER XX.

THE TURNING OF THE TIDE.

A LETTER, in which Miriam repeated Benjamin Booth's story, lay waiting upon a table which had been laid for the breakfast of two persons. A door of the room stood open upon a terrace. There was silence within, and no sounds without save the droning of insects and a heavy human sigh. The sigh was Colonel Payne's, who sat with his eyes fixed upon a reposeful scene, which seemed not to cheer him.

This place, to which he had just brought Mrs. Payne, was hung upon the craggy side of the Alpilles, in Provence. Five years Mrs. Payne had passed in different parts of Europe, the last two in the south of France, for her health, while Roland Weir went on with his brilliant career elsewhere. When assured that she preferred the air of Provence and a quiet life, what was to hinder his pursuing with contentment the sort of life he preferred?

It was surely quiet enough *here*, the colonel was saying to himself, with that heavy sigh.

Just then the sound of footsteps and the rustle of a cambric morning gown roused him, and Mrs.

Payne stood in the doorway with Monte Cristo beside her.

The colonel's face lightened as he rose to meet his wife.

"Why, Anna, how fresh and bright you look this morning," he said.

You would have wondered to hear that pale, thin woman called fresh and bright. She, herself, laughed a little and said, " What a dismal thing I must be, commonly, when a smile makes such an impression."

"But I have n't seen you looking like this since — I can't tell when," continued the colonel.

" I 've had a delicious sleep, and such a lovely dream ! " said Mrs. Payne.

"Only a dream ! But you looked quite happy."

"What is happiness but a dream, Randolph ? You know what Rousseau says."

"Don't tell me any of Rousseau's morbid sayings. Tell me that wonderful dream."

"I must tell you one of his sayings. He says people are only happy just *before* they are happy. I think *I* must be going to be uncommonly happy."

" Well, come to breakfast, and let 's have the dream."

"Oh, it would be nothing, told," Mrs. Payne said, turning and moving slowly towards the table. " It is simply the impression it has left which is so delightful. I thought I was in Nantucket, with that dear Miriam Swain. She seemed to have grown into a woman like the Santa Chiara

the sisters showed us the other day, and I had such
a feeling of heavenly peace and rest, — that was
all.   And, Randolph, it has given me another
whim.   I want to go to Nantucket, and have that
child near me, — the placid little thing!   I feel
as if my dream might become truth.   The little
Quakeress would be balm to my soul."

Colonel Payne dropped the apricot he had taken
in his hand, and it rolled upon the floor.

"Good heavens, Anna!" he exclaimed.   "You
will want to go to the wilds of Siberia, or Africa,
next.   Every new move brings you to a more and
more dismal place!"

"I knew what you would say, but something
tells me, Randolph, that Nantucket would help
me.   Take me there and leave me for a while!
I won't ask you to stay yourself.   It will quiet
this restlessness, at any rate.   And to take up the
broken thread where it was dropped seems, some-
how, more hopeful than searching at random.
Ah, letters!" she exclaimed seating herself at
table.   "*What!*   There! you see a letter from
my little Quakeress has made me glad before I
knew it was in the house.   It has brought its own
atmosphere with it!"

She opened the letter, but in a moment put it
aside.

"Ah, she has made an important discovery!"
she said with agitation.

"Important to the world?" the colonel asked,
while he went on quietly removing the skin from
his apricot.

Mrs. Payne pushed the letter towards her husband.

"Read it for me, Randolph," she said, "and tell me if it *is* — about Rollo."

"How straight all your roads lead to Rome, Anna!" said the colonel. "Now, in reason, does such a thing seem likely?"

He dipped his hands in his finger-glass, and wiped them with an air of expedition, as if this small matter might soon be attended to and dismissed. But as he glanced over the letter, he looked more and more surprised and interested. At length, laying it aside: —

"Your Rollo's story is told, Anna," he said slowly and carefully. "You will be glad to know that he belongs to very respectable people. He is the son of " —

"Belongs to *whom?*" interrupted Mrs. Payne, breathing quickly, and raising her head so that her slender neck looked abnormally long. "He is *mine!* He is my *own!* He grew up out of my arms. No matter where he came from, he belongs to *me.* Who wants to claim him?"

"Why, no one, dear. His father and mother " —

"No, Randolph, I don't want to know about his father and mother."

"But they died, long ago," said Colonel Payne.

Mrs. Payne looked relieved, and presently consented to hear the story. But she took her breakfast rather silently. Apparently the letter had not delighted her.

Upon rising from table, she turned suddenly to her husband.

"Who knows," she said, "but he has found some of these — these new people. His lonely heart would turn to them, of course."

"I never knew you to borrow trouble before," said the colonel.

"And I never had such a rich fund to borrow from. Randolph, I want to go to Nantucket more than ever. That seems to be the place where everything comes to light. I feel *impelled* to go, and Miriam's invitation is as urgent as my longing. Yes, you dear old fellow," she added to Monte Cristo, who had started up eagerly at the name of Rollo, "*you* are invited. They know I would n't think of going without *you*."

"I don't quite know," the colonel began slowly and meditatively. "You see the chief of the American legation can't start up and leave the country quite so suddenly as this. We 'll try to manage it, but of course I could n't let you go alone."

"Perhaps Roland would go with me."

"*Roland Weir!* — in *Nantucket!*"

"It does seem strange to think of him in such a· place," Mrs. Payne said musingly. "What wonderful things time has done! But I think upon every account he had best go. This reckless extravagance of his will ruin him if he remains in Paris. He always assures me he is ready to do whatever I wish, but I can see how reluctant he is to leave the neighborhood of the Vintons. The foolish boy persists in doing homage to Betty. And somehow Betty does encourage him, at the same time that she sets him at naught."

"A little more absolute manliness, or a *good deal* more, would change Betty's attitude, I assure you," said the colonel, sternly.

"And if Betty would only take a different tone," returned Mrs. Payne, "she might rouse and stimulate him ; she might help me correct the mistake I have made. Ah, my mistakes! They spoil my own life,—how many more I cannot tell!"

"We won't spoil life farther by useless bemoaning," the colonel said, with an attempt at cheerfulness. "Somebody has said that our mistakes are often the best things we can do for ourselves."

Mrs. Payne shook her head doubtingly. "Shall I propose to Roland to go home with me?" she asked.

"Yes, I think that will be best," the colonel answered.

But it so happened that Mrs. Payne was not the one to make the proposition. Before she had written, there came a letter from Roland Weir, expressing the same desire, — to go to America.

"Why, what does it mean?" said Mrs. Payne.

"The Vintons are probably going home? Don't you see?" returned the colonel.

CHAPTER XXI.

THE INCOMING OF THE TIDE.

THE southwest chamber of the Swain house, with its dark old mahogany and snow-white coverings and hangings, was airing and sunning every day, for Nantucket, being all the time at sea, is rather a damp place. The solemnity of that once awful room was moderated to quiet cheerfulness. There were other pictures on the walls besides the old one of Solomon's Temple, for Miriam had been to Yearly Meeting with Aunt Dorcas, and brought home from the Newport shops a few things to soften the severity of pure utility.

And there was a glass bowl of roses on the dressing-table, for Mrs. Payne might arrive any day, and she was to be made cheerful and well.

Back of the southwest room was the one which had seemed so luxurious to Roland Weir when he first came to it from the Dagget cottage. That, too, had been somewhat embellished, yet it was left much the same as in the old times, for Roland would not like to see it changed, Miriam thought.

The brass door knobs, the brasses of the fire frames, the andirons, shovels and tongs, and the knocker on the front door, that all shone enough to put your eyes out, were to have one more rub, the furniture a few more polishing touches, the finest linen and the extra silver were to be brought out, and Sally Martin was to be taken home to her mother.

While Betsy Blossom and Rosanna attended to the works of supererogation, Miriam attended to Sally, who, when she came up to town last, was brought up by John Blossom, so that Miriam has not seen 'Sconset herself for several weeks. What is her surprise, then, when she jogs into its sleepy thoroughfare, to see, in place of the Dagget cottage, such a marvelous little piece of architecture as never stood on the soil of Nantucket before. It is, in fact, the Dagget cottage itself, awakened from its nap, yawning and stretching itself in a fine new dress. It has stretched itself to the extent of larger rooms, and one new one, besides a higher roof with dormer windows. There is a broad veranda running round it, the little greenish panes are removed from the windows and clear bright glass put in their places. The ship's figurehead is no more. The house is covered with coats of Pompeiian red paint, and there are glimpses of dark myrtle green, that show like the facings and linings of a fine gown.

The same group of old women are gossiping in the sandy pathway again that Miriam had seen there when she first noticed the cottage asleep, or if they are not identically, they are pictorially and historically the same.

There is no face better known and loved in 'Sconset than Miriam's. Each gossip offers her a respectful reverence and a beaming smile, and she pulls up Jerry to speak to them.

"Why, who is making such a grand display in 'Sconset?" she asks.

"It's Ma'am Dagget's boy," is the answer. "He's come back so altered as nobody would 'a' knowed him, — a tall, proper-good-lookin' man, with a grand voice when he speaks. He knowed us, and hed the key to the cottage, so I s'pose 't is him, but my! he don't look no more like that boy than hen's eggs looks like hens! I expect he's found the chist of money, for he had n't been here but a day or so before he had the men come and tear down and build up, and putty and paint, and now look a' there! There ain't such a pretty house on the island, and he's gone off island to buy things to put into it. He's been a-follerin' the seas, and he says he wants a home to go to when he lands, and it looks consid'rable as if he'd got one, don't it?"

"Why, ye-s," Miriam said, taking in the whole picture slowly.

"Funny color for a house, ain't it?" said the gossip.

"It's beautiful," said Miriam. "It's so pleasant to look at in the glare of the sand."

At this point, Sally Martin's mother put her head out of the cottage door, having another moment's leisure to bestow in admiration of the great work of regeneration, and seeing her offspring in a position of importance, came out smiling and primming herself to get her share of honor, and Sally's secret sorrow, which she had kept within her own bosom, burst forth amain.

" I wanted to stay and see the company!" she cried.

" Why, the greatest sights are here in 'Sconset, Sally," said Miriam. " I shall bring the company down here."

" Well, of all the naughty girls I ever did see! Come here to me!" said Mrs. Martin, and Sally is dragged down from her high position, and set upon a level with ordinary mortals, where she stands weeping and trying to hide her tears.

A few words of comfort to Sally, a word of kindness to everybody, and Miriam says she must hurry to get home before the boat is in. Sally reaches up a quivering lip to kiss her adored friend, and Jerry, at the sound of the smack, turns and points his nose homeward.

The day was hot, and the sand seemed deeper than ever to the worthy Jerry. He soon began to make little pauses, which were like commas, and colons, and semicolons, in a long, long paragraph.

" Come, come, Jeremiah," Miriam entreated, " what can thee be thinking of now? Thee seems to have lost that lively idea thee started with."

There was one thing that Jerry started with from 'Sconset, which, unfortunately, he had not lost, however. That was a hard little shell in his foot, which gradually worked its way into a place where it gave him much discomfort. He hesitated more than ever, he limped, he came to a full period.

After having brought her to the very most inconvenient point in the whole journey, far from 'Sconset, very far from town, far even from the two or three farm-houses that sat slowly disintegrating, miles apart, on the lorn and lone roadside, he absolutely declined to go on.

Miriam got down and examined his hoofs to find the trouble. There it was, wedged tightly in, and she had nothing with which she could remove it.

Well, then, what was to be done? There might no one pass over the road again that day, perhaps not the next day, possibly not for two or three days. The nearest farm-house was two miles away. Looking over "a weary, thirsty land," she could see it "far beneath a blazing vault," sit sulking in the sweltering heat. Jerry was immovable. His heart was not to be melted by coaxing. It was far likelier to be melted by the fierce July sun. Miriam looked before her, behind her, on all sides of her, and above her. There was nothing — everywhere nothing — but hot sky, hot sand, and parching heather.

It seemed impossible to cross the burning desert on foot with nothing to shade her, so she sat quietly in the chaise and waited for help to happen along, thinking that when it was cooler she would walk on to the farm-house, if no one should appear and Jerry should not change his mind. She waited an hour — two hours.

Meantime the Nantucket boat had arrived at its wharf. Among its passengers was a pale, delicate woman and a distinguished-looking young man, who gave her devoted attention, while every person on board gave attention to him, in the way of noticing how handsome he was and how excessively elegant. It was unusual, not to say unprecedented, for such a dazzling person to be seen in those waters.

These two appeared to be of especial interest to a young man in the office of the captain. He had retired to that seclusion when he had seen them coming aboard with a beautiful Irish setter, who sniffed about in an uneasy way, seeming at occasional instants to get a frantic idea in his head, and then to lose or give it up again. He took no notice whatever of the commands of the distinguished young man to him to lie down and be quiet, but yielded to a touch of the lady's hand, and seated himself at her feet with an alert look, watching everything, and sniffing the air with an appearance of reconnoitring. Our secluded young man waited for them to go ashore and take a carriage before he moved from his position, and then followed their example, except that he took his carriage for 'Sconset, and sat silently within it, while a hundred tumultuous thoughts were seething in his mind. He scarcely saw, away on, in mid-island, a horse and chaise, though he fixed his absent eyes upon it.

"Them folks don't seem to git on much, he-y?" said his driver, and then he noticed that the vehicle stood waiting, waiting, waiting, all the time perfectly still, as they approached and approached.

When they drew up beside it, Miriam explained her difficulty.

"I'll see what I can do," the young man said, alighting, and feeling in his pockets for an instrument. He was not quick in finding one, however, for ruffled and tossed in mind as he was, it seemed to soothe him to look upon the face framed in the old shay-top. The presence of something serene and noble is quieting to agitation, and nothing more serene and noble could by any possibility be imagined than the lovely young Quakeress, serene in spite of the heat and the weariness and the vexation.

Our young man felt obliged to discover something to his purpose in the last of his nine or ten pockets. He brought it out, and in the same moderate manner, investigated Jerry's feet.

It was a simple matter to extract the offending shell. One instant, and it was all over, that pleasant little episode, as he supposed.

"I'm very much obliged to thee," said Miriam. "Now if my horse were only as impatient as I am I should do very well. Some friends may have arrived on this boat, who have come all the way from Europe to visit me, and here I sit in the middle of the island!"

"Your horse looks like a capable fellow. He ought to take you home very soon."

"Oh, he *ought* to, and he 's capable enough," said Miriam. "But I 've allowed him to have his own way so much that he takes advantage of me. He will never hurry when *I 'm* driving him."

"Let 's see what he will do for me," said the young man. "May I ?"

He mounted into the chaise, with Miriam's permission, and took the reins, beckoning his driver to follow.

When the electric current of a young, masculine energy shot down the lines into Jerry's consciousness, he started with a jump which surprised Miriam, for she had never before seen such a disposition in the phlegmatic animal. But Miriam's surprise was nothing compared with Jeremiah's own astonishment. He felt the unaccustomed power and will at the other end of the telegraphic medium, and it roused the same qualities in himself; roused his latent ambition; roused memories of youth, when his fiery soul thrilled with longings to *go.* He perceived that, after all, he was still young, for he felt something of the same thrill again, and rejoicing, as middle-aged people are apt to do, at a return of the waning fires, he forgot himself entirely, and frisked like a yearling colt. He was so eager that his trotting now and then broke into a canter. It was very refreshing after that long, compulsory rest in the desert. Miriam felt admiration for one who could bring such marvelous things to pass. She looked up at him with a smile of gratitude. He was so tall that his head

bumped against the top of the chaise. He laughed
a little at that, and his fine teeth flashed in beautiful contrast with his dark brown skin. Miriam
protested against his troubling himself to go back,
but he said the privilege of driving such a lively
steed was ample compensation. He hoped she
would not refuse him the pleasure. She could
not, of course. He was very obliging. Miriam
declared she had never been in such a dilemma
before, as that one with Jerry, and the young man,
who, by the way, we may as well call Rollo, responded that to be lost in a great city like New
York, he should think would be worse. Then Miriam looked at him in a way which asked why he
said that, and Rollo went on to tell her about having seen a little girl in that predicament once; and
then Miriam remembered that one day, in New
York, when she had wished to go home from
Betty's alone, to enjoy the sensation of a large
freedom, she had turned from the avenue into a
side street to see a Punch and Judy show, and
had crossed the street with it two or three times,
until she was quite turned about, and finally found
herself in the wrong avenue, very much bewildered and distressed, when a sailorish young man
with blue eyeglasses had happened along and
kindly taken her home. And this was the young
man? How marvelous! And how had he remembered her? Miriam wondered a great deal.
She declared Rollo was a true knight-errant; and
Rollo answered that he should find the profession

amazingly dull if it were not for her. All the business he had ever had was what she kindly furnished. They laughed at that, and began to feel almost like friends. They found so much to talk about that sometimes the reins slackened, and Jerry lost communication with the battery, and slackened too. A southwest wind sprang up, and brought delicious coolness. Miriam pushed back her pretty little hat and let it rest at the nape of her neck, as she had used to do with her prim bonnet when she was a little girl. Her bright hair blew about her temples in captivating rings. The distance across the island seemed very inconsiderable to Rollo. But at length it was all accomplished, and he left Miriam at her own door, and walked slowly up the street to meet his carriage, which had not been able to keep up with the animated Jerry.

Notwithstanding her high expectations, Miriam was hardly prepared to see, through the open door of the south front room, as she entered the house, such a transcendent young man as stood there gazing curiously at one of the new pictures. Miriam had never seen such a figure, so smoothly and exquisitely clad; and that lovely hair, parted in the middle, and those ravishing hands with pink, polished finger nails, she would have said they belonged to a girl, if they had not been offset by a highly cultivated moustache and the habiliments of manhood.

And Miriam, with her hair all tumbled and

tossed, as she had repeatedly brushed it back from her heated forehead, an excess of redness in her astonished face, looked like Nature confronting Art.

"Ah! Miriam! Don't you know me?" said the peerless young man.

"It — can't — be!" Miriam murmured slowly.

"Take my word for it.   It *is.*"

"Why so it *is!*" cried Miriam, seeing the old smile in his eyes; and recovering her self-possession, she frankly kissed her old comrade.

They regarded each other with mutual surprise. They exchanged exclamations of wonder at the marvelous work of time.   They were professedly glad.

But what was it that disappointed Miriam? There was more there than she had expected, and yet there was something unfulfilled.   She felt suddenly lowered into a cool, damp place.   But Roland Weir was not at all cool or damp, himself. He was warm and effusive.   He paid Miriam graceful compliments, he said beautiful things, he stood before her with an air of having utterly surrendered himself to her worship and service, in the most perfect Parisian manner, — and yet Miriam felt a vague dissatisfaction, which robbed her of her old delight in him.

Roland perceived something of this in the grave, steady look with which she observed him.

"What is it, Miriam?" he said.   "You look as if you meant to reject me, as an unsatisfactory article."

" I shall reject some things, probably," Miriam answered frankly. " Thee 's — a good deal changed."

" Why, unfortunately, I could n't manage to remain a boy," said Roland. " I 'm an inevitable result ; a poor one, no doubt, but I submit myself to your correction."

" Oh," said Miriam, blushing and laughing. " I only want to find Roland Weir. He 's there, somewhere, I suppose."

" You believe in him, then ? "

" With a faith equal to that of Mahomet's good Kadijah," said Miriam seriously.

" Thanks," said Roland, almost as seriously. "I am in Mahomet's need, — when *only* Kadijah believed in him."

At this moment, the voice of Rosanna was heard from above in a loud whisper.

" Is yo' thar, honey ? Shor ? Safe an' soun' ? Nothin' hain't happened to yo' ? Wal, Mis' Payne say do come up ! "

Miriam responded to this summons, and was shocked to find, resting upon a couch, in place of the beautiful Mrs. Payne of her memory, a thin-faced woman with threads of gray in her hair, and an eager, wistful look where there had once been unruffled calm.

She stretched her arms towards Miriam with the exclamation, " Yes, there she is ! exactly like my dream ! " and when Miriam folded her in strong, gentle arms, she added : —

" My dream has come to pass ! "

And perhaps, if Monte Cristo could have spoken, he would have uttered words similiar to those last, as he stepped out from under the carriage, when it stopped at Rollo's door at 'Sconset.

Miriam had conveniently left her own door open when she entered it, and Monte, looking out to see what sort of a place he had arrived at, had his eyes arrested by the sight of a person walking up the street with an air and a gait which he well remembered. He had trotted behind that footstep too often to forget it. Those haunting notions on the steamboat were accounted for to Monte's satisfaction. He stole down the steps and pursued, — more cautiously this time than before, in New York, — and shooting under the carriage, after Rollo had entered it, followed what he considered to be the line of duty, until it brought him to 'Sconset.

Rollo and Monte looked at each other eye to eye, as they each emerged, the one from within, the other from beneath, the carriage. Monte did not spring upon his master as he had done upon the former occasion, but laid himself down at his feet, making little agitated raps with his tail on the ground, licking his lips slowly, and averting his eyes under Rollo's steady stare like a dog who is uncertain of a welcome.

Again Rollo's heart yearned over the dear, faithful fellow, — faithful in spite of his cruel abandonment ; but the smallest sign of encouragement would make trouble for his owners, so turning to his driver, Rollo paid his carriage hire, and added something for Monte Cristo's fare.

"I wish you 'd take this dog home again," he said. "He belongs at Mr. Obed Swain's. Here sir! get up! Get up here!" he called to Monte Cristo, who, with a patient grief which his dumbness made more eloquent than the most voluble human eloquence could have done, sprang into the carriage, and laid himself down, once more discarded and betrayed.

CHAPTER XXII

THE MEETING AT THE HAUL-OVER.

IT was indeed a question of importance, — especially in his own mind, — what that young exquisite was to do with himself, or what was to be done with him, on the homely island, for his acquired tastes made him incline to count the dull and simple life there among the things he had escaped. He could hardly believe he had ever been homesick for such a tiresome place.

And in addition to some discontent, Roland had one positive woe, which, although it seemed infinite to himself, may be indicated in very few words.

On his last crossing of the detestable Atlantic, as he called it, Betty Vinton had shown more plainly than ever her contempt of a certain defect in Roland, in regard to which he, himself, was apparently unconscious, or utterly indifferent. This was a conspicuous lack of manly stamina. At length, one day, when she was surrounded on deck by what he considered intolerable fellows, who could offer her perpetual attention because of their abominable sea-legs, he had undertaken to pass them, on the way to his state-room, clinging now to a stanchion, then to the bulwarks, and had finally been precipitated almost at Betty's very feet, in consequence of an inconvenient plunge of the ship, and Betty had looked up and laughed,— actually mocked at him, as he sensitively imagined.

Betty's ill-timed laugh, however, had come rushing out to hide her compassion. She liked Roland well enough to prefer to admire, rather than pity him. If pity and love *are* kindred, they do detest to live together, and as for Betty, she refused, professedly, to harbor either of them.

Roland received her after-apology with coldness. Nothing could soothe the sting. That laugh would ring in his ears forever! But he was far too well-bred and too good-natured to allow his trouble to be apparent. It was the secret of his soul, and although he said a good deal to himself about it, he said never a word besides, but submitted with a very commendable show of cheerfulness to the efforts of his friends to give him the pleasures of the island, or what they, simple souls, fondly imagined to be pleasures. He surrendered himself indifferently to anything.

One afternoon Miriam asked him to row her up to Polpis to see some person who was ill at one of the farm-houses there. Though it was hard pulling so far against a strong current, and Miriam was sure Roland would be afraid of his lady-like hands and his complexion, she offered the dose with such firmness as a wise mother maintains in the cause

of a sick child.   It was chiefly moral heroism that
she looked for in her ideal Roland Weir, but it
seemed to her that moral heroism would refuse to
consort with such physical softness, which was not
the result of frail health, as it had been formerly.
Roland's health was fine, but he had become an
enervated, self-indulgent sybarite.   He dreaded
pulling against the tide in any sense, but he ami-
ably took to the oars with apparent willingness,
while Miriam, turning partly away from him, kept
her eyes fixed on the low, sandy shores, fringed
with rank beach grass, that looked like a running
stream as the wind blew over it.   The descending
sun put them into such light that they were beautiful in a meek way.   Miriam seemed to observe
this more than she did her oarsman, and talked a
good deal, with her eyes fixed always upon something far away.   At length the oars ceased to
thump in the rowlocks.   Something was the matter.   The propelling power had given out.   It lay
upon its oars with a decidedly used-up appearance,
making a polite pretense of pausing to enjoy the
scenery, while the boat drifted backward.   Miriam would have been glad to take the oars, but
one cannot take a patient's medicine for him, and
she had decided that her patient needed a few
grains of hardship.   Her oarsman continued to al-
ternate between feeble pumping and pausing to
let the boat slide back again, and they would have
remained just opposite Shimmo to this day, but
that laugh of Betty Vinton's, which perpetually

haunted Roland, seemed suddenly to apply itself to the occasion. It rippled and rang out and returned in mocking echoes, or seemed to, until Roland fairly ground his teeth, and the occasion reached a momentous crisis.

"By Hercules!" he muttered, taking the biggest breath he had ever drawn, and bending to the oars, he never paused to admire the scenery again until he had brought the boat up at Polpis.

Miriam took the heroic performance as a matter of course, as if it had been only what she expected of him, though she was almost frightened at the unaccountable effect of her prescription, the expression of the set lips, and the heaving of the tired wrath-expanded chest.

They floated back with the tide, and the only allusion Miriam made to this wonderful spurt of Roland's was when he gave her his hand as they left the boat.

"We've gained one more believer, to-day, Mahomet," she said.

"Bless you, Kadijah, who's that?"

"Thee's beginning to believe in thyself," Miriam answered.

Roland privately doctored his blistered hands, and looked at his sunburned face in his mirror, as if it were the face of some one he took malicious delight in exposing to such treatment, and day after day he repeated it, taking a boat by himself and pulling up the harbor. His face and hands grew brown, and he began to throw out his chest when he walked, like a commodore, so that Mrs. Payne expressed frequent wonder, and declared that Nantucket was doing him even more good than it did her.

"But wait until I 've done with you!" Roland would say, shaking his fist at his altered self in the glass on his dressing-table.

One day he rowed from point to point, until he landed at the Haul-over, where the harbor at its head is only separated from the Atlantic by a narrow strip of land,—a bare sand-bar, of about a furlong's width, — across which a boat may be hauled. It is a rough clasp between the sapphire of the harbor and the diamond of the sea; or it is the dividing line between home and the wilderness, whichever you will. On one side are safety and peace; on the other, peril and terror and loss. It is a spot of such desolation that it seems to have nothing to do with life, — especially human life. It appears to be there only to keep those waters apart, and yet it is such a little barrier that it might easily wash away and let them flow together.

The place is a few miles north of 'Sconset, on the same side of the island.

Roland pulled his boat up on the sands, and crossing over the little isthmus, threw himself down by the open sea and watched the great rollers come tumbling in and the clean sweep of the terrible undertow. A stronger than he might have been seized with awe at feeling himself the

only human atom in that illimitable space. Not
a suggestion of human life was anywhere within
the circle of the horizon. He was absolutely alone,
on a handful of sand, in infinitude. He might
have been the first man — or the last. He faced
the grandeur with boldness for a time, but at
length, overwhelmed, he closed his eyes to shut out
an awful impression; his human soul shrinking
back to hide itself among the molecules again.

When he raised his eyes once more, he was
gladdened by the sight of a small sailboat approaching from the south. At once he seemed to
have companionship. He watched the sail. It
was like something one fixes the eye upon in
climbing high, to prevent dizziness. It kept just
off shore until it was directly opposite Roland,
when it dropped sail and seemed to be making
straight for him. He was a nervous young man,
and felt as if he were marked and shot at.

"But it's probably only some 'Sconset fisherman," he said.

And indeed it was only they who could catch
those wild horses of the sea, with their flying
white manes, and ride them safely to shore. An
unskilled rider would be thrown and trampled
under. This one came magnificently in upon the
beach, but he was no 'Sconset fisherman. It was
uncommon, perhaps, for two arrivals to occur at
the Haul-over in the same hour, or even the same
day, and, possibly, never since that period of crea-
tion when the land was divided from the waters,

had one man come up the harbor to meet another man coming from over sea with the punctuality of an appointment; yet Roland was more struck with the look which the stranger bent upon him than he was with the coincidence itself.

The two exchanged courteous salutations, and the newcomer, taking a basket from his boat, was about to go on across the bar in silence.

"For Heaven's sake!" cried Roland Weir, "do say something, if it's only 'How are ye,' for I long to hear the sound of a human voice. I think this must be the lonesomest spot in the universe."

The stranger was very tall, with broad, square shoulders, well set back, and he carried himself in such a way as to give the impression of remarkable freedom and firmness, but he turned to answer Roland in quite a hesitating way.

"Yes," he said, "I suppose I've crossed here fifty times, and I never met a soul before."

"Then I'm a remarkable occurrence. I'm one in fifty, at least," said Roland. "When I see a man who can pass by something like that with such coolness, my curiosity is aroused. I say to myself, 'That man has seen tremendous things,' and I want to know more about him."

"I'm sorry to disappoint you," returned the stranger; "there's nothing to know about me except that I'm named Tuttle, and I came from 'Sconset."

"Tuttle! Of 'Sconset! Get out with your modesty!" said Roland. "I know a good deal about you already. I know two fellows who breakfast, dine, sup, and sleep on Tuttle of 'Sconset and his new ship. As to me, I 'm only Roland Weir, of nowhere in particular. Have you ever chanced to hear of him ?"

"Yes, I have," Mr. Tuttle replied, flushing in a curious way, and feeling two letters in India ink stinging his arm.

"Those same fellows have been talking about *me*, then," said Roland, who had risen, and now came towards Mr. Tuttle with his hand extended. Mr. Tuttle, changing his basket, gave his own hand in return.

The youth from the inner harbor looked up at the one from the outer sea with a certain wishfulness, as he took his measure, moral and physical. There was something large and strong there besides the tall person. You could never have thought of Mr. Tuttle as being "alone or poor or exiled or unhappy or a client." He seemed provided against those misfortunes, in himself, though he was a very modest, simple sailor, who was only sure of himself as an honest man and a good navigator.

Roland Weir, who had sighed for Paris, was rather surprised to find himself attracted to this plain man. The gravitation of the weaker towards the stronger nature is as irresistible, sometimes, between man and man, as between woman and man, and there are impressions which strike deeply at the first, and become affairs of the heart in friendship, as well as in love, especially with a person like Roland Weir, whose sensitive nature had something almost feminine to account for it.

Yet do not fancy Roland jumping at friendship and a new ideal from just having a look at a young man. He knew much about him, as he has said, for he had listened to long and fulsome dissertations from Paul Haddon and Perez Howard on " the captain," as they called him. He had heard how " the captain's " bravery, his cleverness in the things connected with his occupation, his modesty, his straightforward truth and honesty, had at first won the good-will, then the admiration, and at last the warm friendship of his captain, who had pushed him on at a pace which, though rapid, did not outstrip his ability; and how a splendid new ship was building down at New Bedford, of which he was to be commander as soon as it was finished. Paul and Perez had been down there ever since Roland's arrival at Nantucket, so that all this had but freshly come to him. He had listened to it with some interest, and had challenged Haddon and Howard to trot out their prodigy and put him through his paces. His interest was immensely increased now that he stood face to face with the prodigy.

" Well, then, here we are, John Dagget's two boys," he said. " What the dickens do you suppose we 've come to a rendezvous here for? There 's something monstrous queer about it."

" Why, I 'm here on my way to market," said

Mr. Tuttle. "I go to town this way sometimes, rather than cross the island. It's easier to me, though it's farther. I keep another little old boat fastened there at the head of the harbor, and when the wind is fair, this is as quick as either way."

"Well, that accounts for you, but it don't account for me," said Roland, poking the sand with the toe of his boot, and looking intently at the operation. "Do you believe in destiny, and that sort of thing?"

"No, not much," Mr. Tuttle responded, gazing down at Roland with far the keener sense of the queerness of the situation, for it was but a whimsical fancy on Roland's part to make so much of the chance meeting.

"Well, I do," Roland declared emphatically. He enjoyed being dramatic and exciting an interest. "We're here for *something*, I'm sure of that, so do sit down, won't you, and let's see about it."

Rollo sat down on the sand, with his basket beside him, in an automatic way, as if there were nothing else to do.

"Does n't it establish a relationship between us, to begin with, that we've both been John Dagget's boys?" Roland wanted to know.

"You're very kind to suppose such a thing," Rollo replied, not with humility, but with a touch of dignity.

"*Kind?* Now that's great stuff," said Roland, flinging the assertion back with a wave of his hand. "*Does* it? That's all I want to know."

"I hope so," returned Rollo civilly.

"Well, it *does*, then. Now, two persons, previously related, meet for the first time in a peculiar way, in the most peculiar spot on the map. Don't you suppose that means something?"

"I'm not much for getting at meanings," said Rol. He was the same old rather-silent Rol that we remember, and he was more than usually dumb upon this occasion. It was Roland Weir who expanded and executed the one-sided conversation, holding forth upon all sorts of things. He had naturally a brilliant, rapid, nervous manner, and he took up one subject after another, in quick succession, even touching upon heroism, and matters of that sort, in a few glowing words, which made him a surprise to himself. Rollo listened and watched him, the earnest look growing in his clear, brown face. It grew into admiration, and that again into an expression of real pleasure. He was beginning to like the charming youth whose initials burned upon his arm.

At length Roland drew in his rattling conversational courser, and Rollo took his turn to speak.

"Do you mean to stay long on the island?" he asked.

"Why, I can't tell," Roland answered. "I came with my aunt, who is an invalid. She fancied it would do her good. It did, at first, but she is beginning to fall back again. She is very restless and nervous, and everything depends upon her."

"I hope it is n't serious," said Rollo, overcoming
a slight hoarseness, and trying to speak in a tone
of simple politeness.

"I think it *is* getting to be serious, yes," returned Roland gravely.

"Why, — can't they *do* anything for her, these
doctors? Have they tried *everything?* There
must be something they have n't thought of!"
Rollo said, with eagerness, while his anxiety looked
plainly out of his honest face.

"What a sympathetic nature you have, have n't
you?" said Roland.

"Ye-yes, I believe I have," Rollo answered, trying to recover the manner of a polite listener; but
he looked so dejected that Roland quite revered
his benevolent spirit.

"What a kind, noble heart he has," he said to
himself. "I don't think it is anything the doctors
can help," he continued aloud. "It is something
she is worrying about, and it just wears her out."

Rollo then looked so wretched that Roland Weir
again said to himself, "Why, he 's an out-and-out
Buddha! How he takes the troubles of the world
to heart!"

And this matter upon which he had begun to
speak was a trouble to himself. Mrs. Payne had
never spoken to him of what was grieving her,
she was so eager for him to know nothing but
happiness, and Roland had never ventured to in-
troduce the subject to her; but the way was open
for guessing, with Betty's help. He had, however,

never mentioned the matter to any one, except Betty, and Betty knew no more than he did.

Now he felt a womanish rush of confidence towards this strong, sympathetic nature. He longed to open his mind. Have you never known an impulsive, warm-hearted girl to say to the friend of an hour, "It seems as if I could tell you *everything!*" Just so it seemed to Roland Weir. He could almost have told Rollo his sorrows about Betty. While he meditated this offer of his confidence, a great white skimmer went flapping by with a cry that sounded like "Speak! speak!" The two young men watched it in silence, as it swooped along from wave to wave. Was it only a gull, or was it the spirit of that destiny in which Roland Weir professed to believe?

Presently Roland started out with his confidence.

"It is a trouble of conscience that affects my aunt," he said. "She fancies she has wronged somebody, and driven him off to nobody knows what, by some little unkindness or neglect. It could n't be so, you know, for she 's the kindest, gentlest person in the world."

"Yes, — yes," said Rol.

"It seems strange for me to be telling you our family affairs, does n't it?" Roland asked.

"No — yes — I don't know," Rollo answered, with complete confusion of mind and manner. "Of course," he added, catching his breath, "I 've heard about that strange boy, who was put into your place.   Is it — is *that* the person she has the fancy about ? "

" Yes."

" Well," Rollo went on, swallowing hard.   " I know that person.   He 's a sailor, like myself, and he makes quite a friend of me.   I wish you would tell your aunt that I have heard him say she *never* was unkind, *never.*   He 's as grateful to her as can be.   He only went away because he did n't want to be a trouble to her.   Come, go and tell her that, won't you?   Don't — *don't* wait !   It might make her better at once to have that off her mind. I 'm in a great hurry myself.   I must go on.   For Heaven's sake, don't let 's sit here any longer gabbing, when she 's worrying about *that !* "

Rollo got up and started on, forgetting his basket, and panting with impatience and emotion. " Come, I 'll take you down the harbor," he said. " Come !   Come on !   Do come on ! "

CHAPTER XXIII.

CAPTURED.

It was not until he had parted with Rollo at the market, and was wending his way up town, with a cautious eye on the ups and downs of the sunken old flagging of the Nantucket sidewalks, that Roland reflected carefully and soberly upon this emotional lover of the human race, — that was how he still considered him, for it would be a slow process, naturally, which would bring him to connect the emotions of Mr. Tuttle of 'Sconset solely with his aunt.

He was still dwelling perplexedly upon this divine compassion, when he reached home and presented himself at the door of the south room, where he found Mrs. Payne in the large cushioned chair in which she usually sat, with her thin hands lying listlessly in her lap. This time she was face to face with Monte Cristo, and the two seemed to have been having a discussion without coming to an understanding.

"What ails the dog?" Mrs. Payne exclaimed as Roland entered. "It is really frightful to see how frantic he gets." Then in a confidential tone she added, "He does n't like to stay here. He is constantly urging me to go."

" Go where ? " asked Roland.

" I 'm sure I .don't know.   He has been like my shadow, you know, but since we came here he is just a vagabond, — goes away and is gone all day, and comes back quite used up and half starved."

" Goes where, do you suppose ? "

" Indeed, I can't suppose.   The very afternoon we arrived, he started off before we were fairly settled in the house.   A public carriage driver brought him back, and said Monte had followed him across the island."

" To where, — in what direction ? "

" To that fishing village, — Siasconset."

Roland held himself still, to give his mind a chance to settle, and presently that turbid mixture of uncertainty and perplexity with which he had come home cleared into limpid enlightenment. Still, as Roland recognized the patent fact that more than half the people who think they have discovered the truth are very much mistaken indeed, he kept his light to himself for the time, and seating himself on a footstool at Mrs. Payne's feet said : —

" I met a young man this morning who knows — Rollo."

Mrs. Payne started forward in her chair.   " Who is he ?   Where is he ? " she asked in one quick breath.

" He 's that remarkable young man Paul Haddon was telling us about — Dame Dagget's heir."

" And he lives at Siasconset ? "

" Yes."

" Roland," Mrs. Payne cried, clasping her hands, " don't you see ?   Rollo has probably been to this place.   Monte has fallen upon some clue and wants to tell me.   Oh, I was inspired when I insisted upon coming here ! "

Mrs. Payne looked highly excited, and caressed Monte Cristo, who flounced about, panted, and sneezed at every mention of Rollo's name, like a dog who hopes he is beginning to be understood.

" But where is Rollo ?   What did this young man say about him ?   Should you think he had seen him recently ? " Mrs. Payne continued with trembling eagerness.

" I — I should rather think he had," Roland answered.

" Is it some one who knows him well, or only a casual acquaintance ? "

" Oh, I should think he must know him uncommonly well," Roland answered with assurance.

" I must see him, then, though he is of the species I dread."

" What species ? "

" The self - made, self - congratulating sort, — strong of their successes, and so unconscious of their ill-breeding."

" Why he 's not at all that kind, aunt.   He 's a noble fellow — quite a splendid fellow — as gentlemanly as you please, and as modest as a dove. And besides all that, he is so tender-hearted that he could not rest when he heard of your concern about Rollo, but sent me home spinning, to ease your mind."

" I shall go to see him," Mrs. Payne said rising and moving to the window, from which she looked out with wistful eyes, as if she would have gone on the wing and on the moment. "I must go to-morrow," she added; "I feel uncommonly well."

" It is a tiresome drive, aunt. You 'd better let him come here and see you."

" No, I should like to be tired for some reason. I am always tired. Nobody knows why."

It was then dinner time, and during the dinner it was fully settled that Mrs. Payne and Miriam would drive over to 'Sconset the next day.

" And I shall take a horse and canter across in advance, to be sure the young man has n't gone a-fishing, and that his mind is prepared," said Roland. " He seems rather a shy fellow, and probably is n't accustomed to receiving visits from ladies. It would n't be fair for you to spring such a surprise upon him."

There seemed no doubt but that Rollo would be taken, when on the following morning Roland Weir went galloping over the moors, as eager as a huntsman with his eye on the game, and afterwards Mrs. Payne, who was like a ferret in her keenness and eagerness and tenacity of purpose, and with her the Quaker girl, full of the spirit of the occasion, which she caught sympathetically, as one who rides with the hunt as a looker-on catches the enthusiasm of the hunters.

But Monte Cristo was left behind!   It was too long a run for him on a summer's day, Mrs. Payne thought, and so the poor, patient fellow, who had trotted down to 'Sconset again and again to watch his old master from afar, and try to make out what ailed him that he should be so cruel and strange, who had told his story to Mrs. Payne over and over, and lost himself repeatedly in wonder as to what ailed her, too, that she should be so dull,—poor Monte Cristo was shut up in the wash-room, to consider with discouragement how much was needed to be done for these humans in order that they might see things with the clear understanding of a dog.

Ah, what bitterness it would have been to this wise and worthy animal if he could have known that the Pretender — so he contemptuously regarded Roland Weir — was leading the way where he had longed and begged to lead, while he was a prisoner in the wash-room!   He got up with his paws on the window-sill, and saw Mrs. Payne depart in the chaise, — yes, and in the right direction, too!   Could it be — *could* it be that she was going *there*, and he left out?   He turned and turned in a frenzy, calling for help with his loudest yelp, and protesting with his fiercest bark; but no help came.   He passed through every stage of anguish and wild despair which a prisoner suffers, when he knows the hour has come, — some blessed hour for which he has waited long, — while he is cut off from its joy by only the thickness or thinness of a wall or a door, which is yet as impassable as the gulf between world and world.

Monte was, in the main, a reasonable dog, however, and when he had succeeded in making himself hoarse, he sank downwith a long sigh upon the wash-room floor and waited, while Roland Weir was flying over the moors, drawing near 'Sconset, and coming at length within sight of the precious game.

As Roland swept down upon 'Sconset, the wind from the sea swept down upon him, and blew away his light straw hat. He did not even stop to look back at it, for there on the veranda sat Rollo, playing his violin.

"Here we are, violin and all, my tender-hearted young man," said Roland. "I don't dare to be sure, even yet, that you are the very one, but I 'm bold to believe you are."

Rollo turned and saw him coming, galloping on, bareheaded, flushed, heated, and very wild looking. He started to his feet and turned pale.

Roland dismounted with a bound, came up the steps with another, and there, for a moment, they stood, confronting each other, — Roland speechless and red, Rollo speechless and pale.

"Did n't I tell you," asked Roland, panting, "that we met for something up there yesterday?"

"I — I — believe — you — did," gasped Rollo slowly, like a waking sleep-walker in growing trepidation.

As he looked up at the great splendid fellow, that feeling of attraction which had possessed Roland the day before was doubly, trebly strong. With his new longing after manliness, it seemed to him that this example of manliness had come to him as the gods of old came to men's help in times of need. A moment they looked in each other's faces, then the one word that was wanted came from Roland Weir.

" *Rollo?* " — and in his warm-hearted, impulsive, facile, Frenchy way, he threw his arms round the confounded Rollo and gave him — there was no mistaking it for anything but a cordial hug.

" There ! So I take possession of you, deserter," he cried.

Rollo choked with the suddenness of this gust. But that idea of Roland Weir's possession was not unfamiliar to him. There had been scarcely a day in which he had not looked at the brand upon his arm with some thought of the secondary significance he had given it. When he had sufficiently recovered the breath and the senses which Roland Weir had quite taken away by his outburst of demonstration, "I own your claim," he said, pushing back his sleeve. "See? There's your mark."

" Good, good ! " returned Roland, bubbling over with satisfaction !

" But what does it all mean ? " Rollo begged to know. " How did you find " —

" Find you out ? It was very simple. We had

a hint from Monte Cristo, and as for you, you 're
a piece of clear, plain glass. I was very dull not
to see through you at once. I have only told my
aunt that there is a young man here who knows
Rollo, and she was for starting on the moment to
see him. She is on her way down here now with
Miriam Swain. There 's no escape for you, sir ! "

An energetic person will not rest physically
passive under strong mental commotion. Rollo
moved up and down the veranda with long
strides, — not rapidly, — he put all his possibility
of repression into the effort to go moderately, and
shut his hands in his coat pockets as if he were
reining in a violent horse, or as if that were a
means of self-restraint.

Roland soon came to his side, took his arm, and
walked with him, Rollo checking his great steps
to accommodate them to the lesser man.

" I have remembered a hundred times the lonely
boy you seemed when you started away that morning, Rollo, with nothing much but your soul and
body to call your own," Roland said. " I want
to hear the whole story — the most minute history
of those years of exile. What became of you that
day ? Where in heaven above or on the earth beneath or in the waters under the earth did you go
to ? "

" Oh, there 's no story to tell. I came here."

" *Here ?* To John Dagget's, at once ? Well,
upon my word, that was *quid pro quo !* Did you
mean to hold your head high and show me that

either place was all the same to you ; to give me
all the odds and then come out winner ? "

" Nonsense ! " said Rol.

" Well, tell me, like a good fellow, how I can
lay hold of a manly life as you have done," pursued Roland. " You make me feel as if I might
be something yet. I long to be a true man. Steer
me a little, won't you ? Show me the straight
course !   Tell me how to begin ! "

" Why, we 've already begun to be what we long
to be, have n't we ?   Go on longing, and do whatever ought to be done, — whatever you can do best.
Is n't that a fair idea to start with ? " Rollo blushed
to find himself taking the part of Mentor.

" The idea is well enough, yes," Roland assented ; " but as a fact, you seem to be the fellow
who has had the chances, and I the one who has
missed them. It was you, after all, who stepped
into a place in life. Yes, hang me if you have n't
escaped the drawbacks and made a man of yourself at my expense, thrusting me into abject luxury, and seizing the advantages of penury yourself !
Do we need to have our props knocked away, I
wonder, in order to discover ourselves, and stand
upon our own strength, or get strength to stand
upon ?   Who knows whether you would ever have
been the fine fellow you are, sir, if you had remained Roland Weir ? "

" Oh, come," cried Rollo, by this time, in a tone
of strong deprecation, stopping short in his walk.
" I can't stand and hear myself called a fine fel-

low! No such names as that, now. Just come with me, won't you, while I catch my fish for dinner. How soon will my other guests arrive?"

"In not much more than an hour, I should think."

Rollo felt that the only way he could get becomingly through that hour would be to do something. He led Roland's horse to the barn, brought out his basket and line, and Roland followed him across the road and down the cliff to the beach.

The manner of taking the fish was the 'Sconset fashion of throwing the line from the shore.

Rollo unreeled the long cord and coiled it at his feet, then swung the hook and the heavy sinker in more and more rapid circles above his head, until it had acquired tremendous velocity, when he threw it forward, and it splashed into the sea at a magnificent distance. The fish answered his invitation without much delay, and he presently had a fine bluefish flapping on the sand.

Roland was eager to try his own hand at this sport. It looked most easily done when Rollo's strength gave the momentum, and his skill a grace which seemed lightness of hand.

Again and again Roland made a venture with no success. Again and again he begged Rollo to give him one more example. He was big with determination, swollen with ambition; he would not give up, and so the time passed on, until Rollo excused himself to go and deliver his fish to Manuel, the important native of Fayal who had been carefully trained to be cook and steward of the new ship, and who, with the occasional assistance of Mrs. Martin, performed the domestic service of the cottage. Roland asked to be left to practice by himself, promising to come up before it should be time for the ladies to arrive.

When Rollo had ascended to the road, however, he started at the sight of Jerry and the old chaise already at the cottage door, and the ladies, who had made more haste than Roland expected, were just entering the little hall at Manuel's invitation. Rollo hesitated, as if about to turn back. But why should he? he asked himself. He was on the eve of that great moment towards which his ambition had continually pointed for six years. He was about to present himself to Mrs. Payne, unashamed. This was all just as he had hoped, and yet his courage failed him. But putting his will in the place of his courage, he kept on without calling Roland Weir, went round to the back door with his fish, and received Manuel's breathless announcement that there were "ladies in the parl' who had come to see Meest Tuttle," with as much apparent composure as if he were giving receptions to ladies every day, though his big heart pounded like a sledge-hammer.

During the minutes up-stairs in which he washed his hands and minutely and carefully restored himself to freshness, he seemed, as, one often does, to be exactly repeating an experience, to find the same act and the same thought occurring simultaneously as they had done long ago. It was as if he washed his objectionable hands, and changed his cuffs again, at Newport, and again, as at that time, he turned those grievous words over in his mind, "It seems as if you were not my boy!"

At length he was quite ready, and turning into the little entry went quickly down the short, angular staircase, which creaked under his tread, and in a moment filled the small doorway of the parlor with his large presence. The light in the room was dim, for the blinds were all closed to keep out the glare of the sun and the sand, and it did not at once occur to Rol that more light was needed on this matter. His eyes were strong and clear and able to discern the two faces that looked out upon him; but Mrs. Payne, in advance of her day, had astigmatic vision, and the blur of imperfect sight, in addition to the dimness of the room, made it impossible for her to clearly distinguish Rollo's features. She saw only the outline of an erect, manly figure, which was quite imposing in the frame of the doorway. It gave her the impression of a man of thirty.

"Mr. Tuttle?" she asked, rising.

"Yes," was all Rollo could answer.

Miriam, with her old-fashioned Quaker manners, rose too, and shook hands with Rollo, reminding him that she was the forlorn maiden whom he had occasionally rescued.

"I thought we should find my nephew here,"

said Mrs. Payne, when they were seated. " He started to come in advance of us in order to speak for the privilege of this visit for me."

Rollo accounted for Roland Weir's absence.

" Then you do know the errand which brings me here?" said Mrs. Payne. " But you can hardly understand, Mr. Tuttle, the importance it is to me to have found some one who knows about my Rollo. Tell me at once, if you please, how we should be most likely to reach him."

" I think," said Rollo, " you would be as likely to reach him *here* as anywhere."

" *Here?* Then he does come here? How soon might I expect to see him? Oh, Mr. Tuttle! you cannot guess how much he is wished for and needed! Is there any way of bringing him at once ?"

" Nothing could bring him sooner than your commands, madam." Rollo's deep voice said this with a specific earnestness. He felt Miriam's eyes resting upon him with grave scrutiny. " You have only to say the word, and he is here," he added.

" Ah, no one can know better than I do the un-selfish, obedient spirit of the boy," said Mrs. Payne. " He was as good as gold, as brave and true and kind as any boy could be, and I hope he is the same to this day."

Rollo believed Mrs. Payne's desire to be mag-nanimous was carrying her far. It was to ease her too-tender conscience that she spoke of him in that tone, he thought. She meant to do him more than justice, rather than less, in future.

"Oh, he's quite a common sort of person, every way," he said, "not remarkable for anything in particular."

"I see you do not know him well," Mrs. Payne said with a certain stiffness of manner, a complete withdrawal from the gracious attitude she had at first thought proper. "You are either unacquainted with him, or you are unfriendly to him."

"He never had a better friend," said Rollo, — "excepting yourself."

"Still," said Mrs. Payne, "I do not find the satisfaction I expected in hearing you speak of him. If you will kindly give me his address, I need not trouble you farther."

Mrs. Payne waited for a reply with nostrils expanded and lips parted. It was not to ease her conscience that she breathed in that quick, agitated way. Rollo's heart swelled at the sight.

"I can tell you this," he said, "if there is any good in him, he thanks you for it. Among all his faults there is not a trace of ingratitude to you. He has worked up to a place that he is not ashamed of, and it was the thought of you that helped him. He longed to be something that you would approve."

The tone in which these words were said, not less than the words themselves, melted Mrs. Payne's iciness, so that there was a warm mist in her eyes, which threatened to turn into rain.

"Ah, my dear boy!" she said, quite to herself, almost inaudibly, but Rollo heard it, and flushed scarlet with surprise and incredulous joy. He leaned forward with a gesture of absolute surrender, the old true affection thrusting the impostor pride quite out of the way.

Miriam saw the whole truth, and rose quickly, with a mist in her own eyes, to leave those two to their very personal interview, when she was frightened back by the sound of quick hard breathing, a dash upon the veranda, a plunge through the hall, and Monte Cristo, ready to drop dead, flashed into the room, halted an instant to review the situation, the frantic fear of having arrived too late making his wild eyes gleam like balls of fire in the obscurity of the room. Catching the look of the dear old by-gone days in Rollo's face, he blessed the good dog-star that at last, at last his master was himself again, and with all the breath he had left, gave one cry of exultation, flew at Rollo, and if ever a dog said what he had to say, if ever a dog wept for joy, it was then and it was there. Never, perhaps, had there been such a manifestation from dog to man since there were dogs and men on the earth. Mrs. Payne stared, benumbed. Who was this, who could bring such cries and tears from Monte Cristo?

She moved her lips to speak, but no sound came. Then, rising slowly, in a dazed, unsteady fashion, and stretching her hands before her, like a blind person seeking the lost way,—

" Rollo!" she hardly more than whispered, as if she feared to say it, dared not believe it.

Again, faint as the voice was, Rollo heard it, and quicker than a thought, made one step and took the groping hands in his, while Monte Cristo found that he had just life enough left for one mad demonstration more.

" Forgive me!" said Rollo; "I was waiting for courage. See how poor I am! I have n't the courage of a man!"

Mrs. Payne brought Rollo to the light, looked long at the face which told such a different story, and as she felt the gentleness of the strong, young arm which offered her support,—

" Ah, but *I* am rich enough," she said, " and I have the courage of a whole race of men!"

CHAPTER XXIV.

KITH AND KIN.

I SHALL not invite you to be present when the story was told which revealed to Rollo his true name and place in life, when all that he had ever wished for and more than he had hoped for was poured in one flush stream upon him. Profound joy is as sacred as profound sorrow.

And if I should show you Amos Tuttle, when he stood with trembling hands on Rollo's shoulders, looking into Lydia Macy's blue-gray eyes, while the good-natured creases in his cheeks were turned into water courses, you young people, who know nothing of lonely, unsuccessful old age, and the dearness of the links by which it possesses some remnant of the hopeful past, would call him a foolish old fellow. Ah, but he was a gentle, loving, faithful old fellow, and this was the one great joy, the one true and perfect satisfaction, that had ever come into his patient life.

It is impossible for a transplanted offshoot of an old Nantucket family to remain transplanted long enough to find himself without relationship on the island. A little genealogical research will supply him with a large family connection, with blood somewhat mixed and diluted, it is true, but while one has a single drop of the original current in his veins, he is analytically a Macy, a Starbuck, a Coffin, a Swain, a Gardner, or a Folger. As soon as Rollo's history became known, he was cousin to half the people on the island, and they all discussed and compared, at their meetings in the sail loft, or in the old counting-rooms down by the wharves, or at their tea-drinkings, to find who was nearest. Amos was not behind any one of them, I do assure you. When it was seen that Rollo was more attached to him than to any of his new connection, he was frequently asked what relation the young captain was to him.

"'To *me*! Why he's my own *prottyjee!*'" Amos would reply with as much arrogance as was possible to his mild nature.

And at the close of a heavenly day, when the sparse cedars cast long, peaceful shadows in the north burying-ground; when Mrs. Payne and Roland Weir, and all the friends and relatives unto the sixteenth cousin, stood there with bowed heads to give hail and farewell to some sacred dust, — it was Amos, with Rollo, who lifted and placed it on the spot where the motherly old island had opened her bosom. It was Amos who stood side by side with Rollo when the prayer was said. It was his tear that consecrated the earth where Lydia Macy's dust was to lie.

It was a sweet and hallowed rest, at last, which she found at whose first burial only Ezra Hodges and Benjamin Booth were present as mourners.

And Pel'tiah, with his long, snowy curls uncovered, and shining like a glory round his innocent face, laid the warm earth on gently, for in forty years he had not learned to do this service irreverently. He covered those profound sleepers as if a sound might wake them.

And by and by they had all gone, and there were no sounds above Lydia's grave save the creaking and zizzing of insects, the murmur, murmur, murmur of the sea, the cry of a wandering plover, and the low voice of her son that said, "Goodnight, mother!"

CHAPTER XXV.

ROLLO'S errands to town, during those fast-flying days, were more than could well be accounted for by anybody but himself. He rode in that direction on a lovely cool morning of September, with Monte Cristo at his heels. Monte, by the way, never lost sight of his master again, and all his life, poor dog, seemed to suffer anxiety and fear least he should take himself off again.

Rollo's face, that was always aglow, now, with gladness, wore an unusual look of gravity that morning. As he approached the town, he drew his horse into a walk and appeared to consider.

He was wondering what pretext would take him to the Swains again. He had been there repeatedly with Roland Weir; he had stopped to get Mrs. Payne's smelling-bottle, of his own accord; he had taken a note to Miriam once, from Mrs. Payne, who, with Roland, was passing the last weeks of Rollo's stay on shore at the cottage at 'Sconset, and returned with a feeling of great satisfaction at having the reply in the breast-pocket of his coat, from whence he had withdrawn it several times to stare at the address in a thoughtful way. Each time he had had a little chat with Miriam, quite at his ease, for he felt the sustaining sense of having a reasonable and evident purpose, and every time he went he wished to go again, each time more than the last; but now, as he rode towards the town, he was destitute of ostensible purpose, but well furnished with a desire to see the Quaker girl, and hear her smooth, rich voice again.

Rollo, however, was very shy. He had made trips to town before, with bold intention, but the boldness had completely forsaken him when he came within sight of the Swain house, and he was wondering if he should disappoint himself this time. He was but twenty-one, you know, and had passed five years on shipboard, where there had never chanced to appear such a girl as Miriam, and, indeed, according to his own view, such an one had never appeared in history at all, and the sailor boy had never before been brought to consider an undertaking so important as a formal visit to a young lady, for the sole and definite purpose of seeing her and having something to say to her. He was sure he should have not a word to speak under those circumstances. Confusion seized him at the thought, for he was far from ready to tell her how he had become saturated with beautiful thoughts of her, though that was exactly Rollo's case. A young man of twenty-one would not need much time to arrive at such a situation, even if he were more reasonable and sensible than Rollo, who was quite reasonable and sensible enough, and Rollo had been considering, with a mixture of wonder and delight, for several weeks, this lovely girl, and the thoughts and sensations that filled his mind in regard to her were conditioned upon something more beautiful than Miriam's beautiful person even, and that was a perception of her beautiful, strong, tender spirit.

But Rollo had said more than he knew in those casual meetings with Miriam, not in words, of course, but his honest look and manner had revealed so much that Miriam perceived, with a shock of surprise, that every vestige of her childhood was gone, that she was getting really old, and one day she brought out Friend Polly Hopkins and whispered one more confidence to her, and shed one more tear on her neck. And she took to wandering in her old childish haunts again. She went often to sit by Rachel Gardner, and flattered Pel'tiah and Amos by frequent visits to them. She held on to Sally Martin, too, as if she were the embodiment of her lost youth, and meant never to take her back to her mother again.

On the same morning of this day of September, Miriam was in the Friends'' burying-ground with Sally. She had taken her to see Rachel Gardner's grave, for she had told her the story of this friend she had lost when she was a little girl like Sally herself. As they went slowly on in the narrow paths, bordered and overgrown by weeds, she lingered upon that memory with her eyes fixed dreamily on the untrodden way.

It was just at that moment that Rollo was passing, and he could see the little Quaker bonnet above the palings of the fence, and the curly head of Sally bobbing along below it. That settled his question for him. He would go boldly into the burying-ground, and meet Miriam, and have a chat with her there. If conversation failed, he could always address a remark to Sally. He was very fond of Sally. Day after day he had seen her sitting in the doorway of her home, watching the road to town, and when he had asked her, " What are you looking for, little one ? " she had always answered, " I am looking for Friend Miriam," and Rollo had looked for her too ; they had watched together ; and so he had grown into sympathy and friendship with Sally Martin.

He fastened his horse to the fence, and marched courageously on, crushing deep prints in the moss-covered ground as he went. Miriam saw him coming with a feeling which could not quite be called pleasure, and was not altogether dread.

She blushed, and so did Rollo, but she expressed no surprise at finding him in that unwonted spot, and Rollo gave no explanation, made no excuse. It was as if they had met there every day.

Rollo sat down on the grass by Miriam, near Rachel Gardner's grave, after they had exchanged greetings, and at first there was an awful hush. But presently Miriam, laying her hand on the little mound with a caressing touch, stroking the earth which she had always kept smoothly rounded with her own hands, told Rollo about that child friendship, and how she had always loved to come and sit beside little Rachel. There was great tenderness in her look and tone as she spoke. Rachel Gardner had never seemed so dear.

" Thank you for telling me that," Rollo said, when she had finished. " I was wondering how you could like to come *here*. But I 'm glad you happened to, this morning "—as if the Friends' burying-ground had been his destination and Miriam had accidentally fallen upon it. " I 'm going to China so soon, now, that I want to see my friends all I can, you know, in the mean time."

·That was quite a little venture for Rollo — to call Miriam his friend.

" I was on my way to China when I brought up at Newport," said Miriam. " Does thee remember that ? "

" Oh, yes ! " Rollo answered. " My memory is pretty good about some things. What were you going to China for ? "

" I 've always longed to go there since I was a little girl," said Miriam.

As Rollo had no moustaches to twirl, he was busy pulling and twirling the wild turnip heads.

" Things must be so curious there," added Miriam.

" Yes, so they are."

Rollo was uncertain whether to say something

that was in his mind.   He was already so uncertain what to say at all that he looked for refuge to Sally Martin, who was petting Monte Cristo. Much as he had depended upon her, he had not fully calculated her power to help him.

" You like dogs, don't you, Sally ? " he said, with wretched stupidity, he knew.

" Yes, I like them *pretty* well," Sally answered, leaving Monte and leaning back against Miriam again ; " but I like Friend Miriam best of everybody.   Do *you* like her ? "

Rollo felt as if caught up and borne on by a strong wind.   He was ready to answer earnestly, " Yes, I do ! "

" What does thee hold my hand so *tight* for, Friend Miriam," pursued Sally, in her drawling child's tone, looking up at Miriam with immense surprise.   " I don't want to run away, for I love thee very much, thee knows," and she nestled close within Miriam's arm, looking out upon Rollo from that freehold with the assurance of an established right.   She watched him sharply, and then, " *Do* YOU *love her ?* " she asked, mixing the Friendly manner of speech, which she had caught from Miriam, with her usual worldly fashion.

Sally touched a match, this time, to the well-guarded powder that Rollo had stored away.   A lighted match and explosives ! You know how they work.

Fizz — bang !   It is all soon over.

" Ah, that is something I must say only to

Friend Miriam herself," Rollo answered. "May
I say it? May I tell you the truth, Miriam?"

"Not now — not now," entreated Miriam, clinging to Sally Martin.

"Some day, may I? Some other day shall I
tell you all I am thinking now? And won't you
go with me the next time you start for China;
let *me* guide the ship for you — *always?* Will
you, Miriam?"

Though Miriam did not answer in words, Rollo
was just as content, just as exultant, as if she
had; and when they went away from the burying-
ground, the childhood which Miriam had buried
there with Rachel Gardner had had its Easter
Day, for out of its ashes had risen her happier
womanhood.

CHAPTER XXVI.

THE LAUNCHING OF THE SHIP.

IT will be impossible to give any just impression of the immense importance of *The Ship*. Though you have heard of the Armada and the Mayflower and the Great Eastern, these were of no consequence whatever in comparison with *The Ship!*

Paul's father and Perez's grandfather were its owners, and Rollo and Paul and Perez were to be interested together in its cargoes, and to have the privilege of buying it, in time.

The conversation of these young men during the year that ends the events of these little annals was solid ship. You would have said that all the commercial and maritime interests of the nation were in their hands.

The day for the launching of this precious bark was drawing near; it was close at hand.

It had been left to the future owners to choose its name, yet out of a yard-long list, and out of innumerable hours of discussion, no satisfactory name had as yet been extracted.

At length Paul and Perez came down to 'Sconset one morning, with a solemn, official air, to say

that the matter was to be left entirely to Rollo.
Rollo's surprise was only half equal to his pleasure,
for he had longed to give the name to his ship.

"A thousand thanks," he said. "You shall
know my choice at the christening."

The great day at length arrived, — that last day
of September, — a glorious day, from which all
clouds had fled, except the one remaining in Roland Weir's sky.

The ship was to be launched at twelve o'clock.
Perez Howard's grandfather had all our friends
from Nantucket staying at his charming house on
the top of the hill at New Bedford.

At a little before eleven o'clock this dear old
mansion began to give up its occupants with reckless abandon. Mrs. Payne came first down its
smooth-worn granite steps with Rollo. Her happy
eyes and returning color made her almost as beautiful as when she was the enchanting chaperon
who sailed down Buzzard's Bay on board the Juno.
Then there were Roland, Miriam and Obed Swain,
Uncle David and Aunt Dorcas, Paul and cousin
Ruth, Perez Howard's whole troop of relatives,
and Perez himself, with a little flotilla of pretty
New Bedford girls.

These the waiting carriages whirled away down
the gently-sloping, elm-shaded streets, that give
glimpses of the water at the foot of their long vis-
tas, and brought them, all beaming and chattering,
to the great shipyard, with its piles of huge timber, its fragrance of the sea and newly-made chips.

There the beautiful creature was waiting, with her flags and streamers flying, and Rollo's heart swelled with pride as he thought that he was her master — him she would obey. Just beyond, in the stream, a smart little tug was getting up steam to take all that beauty and that worth, that glory and that loveliness, out across the bay.

One after another, as they climbed the steps and came upon deck, each person gave an exclamation of delight. The great smooth, white foothold´ was like the floor of a palace, upon which were scattered about under the awnings light chairs and settees, and everywhere were flags, festoons and streamers, knots and garlands, bowers and embankments of flowers, and in the after-part of the ship tables set out to be laid for dinner, in the afternoon, down the bay, and great basets and hampers furnished food and refreshment to the imagination in advance of any lawful claims.

As many old Quakers as had been beguiled into this unaccustomed path indulgently closed their ears, or tried to, to the music of a choice band from Boston, which offered joyous welcome to the guests as they kept coming and coming. Paul and Perez and Rollo received them. They were the coming men; they held the future by the forelock, and had everything their own way.

Perez Howard's face wore a look of distinct and evident consternation as he watched Miriam and Rollo. He had long and assiduously observed the little Quaker girl, who had danced with him at the birthday party, but he had never before felt obliged to include Rollo in his contemplations.

At length, catching Rollo by a buttonhole of his coat as he flew by, he looked him steadily in the eye.

"I recognize you, Vespucci," he said. "Do you know me?"

"Well, I don't know," Rollo answered doubtfully.

"I am Christopher Columbus!" said Perez; "and I mean to haunt you, for I see you intend to claim my own discovery. I knew long ago where the best and loveliest part of this world was situated. Ah, well! Go along with you! There is more than one America that ought to have been Columbia."

Perez said this gayly, and he seemed happy with his pretty New Bedford girls, but secretly there was a real disappointment down deep in his heart.

Roland, having anxiously watched the coming guests until it had grown very late, strolled away by himself with a look of doubt and disappointment, too. Paul, seeing him so much at leisure, called upon him to do the kindness of taking a message to the master workman.

The steps were crowded with people coming up or going down. He swung himself over the bulwarks, dropped to the staging, and ran down a ladder, skipping all the lower rounds and coming to the ground with a bound, like a man who had been long engaged in shipbuilding, or some such active enterprise. He jumped so near a young girl who had just arrived from Newport, and who, looking up to admire the new ship, had watched his whole descent with some admiration, too, that she retreated with a little "Oh!" Roland turned to ask pardon, and found himself face to face with Betty, who looked up at his brown face and his more stalwart figure with grave wonder, and instead of her old, light, nonchalant greeting, instead of that laugh, she looked just as Roland had often wished she would, hesitated a little, and then put out her hand.

"I scarcely knew you," she said. "Papa, do you see, here is Roland Weir?"

And Mr. Vinton himself looked surprised.

Roland had but a step to go with his message. He hastened with it and returned to Betty's side. The bewildered Betty, strangely enough for her, appeared to have few remarks to offer, and Roland addressed himself chiefly to Mr. Vinton. He poised himself upon his new purposes with a new dignity and a virile security that were strange phenomena to Miss Betty.

When Betty reached the deck she was seized and borne away by Mrs. Payne and Miriam, but Roland, from time to time, saw her eyes fixed upon him from afar, with a look of penetrating scrutiny that she had never thought it worth while to expend upon him in the past.

To let her see, as he said to himself, that there was none of the small pique remaining which he had disclosed at parting with her a few months before, he went to her at length, and offered to show her how the vessel would be launched, what blocks held her in place, and how the removal of these left her free to go on her way. They stood looking over the vessel's side, watching the row of men hammering at the blocks, in the fresh white shirt sleeves with which they had honored the occasion, and Betty had received Roland's information with marvelous respect, as if it had been of immense importance, and then they both dropped into silence, which lasted long enough for Roland Weir to take the full impression of Betty's extraordinary new manner, which was incredibly gentle and subdued.

"How you are changed, Betty!" he said, in a tone of slow consideration.

"Oh, but how *you* are changed!" returned Betty, quickly.

"Do you — a — do you like the change in me?"

"Yes, *very* much," answered Betty, promptly; and then, with more hesitation, and a little blush, — an actual *bonâ fide* blush, — "Do *you* like the change in *me?*" she asked.

"Oh, im-*mensely!*"

And as Roland looked down at Betty, and Betty looked up at him, that one last woe vanished altogether and forever.

At that moment the sound of the pounding

ceased.   There was a cry of "A—ll ready!" everybody ran forward, the hammers beat the parting blows, and Mrs. Payne proclaimed, in a voice which sounded triumphant, as she broke a bottle of Veuve Cliquot on the bow, — "I name this ship *Miriam!*" while Rollo's own hand ran up a flag with that name in blue letters on the white bunting; and that blessed ship, laden with joy, slipped down the ways amid shouts of applause from deck and shore, and strains of music, which even the old Quakers listened to with bland, tolerant smiles.   The little tug puffed and whistled with all its might, and out they sailed, over the bay, to a smooth, bright, summer sea; and on such a sea — Heaven be praised! — they are sailing to this very day.

Works of fiction

PUBLISHED BY

HOUGHTON, MIFFLIN AND COMPANY,

4 PARK ST., BOSTON; 11 E. 17TH ST., NEW YORK.

Thomas Bailey Aldrich.

Story of a Bad Boy. Illustrated. 12mo $1.25
Marjorie Daw and Other People. 12mo 1.50
Marjorie Daw and Other Stories. Riverside Aldine
    Series. 16mo 1.00
Prudence Palfrey. 12mo 1.50
The Queen of Sheba. 12mo 1.50
The Stillwater Tragedy. 12mo 1.50

Hans Christian Andersen.

Complete Works. In ten uniform volumes, crown 8vo.
A new and cheap Edition, in attractive binding.

The Improvisatore; or, Life in Italy 1.00
The Two Baronesses 1.00
O. T.; or, Life in Denmark 1.00
Only a Fiddler 1.00
In Spain and Portugal 1.00
A Poet's Bazaar 1.00
Pictures of Travel 1.00
The Story of my Life. With Portrait 1.00
Wonder Stories told for Children. Illustrated . . . 1.00
Stories and Tales. Illustrated 1.00
    The set 10.00

B. B. B. Series.

Story of a Bad Boy. By T. B. Aldrich.
Captains of Industry. By James Parton.
Being a Boy. By C. D. Warner.
    The set, 3 vols. 16mo 3.75

William Henry Bishop.

Detmold: A Romance. "Little Classic" style. 18mo 1.25
The House of a Merchant Prince. 12mo 1.50
Choy Susan, and Other Stories. 16mo 1.25
The Golden Justice. 16mo 1.25

Björnstjerne Björnson.

Works. *American Edition*, sanctioned by the author,
    and translated by Professor R. B. Anderson, of the
    University of Wisconsin.
Complete Works, in three volumes. 12mo. The set 4.50

Alice Cary.

Pictures of Country Life. 12mo $1.50

John Esten Cooke.

My Lady Pokahontas. 16mo 1.25

James Fenimore Cooper.

Complete Works. New *Household Edition*, in attractive binding. With Introductions to many of the volumes by Susan Fenimore Cooper, and Illustrations. In thirty-two volumes, 16mo.

Precaution.	The Prairie.
The Spy.	Wept of Wish-ton-Wish.
The Pioneers.	The Water Witch.
The Pilot.	The Bravo.
Lionel Lincoln.	The Heidenmauer.
Last of the Mohicans.	The Headsman.
Red Rover.	The Monikins.
Homeward Bound.	Miles Wallingford.
Home as Found.	The Red Skins.
The Pathfinder.	The Chainbearer.
Mercedes of Castile.	Satanstoe.
The Deerslayer.	The Crater.
The Two Admirals.	Jack Tier.
Wing and Wing.	The Sea Lions.
Wyandotté.	Oak Openings.
Afloat and Ashore.	The Ways of the Hour.

(Each volume sold separately.)

Each volume 1.00

The set 32.00

New Fireside Edition. With forty-five original Illustrations. In sixteen volumes, 12mo. The set . . . 20.00

(Sold only in sets.)

Sea Tales. New *Household Edition*, containing Introductions by Susan Fenimore Cooper. Illustrated. First Series. Including —

The Pilot.	The Red Rover.
The Water Witch.	The Two Admirals.
Wing and Wing.	

Second Series. Including —

The Sea Lions.	Afloat and Ashore.
Jack Tier.	Miles Wallingford.
The Crater.	

Each set, 5 vols. 16mo 5.00

Leather-Stocking Tales. New *Household Edition*, containing Introductions by Susan Fenimore Cooper. Illustrated. In five volumes, 16mo.

The Deerslayer.	The Pioneers.
The Pathfinder.	The Prairie.
Last of the Mohicans.	

The set $5.00
Cooper Stories; being Narratives of Adventure selected from his Works. With Illustrations by F. O. C. Darley. In three volumes, 16mo, each 1.00

Charles Egbert Craddock.

In the Tennessee Mountains. 16mo 1.25
The Prophet of the Great Smoky Mountains. 16mo. 1.25
Down the Ravine. Illustrated. 16mo 1.00
In the Clouds. 16mo 1.25
The Story of Keedon Bluffs. 16mo 1.00
The Despot of Broomsedge Cove. 16mo 1.25

Thomas Frederick Crane.

Italian Popular Tales. Translated from the Italian. With Introduction and a Bibliography. 8vo . . . 2.50

F. Marion Crawford.

To Leeward. 16mo 1.25
A Roman Singer. 16mo 1.25
An American Politician. 16mo 1.25
Paul Patoff. Crown 8vo 1.50

Maria S. Cummins.

The Lamplighter. 12mo 1.00
El Fureidîs. 12mo 1.50
Mabel Vaughan. 12mo 1.50

Parke Danforth.

Not in the Prospectus. 16mo 1.25

Daniel De Foe.

Robinson Crusoe. Illustrated. 16mo 1.00

Margaret Deland.

John Ward, Preacher. 12mo 1.50

P. Deming.

Adirondack Stories. 18mo 75
Tompkins and Other Folks. 18mo 1.00

Thomas De Quincey.

Romances and Extravaganzas. 12mo 1.50
Narrative and Miscellaneous Papers. 12mo . . . 1.50

Charles Dickens.

Complete Works. *Illustrated Library Edition.* With Introductions by E. P. Whipple. Containing Illustrations by Cruikshank, Phiz, Seymour, Leech, Maclise, and others, on steel, to which are added designs of Darley and Gilbert, in all over 550. In twenty-nine volumes, 12mo.

The Pickwick Papers, 2 vols.
Nicholas Nickleby, 2 vols.
Oliver Twist.
Old Curiosity Shop, and Re-printed Pieces, 2 vols.
Barnaby Rudge, and Hard Times, 2 vols.
Martin Chuzzlewit, 2 vols.
Our Mutual Friend, 2 vols.
Uncommercial Traveller.
A Child's History of England, and Other Pieces.
Christmas Books.
Dombey and Son, 2 vols.
Pictures from Italy, and American Notes.
Bleak House, 2 vols.
Little Dorrit, 2 vols.
David Copperfield, 2 vols.
A Tale of Two Cities.
Great Expectations.
Edwin Drood, Master Humphrey's Clock, and Other Pieces.
Sketches by Boz.

Each volume $1.50
The set.   With Dickens Dictionary.   30 vols. . 45.00
Christmas Carol.   Illustrated.   8vo, full gilt 2.50
The Same.   32mo 75
Christmas Books.   Illustrated.   12mo 2.00

Charlotte Dunning.

A Step Aside.   16mo 1.25

Edgar Fawcett.

A Hopeless Case.   "Little Classic" style.   18mo . 1.25
A Gentleman of Leisure.   "Little Classic" style.   18mo 1.00
An Ambitious Woman.   12mo 1.50

Fénelon.

Adventures of Telemachus.   12mo 2.25

Mrs. James A. Field.

High-Lights.   16mo 1.25

Harford Flemming.

A Carpet Knight.   16mo 1.25

Baron de la Motte Fouqué.

Undine, Sintram and his Companions, etc.   32mo . . .75
Undine and Other Tales.   Illustrated.   16mo . . . 1.00

Johann Wolfgang von Goethe.

Wilhelm Meister.   Translated by Thomas Carlyle. Portrait of Goethe.   In two volumes.   12mo . . . 3.00
The Tale and Favorite Poems.   32mo 75

Oliver Goldsmith.

Vicar of Wakefield. *Handy-Volume Edition.* 24mo,
gilt top $1.00
The Same. "Riverside Classics." Illustrated. 16mo   1.00

Jeanie T. Gould (Mrs. Lincoln).

Marjorie's Quest. Illustrated. 12mo 1.50

The Guardians.

A Novel 1.25

Thomas Chandler Haliburton.

The Clockmaker; or, The Sayings and Doings of
Samuel Slick of Slickville. Illustrated. 16mo .   1.00

A. S. Hardy.

But Yet a Woman. 16mo 1.25
The Wind of Destiny. 16mo 1.25
Passe Rose. 16mo 1.25

Miriam Coles Harris.

Rutledge.   Richard Vandermarck.   St. Philips.
The Sutherlands.   A Perfect Adonis.   Missy.
Frank Warrington. Happy-Go-Lucky.   Phœbe.
Each volume, 16mo 1.25
Louie's Last Term at St. Mary's. 16mo 1.00

Bret Harte.

The Luck of Roaring Camp, and Other Sketches. 16mo   1.25
The Luck of Roaring Camp, and Other Stories.
Riverside Aldine Series. 16mo 1.00
Tales of the Argonauts, and Other Stories. 16mo .   1.25
Thankful Blossom. "Little Classic" style. 18mo .   1.00
Two Men of Sandy Bar. A Play. 18mo 1.00
The Story of a Mine. 18mo 1.00
Drift from Two Shores. 18mo 1.00
Twins of Table Mountain, etc. 18mo 1.00
Flip, and Found at Blazing Star. 18mo 1.00
In the Carquinez Woods. 18mo 1.00
On the Frontier. "Little Classic" style. 18mo . .   1.00
Works. Rearranged, with an Introduction and a
Portrait. In six volumes, crown 8vo.
Poetical Works, and the drama, "Two Men of Sandy
Bar," with an Introduction and Portrait.
The Luck of Roaring Camp, and Other Stories.
Tales of the Argonauts and Eastern Sketches.
Gabriel Conroy.
Stories and Condensed Novels.
Frontier Stories.
Each volume 2.00
The set 12.00

By Shore and Sedge. 18mo $1.00
Maruja. A Novel. 18mo 1.00
Snow-Bound at Eagle's. 18mo 1.00
The Queen of the Pirate Isle. A Story for Children.
　Illustrated by Kate Greenaway. Small 4to . . . 1.50
A Millionaire of Rough-and-Ready, and Devil's Ford.
　18mo 1.00
The Crusade of the Excelsior. Illustrated. 16mo . 1.25
A Phyllis of the Sierras, and A Drift from Redwood
　Camp. 18mo 1.00
The Argonauts of North Liberty. 18mo 1.00
Cressy. 16mo 1.25

Wilhelm Hauff.

Arabian Days Entertainments. Illustrated. 12mo . 1.50

Nathaniel Hawthorne.

Works. New *Riverside Edition*. With an original
　etching in each volume, and a new Portrait. With
　bibliographical notes by George P. Lathrop. Com-
　plete in twelve volumes, crown 8vo.
Twice-Told Tales.
Mosses from an Old Manse.
The House of the Seven Gables, and The Snow-Image.
The Wonder-Book, Tanglewood Tales, and Grand-
　father's Chair.
The Scarlet Letter, and The Blithedale Romance.
The Marble Faun.
Our Old Home, and English Note-Books. 2 vols.
American Note-Books.
French and Italian Note-Books.
The Dolliver Romance, Fanshawe, Septimius Felton,
　and, in an Appendix, the Ancestral Footstep.
Tales, Sketches, and Other Papers. With Biograph-
　ical Sketch by G. P. Lathrop, and Indexes.
　　Each volume 2.00
　　The set 24.00
New "*Little Classic*" Edition. Each volume contains
　Vignette Illustration. In twenty-five volumes, 18mo.
　　Each volume 1.00
　　The set 25.00
New *Wayside Edition*. With Portrait, twenty-three
　etchings, and Notes by George P. Lathrop. In
　twenty-four volumes, 12mo 36.00
New *Fireside Edition*. In six volumes, 12mo . . . 10.00
A Wonder-Book for Girls and Boys. *Holiday Edi-
　tion*. With Illustrations by F. S. Church. 4to . 2.50
The Same. 16mo, boards 40
Tanglewood Tales. With Illustrations by Geo.
　Wharton Edwards. 4to, full gilt 2.50

The Same. 16mo, boards $0.40
Twice-Told Tales. *School Edition.* 18mo 1.00
The Scarlet Letter. *Popular Edition.* 12mo . . . 1.00
True Stories from History and Biography. 12mo . 1.25
The Wonder-Book. 12mo. 1.25
Tanglewood Tales. 12mo 1.25
The Snow-Image. Illustrated in colors. Small 4to . .75
Grandfather's Chair. *Popular Edition.* 16mo, paper
    covers 15
Tales of the White Hills, and Legends of New Eng-
    land. 32mo 75
Legends of Province House, and A Virtuoso's Col-
    lection. 32mo 75
True Stories from New England History. 16mo,
    boards 45
Little Daffydowndilly, etc. 16mo, paper 15

Mrs. S. J. Higginson.
A Princess of Java. 12mo 1.50

Oliver Wendell Holmes.
Elsie Venner. A Romance of Destiny. Crown 8vo . 2.00
The Guardian Angel. Crown 8vo 2.00
The Story of Iris. 32mo 75
My Hunt after the Captain. 32mo 40
A Mortal Antipathy. Crown 8vo 1.50

Augustus Hoppin.
Recollections of Auton House. Illustrated. Small
    4to 1.25
A Fashionable Sufferer. Illustrated. 12mo . . . 1.50
Two Compton Boys. Illustrated. Small 4to . . . 1.50

Blanche Willis Howard.
One Summer. A Novel. New *Popular Edition.* Il-
    lustrated by Hoppin. 12mo 1.25

William Dean Howells.
Their Wedding Journey. Illustrated. 12mo . . . 1.50
The Same. "Little Classic" style. 18mo 1.00
A Chance Acquaintance. Illustrated. 12mo . . . 1.50
The Same. "Little Classic" style. 18mo 1.00
A Foregone Conclusion. 12mo 1.50
The Lady of the Aroostook. 12mo 1.50
The Undiscovered Country. 12mo 1.50
Suburban Sketches. 12mo 1.50
A Day's Pleasure, etc. 32mo 75

Thomas Hughes.
Tom Brown's School-Days at Rugby. Illustrated. 1.00
Tom Brown at Oxford. 16mo 1.25

Henry James, Jr.

A Passionate Pilgrim, and Other Tales. 12mo . . . $2.00
Roderick Hudson. 12mo 2.00
The American. 12mo 2.00
Watch and Ward. " Little Classic " style. 18mo . 1.25
The Europeans. 12mo 1.50
Confidence. 12mo 1.50
The Portrait of a Lady. 12mo 2.00

Anna Jameson.

Studies and Stories. New Edition. 16mo, gilt top . 1.25
Diary of an Ennuyée. New Edition. 16mo, gilt top . 1.25

Douglas Jerrold.

Mrs. Caudle's Curtain Lectures. Illustrated. 16mo . 1.00

Sarah Orne Jewett.

Deephaven. 18mo 1.25
Old Friends and New. 18mo 1.25
Country By-Ways. 18mo 1.25
The Mate of the Daylight. 18mo 1.25
A Country Doctor. 16mo 1.25
A Marsh Island. 16mo 1.25
A White Heron, and Other Stories. 18mo 1.25
The King of Folly Island, and Other People. 16mo 1.25

Rossiter Johnson.

" Little Classics." Each in one volume. 18mo.

I. Exile.	X. Childhood.	
II. Intellect.	XI. Heroism.	
III. Tragedy.	XII. Fortune.	
IV. Life.	XIII. Narrative Poems.	
V. Laughter.	XIV. Lyrical Poems.	
VI. Love.	XV. Minor Poems.	
VII. Romance.	XVI. Nature.	
VIII. Mystery.	XVII. Humanity.	
IX. Comedy.	XVIII. Authors.	

Each volume 1.00
The set 18.00

Joseph Kirkland.

Zury : the Meanest Man in Spring County. 12mo . 1.50
The McVeys. 16mo 1.25

Charles and Mary Lamb.

Tales from Shakespeare. 18mo 1.00
The Same. Illustrated. 16mo 1.00

Harriet and Sophia Lee.
    Canterbury Tales. In three volumes. The set, 16mo $3.75

Mary Catherine Lee.
    A Quaker Girl of Nantucket. 16mo 1.25

Henry Wadsworth Longfellow.
    Hyperion. A Romance. 16mo 1.50
    Popular Edition. 16mo 40
    Popular Edition. Paper covers, 16mo 15
    Outre-Mer. 16mo 1.50
    Popular Edition. 16mo 40
    Popular Edition. Paper covers, 16mo 15
    Kavanagh. 16mo 1.50
    Hyperion, Outre-Mer and Kavanagh. 2 vols. crown 8vo 3.00

Flora Haines Loughead.
    The Man who was Guilty. 16mo 1.25

D. R. McAnally.
    Irish Wonders. Illustrated. Small 4to 2.00

S. Weir Mitchell.
    In War Time. 16mo 1.25
    Roland Blake. 16mo 1.25

Lucy Gibbons Morse.
    The Chezzles. Illustrated 1.50

The Notable Series.
    One Summer. By Blanche Willis Howard.
    The Luck of Roaring Camp. By Bret Harte.
    Backlog Studies. By C. D. Warner.
    The set, 3 vols. 16mo 3.75

Mrs. M. O. W. Oliphant and T. B. Aldrich.
    The Second Son. Crown 8vo 1.50

Elizabeth Stuart Phelps.
    The Gates Ajar. 16mo 1.50
    Beyond the Gates. 16mo 1.25
    The Gates Between. 16mo 1.25
    Men, Women, and Ghosts. 16mo 1.50
    Hedged In. 16mo 1.50
    The Silent Partner. 16mo 1.50
    The Story of Avis. 16mo 1.50
    Sealed Orders, and Other Stories. 16mo. 1.50
    Friends : A Duet. 16mo 1.25
    Doctor Zay. 16mo 1.25
    An Old Maid's Paradise, and Burglars in Paradise . 1.25
    Madonna of the Tubs. Illustrated. 12mo 1.50
    Jack the Fisherman. Illustrated. Square 12mo . . .50

Marian C. L. Reeves and Emily Read.

Pilot Fortune. 16mo $1.25

J. P. Quincy.

The Peckster Professorship. 16mo 1.25

Josiah Royce.

The Feud of Oakfield Creek. 16mo 1.25

Joseph Xavier Boniface Saintine.

Picciola. Illustrated. 16mo 1.00

Jacques Henri Bernardin de Saint-Pierre.

Paul and Virginia. Illustrated. 16mo 1.00
The Same, together with Undine, and Sintram. 32mo　.75

Sir Walter Scott.

The Waverley Novels. *Illustrated Library Edition.*
Illustrated with 100 engravings by Darley, Dielman,
Fredericks, Low, Share, Sheppard. With glossary
and a full index of characters. In 25 volumes, 12mo.

Waverley.	The Antiquary.
Guy Mannering.	Rob Roy.
Old Mortality.	St. Ronan's Well.
Black Dwarf, and Legend	Redgauntlet.
of Montrose.	The Betrothed, and The
Heart of Mid-Lothian.	Highland Widow.
Bride of Lammermoor.	The Talisman, and Other
Ivanhoe.	Tales.
The Monastery.	Woodstock.
The Abbot.	The Fair Maid of Perth.
Kenilworth.	Anne of Geierstein.
The Pirate.	Count Robert of Paris.
The Fortunes of Nigel.	The Surgeon's Daughter,
Peveril of the Peak.	and Castle Dangerous.
Quentin Durward.	

Each volume 1.00
The set 25.00
Tales of a Grandfather. *Illustrated Library Edition.*
With six steel plates. In three volumes, 12mo . . 4.50

Horace E. Scudder.

The Dwellers in Five-Sisters' Court. 16mo 1.25
Stories and Romances. 16mo 1.25
The Children's Book. Edited by Mr. Scudder. Small
4to 2.50

Mark Sibley Severance.

Hammersmith: His Harvard Days. 12mo 1.50

J. E. Smith.

Oakridge : An Old-Time Story of Maine. 12mo . . $2.00

Mary A. Sprague.

An Earnest Trifler. 16mo 1.25

William W. Story.

Fiammetta. 16mo 1.25

Harriet Beecher Stowe.

Agnes of Sorrento. 12mo 1.50
The Pearl of Orr's Island. 12mo 1.50
Uncle Tom's Cabin. *Illustrated Edition.* 12mo . . 2.00
The Minister's Wooing. 12mo 1.50
The Mayflower, and Other Sketches. 12mo . . . 1.50
Dred. New Edition, from new plates. 12mo . . . 1.50
Oldtown Folks. 12mo 1.50
Sam Lawson's Fireside Stories. 12mo 1.50
My Wife and I. Illustrated. 12mo 1.50
We and Our Neighbors. Illustrated. 12mo . . . 1.50
Poganuc People. Illustrated. 12mo 1.50
The above eleven volumes, in box 16.00
Uncle Tom's Cabin. *Holiday Edition.* With Intro-
duction, and Bibliography by George Bullen, of the
British Museum. Over 100 Illustrations. 12mo . 3.00
The Same. *Popular Edition.* 12mo 1.00

Octave Thanet.

Knitters in the Sun. 16mo 1.25

Gen. Lew Wallace.

The Fair God ; or, The Last of the 'Tzins. 12mo . 1.50

Henry Watterson.

Oddities in Southern Life. Illustrated. 16mo . . . 1.50

Richard Grant White.

The Fate of Mansfield Humphreys, with the Episode
of Mr. Washington Adams in England. 16mo . . 1.25

Adeline D. T. Whitney.

Faith Gartney's Girlhood. Illustrated. 12mo . . . 1.50
Hitherto : A Story of Yesterdays. 12mo 1.50
Patience Strong's Outings. 12mo 1.50
The Gayworthys. 12mo 1.50
Leslie Goldthwaite. Illustrated. 12mo 1.50
We Girls : A Home Story. Illustrated. 12mo . . 1.50
Real Folks. Illustrated. 12mo 1.50

The Other Girls.   Illustrated.   12mo $1.50
Sights and Insights.   2 vols. 12mo 3.00
Odd, or Even ?   12mo 1.50
Boys at Chequasset.   Illustrated.   12mo 1.50
Bonnyborough.   12mo 1.50
Homespun Yarns.   Short Stories.   12mo 1.50

Kate Douglas Wiggin.

The Birds' Christmas Carol.   Square 12mo 50

Justin Winsor.

Was Shakespeare Shapleigh?   A Correspondence in
   Two Entanglements.   Edited by Justin Winsor.
   Parchment-paper, 16mo 75

Lillie Chace Wyman.

Poverty Grass.   16mo 1.25

www.ingramcontent.com/pod-product-compliance
Lightning Source LLC
Chambersburg PA
CBHW031142120726
47905CB00006B/1780